SCV

SHELTER FROM THE STORM

Rowena Summers titles available from Severn House Large Print

This Girl
The Caldwell Girls
Daisy's War
Dreams of Peace
Taking Heart

SHELTER FROM THE STORM

Rowena Summers

Severn House Large Print
London & New York

This first large print edition published in Great Britain 2006 by
SEVERN HOUSE LARGE PRINT BOOKS LTD of
9-15 High Street, Sutton, Surrey, SM1 1DF.
First world regular print edition published 2005 by
Severn House Publishers, London and New York.
This first large print edition published in the USA 2006 by
SEVERN HOUSE PUBLISHERS INC., of
595 Madison Avenue, New York, NY 10022.

British Library Cataloguing in Publication Data

Summers, Rowena, 1932 -
Shelter from the storm - Large print ed.
1. Hotels - England - Somerset - Fiction
2. England -Social life and customs - Fiction
3. Domestic fiction
4. Large type books
I. Title
823.9'14 [F]

ISBN-10: 0-7278-7517-5

Printed and bound in Great Britain by
MPG Books Ltd, Bodmin, Cornwall.

One

1935

Everything was hustle and bustle that sparkling May morning, with some new arrivals expected at the small hotel on the Somerset coast of Braydon. The Retreat was owned and managed by the Elkins family, who, being property owners, rather fancied themselves as being somebodies in the town. It was a busy but fruitful life, and on this particular day Donald Elkins and his wife Ruth had no time to spare for the squabbling of their two younger daughters, Josie and Milly, nor for their grandmother's attempts to separate them.

'Come and help your mother, you girls,' Donald called impatiently. 'There's time enough for all that when you've got the bedrooms swept and the linen changed. The new folk will be here on the afternoon train, and they'll expect to see everything spick and span, the way it should be.'

'She's got my diary!' Josie shrieked. 'She knows it's private. Tell her to give it back to me, Mum.'

'Who's she, the cat's mother?' Ruth said mildly, none too concerned with their backbiting and more intent on spreading snowy-white sheets on the beds, and whisking away every speck of dust before the new people arrived. Ruth was used to smoothing things over within the family, too, and she prided herself on presenting a pristine hotel, even when the frequent blustery winds from the Bristol Channel blew in smuts and leaves and threatened to do away with all her good intentions in a flash.

'Mum, tell her to give it back to me,' Josie shrieked again.

Ruth straightened up from bending over the double bed she was getting ready for the Parker couple from Gloucester, and glared at her youngest daughter.

'Milly, how many times have you been told to respect other people's belongings? Give Josie back her diary at once. I'm sure there's nothing in there she wouldn't want you to see, but that's not the point.'

Her ten-year-old daughter hooted, her blonde plaits flying about her face as she skipped around the room.

'That's all you know, then! She's jealous of our Charlotte, 'cos Charlotte's old enough to go courting, and she's not. She says so, right here!'

Millie stabbed her fingers at a page in the diary and, as she held it out, Josie pounced on it at once, grabbing it out of her sister's hands, her face as red as fury.

'She's a little beast, Mum, and she's got no right to ridicule me.'

'The girl's quite right,' said a new voice.

Their grandmother, Clover, had been half-amused at the squabbles, but now she stepped forward, a bird-like little figure with bright, restless eyes. People considered her odd, but to her family she was merely eccentric, the way many old people were. But she wasn't above putting her spoke in the family wheel, as her son frequently said irritably, and she did so now.

'You should be ashamed of yourself, Milly. Josie's growing up now, and deserves some privacy.'

'She's only five years older than me, and that doesn't make her grown up yet,' Milly said, scowling.

Her father appeared again, having shown out the last of the weekly guests. His face was angry, and Milly was quietened at once.

'I'll remind you girls that we have a reputation to keep up in this establishment, and I won't have you shouting all over the place. Clover,' he turned to his mother, 'why don't you take the pair of them for a walk along the beach and let Ruth and me get on with things here?'

'I don't want to be taken anywhere like a dog,' Milly wailed, but one more look from her father and she gave in.

'I don't want to go for a walk with you, either,' Josie threw back at her as they went back to the bedroom they shared to fetch their walking shoes, 'but it's better than changing sheets.'

'Not listening to Gran's old stories, it's not. Sorry, I mean *Clover*. I don't know why she insists that we call her that, anyway.'

'It's because it's her name, and because she says it makes her feel young.'

Milly was in the mood to be awkward. 'Whoever heard of a name like Clover, anyway? And she's not young. She's old. And she's potty.'

Josie grinned. 'Gran's not potty, just a bit forgetful sometimes. Are you planning on being difficult all day? You're getting to be a real little snob ever since your teacher said you might be good enough to pass the scholarship and go to grammar school next year.'

Milly tossed her head, and the plaits slapped around her cheeks again.

'Well, if I'm a snob, you're soppy for being so jealous of Charlotte just because she's got a young man and you haven't.'

'You might feel the same when you grow up a bit and stop being such an *idiot*. And fifteen's plenty old enough to have a boy, whatever Dad thinks.'

Milly's brown eyes opened wider, and after all the shenanigans of the morning the eager child in her came to the fore. 'Have you got one already then? I won't tell, honest I won't.'

'No, you won't, because there's nothing to tell.'

They could hear their grandmother calling

to them impatiently, and they ran downstairs to where Clover was waiting, buttoned up into a warm coat with a bright knitted hat on her grey head, even though it was the beginning of summer. She hardly looked like the matriarch of a successful business concern, but the way she looked was never a priority for Clover.

She dressed how she liked ... and *when* she liked, too, she thought with a wicked grin. And right now she chose to be buttoned up.

It was because of her old bones, their dad said, whenever they teased her about it. Ancient ones, more likely, according to her three granddaughters.

Charlotte had been excused hotel chores that morning, having offered to go into the town with the regular grocery order that would be delivered to the hotel that afternoon. And on the way back, provided she went by a roundabout route – a *very* roundabout route – she could call and see her sweetheart.

Her heart gave a little flip of delight. She was the prettiest of the three sisters, although she acknowledged that Milly would be pretty enough in time, once she stopped her pointless grousing at being the youngest. Josie was already blossoming in all the right places. She would be a stunner in a year or so with the darker hair that set her apart from her fair-haired sisters.

That held no jealousy for Charlotte. She was perfectly happy in knowing she had captured the heart of the local blacksmith's son, who said she could rival those glamour girls at the flicks any day. She felt the familiar little surge in her heart again. Melvin Philpott was a catch in any girl's eyes, with his broad shoulders and brawny muscles that were as hard as the iron he worked with. Working in the open smithy as much as he did, whether it was shoeing horses or fashioning iron gates for the local gentry, his skin was always tanned, summer and winter.

It wasn't only the excitement at seeing the sparks from the anvil that made Charlotte's blood sing every time she thought about him. She bent low over the handlebars of her bicycle now, remembering she had to give in the grocery order at Hallam's Food Supplies as soon as possible, before she let herself dream of a snatched half-hour with her young man.

She pedalled hard until she arrived at the town centre, where the small tower divided the narrow streets and where the hands of the clock-face had stopped permanently at half-past four. Some of the old lags said it was the exact time that a battalion of young Braydon lads had been wiped out at Ypres in the Great War, but that was something a young girl didn't care to think about.

Charlotte entered the shop, which was like an Aladdin's Cave with its hotchpotch of supplies from food to hardware goods. The shop had a special and not unpleasing aroma that came from such a mixture of goods, from ham on the bone to fresh-baked bread, to disinfectant supplies and shoe polish. Whatever you wanted, it was either here or Arnie Hallam could get it for you.

‘ ’Morning, Mr Hallam,’ Charlotte said cheerfully, smiling at one or two local matrons browsing around the shelves.

He beamed back at her, his chubby pink face, which Josie always likened to that of a prize porker, brightening at once.

‘ ’Morning, Carlotta,’ he said as usual, having once fancied himself as a bit of a ladies’ man with a penchant for the exotic. ‘And what can I do for my very favourite young lady on this lovely day?’

Charlotte grinned, taking no notice of his nonsense, even though they both heard the older ladies clicking their teeth in disapproval.

‘Just the weekly grocery order, thank you. Oh, and Dad says can the boy be sure to deliver it before teatime because we’ve got new people coming in today, and he doesn’t want to be unwrapping goods and putting them away while he’s greeting them.’

Hallam laughed. ‘Your dad was always a stickler for the niceties, and quite right too. You don’t get on in business without paying attention to details, my dear, and especially looking after your customers.’

Charlotte was thankful her sister Milly wasn’t here to hear this. She’d be sticking her ten-year-old nose right up in the air at the thought that a shopkeeper could be compared with a hotel owner. They were going to have to watch Milly, Charlotte thought fleetingly, or she'd be turning into a real little snob.

But she couldn't be thinking about her now. She was too anxious to get out of here and off towards the edge of the open moors, where Melvin and his father had their smithy. First of all she had to submit to Arnie Hallam going through every item on the Elkinses' grocery list, his fat finger running down each one with infuriating slowness, as if to keep her there as long as he could. She knew he was harmless. It was just his way, as everybody knew. They also knew that the minute his wife appeared from the back of the shop he'd be all efficiency, so Charlotte didn't blame him for what he called his little bit of naughtiness in smarming up to the lady customers.

'How's your grandmother, my dear?' he said chattily. 'Still going for her midnight walks along the sea front, is she? She'll catch her death of cold one of these nights, especially in her style of dress, if you get my meaning.'

Charlotte didn't miss the way the other customers were pressing a little nearer now, as if to catch any bit of gossip that they could pass on. Charlotte was very fond of her grandmother, despite her odd ways, and with these two old biddies trying to hear her every word, she felt suddenly defensive on Clover's behalf.

'I daresay it comes from living abroad all those years in a hot climate, when the nights were as hot as the days, and she still feels stifled by being indoors all the time,' she said sweetly. 'She's gone for a walk with Josie and Milly this morning, though, and she's so bundled up in clothes that you can hardly see her, poor love. I'm not really sure who's taking who.'

The women in the shop moved away, disappointed at not hearing anything more, and Arnie grinned at Charlotte.

'You're a good girl, Charlotte. It's good to see young 'uns caring about the old folk. I wish I had a granddaughter like you to look after me in my old age. If you're looking for a job by then, I'm sure we could come to some arrangement.'

She laughed as he winked, having seen his wife hovering behind him, although he was unaware of her as yet.

'I think Mrs Hallam might have something to say about that!' she said, and said hello to Laura Hallam swiftly, before she turned to leave the shop with a small sense of relief. It wasn't that he meant anything, and she knew that, but sometimes he gave her the creeps. She wondered if all men became mildly lecherous as they got older, and immediately knew it wasn't true. Her father hadn't done so but, then he had always had a houseful of women to keep an eye on him, she grinned. Arnie only had Laura and no children of his own.

She got on her bicycle again and cycled through the streets of the town and out to the lanes and the surrounding countryside. Braydon had the best of both worlds, with its coastline bordering the Bristol Channel and the small sandy beaches that attracted the holiday-makers; and the open countryside so near at hand with its many farms and rural pursuits. The nearest city was Bristol, but none of them cared to go there any more than they needed to. Once a country girl, always a country girl, thought Charlotte happily, feeling the breeze lift her hair, and the sun on her face.

Melvin Philpott considered himself a countryman, too. He would have hated a town job and rather despised those young men his own age who were content to be cooped up in an office just so they could draw their wage packet every Friday.

Melvin liked the unpredictability of his work, never knowing what job was going to turn up from day to day. It gave an air of excitement to it, and he could think of nothing better than to be working in the open smithy, shoeing a horse, which was far more skilled a job than many folk believed; or doing something as creative as making a weather vane to order; or just repairing something the way he was doing now, making the iron gates of the church look as good as new.

His father had instilled in him the pride in his craft, doing something that was unique in the area and never being short of work. A blacksmith was a respected member of the community and, as well as that, he had the good looks he'd inherited from his family.

Philpott senior had met Melvin's mother when she was nursing in France during the Great War and, when it ended, he'd brought her home to Somerset to marry her. His father had always been an impulsive and passionate man, and Melvin had inherited that, too, he thought, catching a glimpse of someone blonde and pretty heading his way on a creaking bicycle.

He paused for a moment, glad of a breather in the intense heat of the smithy, and walked outside into the fresh morning air.

'What brings you here today?' he greeted Charlotte, appreciating the way her yellow cotton dress clung to her firm young breasts, and how her fine blonde hair curled so softly around her face. She was a bit like sunlight herself, he thought, with a rare moment of poetry. 'I thought your father would have had you turning out bedrooms and sweeping floors ready for the next invasion of tourists.'

She laughed. 'I've been let off to send for the grocery order, so I thought I'd drop in to see you on my way home.'

'I doubt that he'd have thought it was on your way home, out here in the sticks. Do you want to go for a walk?'

'I can't stop long.'

'That's not what I asked,' Melvin said, his dark eyes bold. 'You didn't come here just to admire the view, did you?'

'All right. Just a little walk then.'

She didn't mean to be coy, and she wasn't normally. But she was shiveringly aware of the sheen of sweat on his powerful, bronzed arms right now. If she dared to admit it, she was a little scared of him when he looked like this, rather as she imagined a gladiator would look. Scared, and excited, too. Not that she ever thought he would ever hurt her. He was an honest young man and he respected her. It was almost herself that she was scared of; of the feelings he stirred up in her, the like of which she had never known before and didn't fully understand. There was no one she could ask about them, either. Not her father, and certainly not her mother, who thought all matters pertaining to the flesh, as she called it, were delicate and private.

Charlotte remembered how difficult it had been for Ruth to tell her eldest daughter about the facts of life a year ago, having considered it her duty to do so when Charlotte reached sixteen. It would be Josie's turn next, she thought with a grin, knowing how her sister would squirm, already thinking she knew enough. As for Milly ... she would probably know it all by instinct before she was twelve.

'You're miles away, love,' Melvin said, catching hold of her hand as they walked away from the smithy. 'Come back, wherever you are. This is what you came for, isn't it?'

He had been wheeling her bicycle for her

and, as they reached the narrow lane bordered by hedges, he dropped the machine and pulled her into his arms. The next moment he was kissing her mouth and her arms were winding around him, regardless of the state her dress would be in by the time she went home.

'How was that then?' he said with a smile, moving slightly back so that he could look down into her eyes. She could feel the strength in every part of his body, and she felt herself blush, knowing exactly what she was feeling.

'Lovely,' she stammered.

She knew his next move would be to let his hand rest lightly on her bosom. He never did more than that, and she wasn't sure that she wanted him to. It felt daring enough that she allowed him to do it, remembering how her scarlet-faced mother had impressed on her that it was a young girl's duty to keep her body to herself and to remain chaste for marriage. Though it was surely not heading for damnation to let a young man that she loved put his hand over her bosom while her dress and petticoat and bodice provided such a barrier between them, Charlotte thought.

But before he could make such a move they heard his father's bellow, carrying on the breeze towards them.

'Melvin, where the hell have you got to, boy? You know damn well the vicar needs this work done by this afternoon.'

Melvin grimaced. His hand, that had been

straying already towards Charlotte's breast, dropped reluctantly now.

'No peace for the wicked, eh?' he said with a grin. 'Will you be able to get out tomorrow afternoon, or will your slave-drivers be getting at you, too?'

'They're not slave-drivers, but I don't really know how busy we'll be with the new people coming in to the hotel,' Charlotte said.

Melvin shrugged his shoulders. 'Oh, well, if you're out and about, I'll see you by the memorial at the beach. If not, another time.'

She spoke quickly. 'I'm sure it'll be all right. I'll do my best, anyway.'

And if she didn't, she had no doubt there would be other girls walking up and down the sea front on Sunday afternoon, ready to catch the roving eye of the brawny young blacksmith. She wished she could be as sure of him as she pretended to be to her sister, but she wasn't, and that was the truth of it.

He gave her one last rough kiss and shot off to do his father's bidding, while Charlotte tried not to notice the dirty marks on her dress as they separated. She'd be in for a tongue-lashing if she didn't manage to change it before her parents saw it and guessed where she had been, and with whom.

Her sister Josie was just as frustrated. Walking the sea front with an old lady who didn't seem to be there half the time was bad enough, even though Milly was keen enough to listen to her daft old tales, despite how she pretended otherwise. Probably to write them all up in that school exercise book of hers, Josie thought scornfully, with the idea that she was going to be a famous writer and make her fortune.

Josie was as fond of her gran as any of them, even though she could be such an embarrassment at times. Even her dad had to admit that, on the nights when they'd had to go looking for her, wandering along the sea front in next to nothing. Well, not quite. At least, she usually wore a nightgown and dressing-gown, Josie conceded, and sometimes a winter coat and hat as well, but it was hardly the way a sane and elderly woman was expected to behave.

'What's going on in that busy young head of yours, Josie?' Clover asked. 'I've asked you a couple of times if you want to run on and buy some sweets from the beach kiosk with Milly, but you haven't bothered to answer.'

Josie scowled. 'I'm not a child, Clover, and I don't want to run on and buy sweets! Let Milly go if she wants to.'

As usual Milly took the money and ran. She wasn't so sophisticated yet that she was going to refuse a treat from her gran, and Josie felt a hand on her arm.

'You're not a child, my love, but you're not quite a woman yet, either. Is that part of the trouble?'

Sometimes Clover seemed to live in a world of her own, and sometimes, Josie thought savagely, she saw far too much.

'Perhaps,' she said sulkily. 'Oh, I don't know, but I do know that I get fed up with always cleaning and waiting on tables.'

'Charlotte does it as well, and she doesn't complain.'

'So where is she now then? She was sent off to put in the grocery order, and I'll bet that's not the only place she's gone.'

'Your sister is a young woman,' Clover said, starting to pant a little as Josie's footsteps gathered speed to match her annoyance. 'But if you don't slow down, I shall probably expire on the spot and then you and Milly will have the job of carrying me back to the hotel. At least that'll give you something else to do, though I don't imagine your father will be too pleased at having a corpse on his hands on his busiest day of the week.'

Josie stopped abruptly, nearly falling over her own feet in her haste as she grabbed at Clover's arm.

'Don't say such things, Gran! It's bad luck, and you're good for a hundred years yet.'

Clover laughed at her dismayed expression. 'Well, seeing as I'm well over three-quarters of the way there already, I'm not doing too badly, am I? Come on, you goose, I'm not ready for my box yet and I was only joshing.'

'It's not a good thing to joke about your own death,' Josie muttered. 'There was a play on the wireless a couple of weeks ago where this man foretold his death, and then it happened, just the way he said it would.'

She shuddered at the memory, wishing it

would go away. But Clover looked healthy enough, she thought, eyeing her carefully as they walked more slowly to where Milly was rushing back to them now.

'If you don't stop inspecting me sideways, Josie, I shall begin to think you're wishing me away, and wondering just how long I've got left before I go to meet my Maker in the great beyond,' Clover commented, making her jump.

'I wasn't doing any such thing. And, even if I was, it's only because I love you. We all do,' Josie said clumsily, 'and we don't want anything to happen to you for years and years yet.'

Although it was blooming creepy how Clover seemed to read just whatever was going through a person's mind, Josie thought uneasily. Captain Bellamy, one of the permanent residents at the hotel, had once informed her that very old people could do that, as if they were already halfway to immortality. She shuddered again, willing the unwanted thoughts away and grabbing one of Milly's sweets without being offered.

Milly howled at once and began chasing her along the sea front, with Josie laughing. Anything to make her feel that this was just a normal day, without any ghoulish images about the future entering her mind.

Two

Melvin Philpott was pretty keen on Charlotte, even if he didn't think of her in exactly the same way that she thought of him. He wasn't ready to settle down yet, not by a long chalk, and if that meant that he saw nothing wrong in giving the glad eye to other girls, well, to his mind, that was the way young men were meant to behave. His father had certainly been of the same opinion, all those years ago in France, and if his mother hadn't been such a strong-willed character, Melvin was pretty sure his dad would still be footloose and fancy-free.

But Melvin admitted that it gave him a hell of a kick to think of Charlotte Elkins as his girl. The Elkins family was well thought of in Braydon, owning a hotel on a prime part of the sea front and all, and it didn't hurt his own smithying business to be well connected. If for no other reason, that made him cautious enough never to let his roving eye rove farther than was decent.

Maybe sometime next week, he thought, bending to his task over the church gate repairs now, he'd see if there was anything showing at the flea-pit, and take Charlotte to the flicks. She always liked that, and the back row of the smoky little cinema was tailor-made for courting couples.

Charlotte was humming to herself as she cycled home, knowing her parents would still be busy getting the rooms ready for the incoming guests, and hoping that she could slip upstairs and get out of her soiled dress before anyone saw her.

She had reckoned without the astute gaze of Captain Bellamy, the ex-military gentleman who had now made The Retreat his home or, as he liked to refer to it, his permanent billet.

'Ho, ho, now, little lady, what have you been up to? Been in the wars, have we?' he said in his blustering voice.

'Something like that, Captain,' Charlotte replied, following his lead. 'I had a bit of a tumble, but I'm not hurt. If you'll excuse me I'll go and change before anyone else sees the state I'm in.'

'That's right,' he said, tapping the side of his nose. 'Mum's the word, eh?'

She moved neatly away from him. Her dress was really only a bit grubby, but trust him to notice it, with his stiff attention to highly polished shoes and always dressing smartly for dinner, and the regimented way he kept his belongings on his dressing-table.

'It comes from being an army man all his life,' Clover had told her approvingly. 'We should be thankful that he's a very clean gentleman. We couldn't be doing with having layabouts in the house. We're fortunate in our regulars.'

It wasn't only for that reason that Clover approved of the word 'regular', either. Clover liked anything military, especially chaps in uniform, she had once told her giggling granddaughters airily. Her own husband, whom the young Elkins girls never knew, had been a regular soldier, finally serving in the Boer War. They had all heard many times how Clover was immensely proud of the way he had died for his country, even though he had left her widowed with a young son, Donald.

In the safety of her own room now, Charlotte felt a great affection for Clover, living half in the past and half in the present. She had to agree that they were fortunate in their regulars at the hotel, even if sometimes it seemed as if the young girls were surrounded by old folk. Clover never considered herself one of them, of course, Charlotte thought with a grin, easily ignoring the fact that she herself was an octogenarian.

But what with the Captain and the two elderly spinsters, the Misses Hester and Daphne Green, who made up the rest of their permanent guests, it was always a breath of fresh air to the Elkins girls when younger guests booked into the hotel, especially the youngish sales rep who came for a few days every three months.

She wondered what these people would be like who would be arriving this afternoon. All anyone knew was that they were a Mr and

Mrs Parker from Gloucester. Milly had gone around gleefully singing about a Doctor Foster who came from Gloucester, and been told on pain of a hiding never to breathe such a thing in front of their guests.

Charlotte hoped they would be young but knew that they probably wouldn't. Braydon was a pleasant but rather staid seaside town with a sea front that had a wide promenade, several small sandy coves, a war memorial and a Victorian pier that was only of interest to birds and fishermen. It was a place that seemed to attract retired and elderly people.

Apart from the usual shops and a couple of churches and schools, there was little night-life. There were a few pubs, a dancehall and a tiny theatre for local productions and one small cinema that opened spasmodically. No wonder so many young people wanted to move away to Bristol and even farther afield. Charlotte never did. She had been to Bristol a couple of times and hated the brashness of the city and, besides, she would be too far away from Melvin if she ever left Braydon.

'Is that you, Charlotte?' she heard her mother call. She answered at once and ran downstairs, assuring her that the grocery order would arrive that afternoon.

'I can't think what took you so long,' Ruth said, eyeing her daughter. 'You could have gone to Bristol and back – or did you go somewhere not quite so far?'

Charlotte decided that evasion was the best reply. Melvin was welcome enough here, provided he didn't disrupt the smooth harmony of the hotel, she thought. Nothing was allowed to do that.

'It was too nice a day to rush about, and I'm here now, Mum, so what do you want me to do?'

'Put some fresh flowers in the Parkers' room, and make sure there are clean towels on their bed. Apart from that, you can help me get the lunch tables ready. Lord knows where Gran and the girls have got to now, and you know how the regulars like their salad on time on a Saturday.'

'The regulars like their food on time every day, don't they?' Charlotte muttered, thinking that when she had a home of her own, her life was never going to be regimented by mealtimes the way a hotel was. It must be wonderful to eat when you wanted to, and sleep when you were tired, and never even have a clock in the place! Her mother never seemed to mind it, though, and her dad and Captain Bellamy were practically two of a kind in that respect.

Charlotte wasn't really cut out to be a rebel – not the way her sister Josie could very well turn out be – but there were times when she wondered what it must be like to live in a house that didn't have a succession of outsiders expecting to be waited on – and regulars who were probably going to live out theirs days here. And then there would be other formalities to deal with, she thought with a shudder.

It was a gloomy prospect, and one that a seventeen-year-old girl didn't care to dwell on too much. She turned her thoughts to Melvin instead. When he proposed marriage to her, she would be away from this drudgery for good.

'Can I get away tomorrow afternoon, Mum?' she said swiftly, before she let herself think that it might not be when, but if. 'Just for an hour or so, anyway.'

Ruth considered her daughter, noting her flushed cheeks, and the way her body was rounding out so attractively, and she didn't need three guesses to know exactly where she had been to make her come rushing back all of a fluster.

'Are you seeing that boy?'

'He's not *that boy*. He's Melvin Philpott, as you know very well. I thought you liked him. Dad doesn't have any objections to him, and that's a miracle, if you like. Melvin's a responsible young man with good manners, and he comes from a well-respected family—'

'For goodness' sake, Charlotte, I don't want to interview him for a job! I have met the boy, remember, and I like him well enough. I would just ask you to be careful, that's all.'

'Careful?'

She didn't twig for a moment, and then she saw her mother's face redden. The memory of the times when Melvin had pressed his hand so lightly on her breast, and the turbulent feelings the small movements of his fingers had produced in her, sent a flood of colour to her own cheeks.

'I see that you know what I mean, Charlotte, so I don't need to say any more, do I? It's a fact of life, though, that a young man has certain urges that need to be kept in check, and a young lady needs to be aware of the need for modesty at all times. It's not wise to be alone with him any more than necessary. Just remember that, and remember the reputation of your family and the hotel.'

Listening to her mother's halting speech that held such embarrassment at having to say such things aloud, Charlotte thought wildly that Victorian values hadn't died along with the old queen at the turn of the century. They were alive and well in Ruth Elkins and The Retreat. And then she saw the slight distress in her mother's eyes and felt a wealth of love for her, and the way that she was a product of her own times, just as Charlotte was. Impulsively, she gave her mother a hug.

'I'll never let you down, Mum,' she said swiftly.

And, just as swiftly, she knew there were things that went on between a young man and a young woman that she was just as eager to explore.

Clover had finished telling her two granddaughters about the time she and their grandfather had lived in South Africa, and of the dramatic day when they had escaped the hands of the Boers by the skin of their teeth. The graphic descriptions of dark-skinned men holding knives between their teeth, shrieking and bellowing blue murder while they rained terror on the British battalion had had Milly goggle-eyed for more than ten minutes.

'She makes half of it up,' Josie mouthed to Milly, when Clover finally paused for breath. 'Dad never talks about it, does he?'

'I do not make half of it up! In any case, your father was at school in England at that time, but if you girls had lived half the life that I have, you'd know better than to scoff at your elders,' Clover said smartly.

'Well, fat chance we've got of that, Gran, stuck here in dreary old Braydon.'

'It's not dreary at all. There are wonderful sunsets over the water every evening, and when it's not raining you can see the coast of Wales. It's almost like being abroad, though it couldn't ever compare with living in a hot country, of course,' she went on dreamily.

Both girls hooted with laughter now, and she frowned. 'All right, so what would you like to do with your life, Josie? You know your parents need you all to be part of running the hotel, and it's a good and honest profession.'

'What, waiting on other people for ever more? I don't think so, Clover. I'd quite fancy running away to join the circus – or the annual fair. That would be an exciting life, and I'd have thought you'd approve of that.'

Clover gave a wry smile. 'Maybe I would, but don't tell your mother I said so. Maybe there's a lot more of me in you than I give you credit for, Josie.'

'Cripes, I hope not! I don't want to end up a dippy old bat,' Josie said in mock horror, and then wheeled away from her grandmother and Milly, who was clinging to her arm, to go racing back along the sea front towards the hotel.

'Cheeky young madam,' Clover said, but her lips twitched all the same.

Milly looked at her curiously. 'Did you ever want to join the circus, Clover?'

'No, but I can understand what wanderlust means.'

'What does it mean?'

Clover got that sweet, dreamy look on her face again that some thought was charming and others considered to be cuckoo.

'It means the way you can't settle in one place, Milly. Military men have to have it when they're sent to faraway places to fight for king and country, of course. And army wives discover that either they've got it or they haven't.'

'Did you have it?'

'Oh, yes,' Clover said. 'I'd have followed your grandfather to the ends of the earth. We had some fine old adventures together, Milly.'

Her face clouded a little. The fine old adventures were all in her head now. They were in her dreams, too, and sometimes she could still hear her Tommy, still see his handsome face and his upright military figure beckoning her to join him in some wicked lark or other.

These young 'uns knew none of it, she thought, her throat catching with a rare moment of scorn; none of the excitement, the danger, the comradeship and the *love*, for each other and for their country, that they all shared in those dangerous times.

'You've gone away again, Gran,' she heard Milly say crossly.

She squeezed the girl's arm and gave a laugh. 'So I have, love, but only for a little while. I'm back now.'

One day, she thought cheerfully, *I'll go to meet my Tommy in one of our secret places and I won't be coming back at all. I'll miss you all, of course, but I'll have the joy of being with my Tommy again – for ever and ever, amen.*

She felt a small pang for the day that must surely come eventually, when she would have to leave her family and begin the final, greatest adventure of all. Donald and Ruth were such a self-contained and well-adjusted pair, and she knew that they would do their dutiful and loving mourning at her passing, and move on.

There was no sense of morbidity in these thoughts. Death was as natural as breathing, except in the case when a man was cut down years before he was ready, the way her brave and stalwart Tommy had been.

Leaving the girls would be a wrench, though. Charlotte was on the brink of becoming a woman, with all the problems and delights and fulfilment that it entailed; Josie had all the makings of a wild one, and Clover couldn't deny that she felt more than a certain empathy with that. Hadn't she wanted to spread her wings and fly away too? Hadn't being with Tommy allowed her to achieve that? Hadn't wherever he had been sent in the cause of duty been the most wonderful part of her long life?

And then there was Milly. Clover gave a soft, indulgent sigh. Milly was a bright, intelligent child who could go far, provided she didn't let her thirst for knowledge make her unbearable for the rest of them to live with.

Clover had never flinched from the unpredictable, even though she had been urged eventually to settle here in Braydon with her remaining family. But when you were growing old, the most amazing, unpredictable time in a person's life was the moment when it was all over, even if the young 'uns would never understand such a thought, and she knew they would think her completely crazy if she ever voiced it aloud. Clover didn't mind in the least being thought eccentric. In fact she revelled in it. It was better that being a doddery old soul sitting in an armchair and staring at the waters of the Bristol Channel all day.

But right now, seeing Milly's frown at realising that Clover wasn't *quite* back with her again, she decided she had thought about the greatest adventure of all for long enough for one day.

'Let's go back and see what your mother's prepared for lunch,' she said breezily, knowing that this was the *most* predictable thing for a Saturday.

Josie didn't consider herself a bad girl. She just didn't want to be forever at the beck and call of strangers (well, the regulars weren't that any more); nor did she want to think about a future when one or other of them would die and make room for another one, welcomed by her parents. They were their bread-and-butter guests, her mother always said, and must be treated with respect. The summer visitors came and went, but the regulars were part of the substance of the hotel.

To Josie, at fifteen, it was just an endless cycle of work. She had liked being petted by the older guests when she was younger, but she found them cloying now with their constant repetitions and dreary reminiscences. Her mother had infinite patience in listening to their stories but, guiltily, Josie knew that all she wanted was to break away and be free, even if she wasn't fully sure exactly what she meant by that, either.

She felt a sudden lurch in her heart. Last summer, when the fair had made its annual visit to Braydon in one of the fields on the edge of the moors, she had met a dashing young chap who worked on the Dodgem cars. She had been mesmerised by the way he leapt on and off the moving cars with their sparks flying, and by the smell of rubber so pungent in her nostrils.

'Do you want a go, love?' he'd called out to her. 'I'll give you a free one, if you like, providing you tell your mates how exciting it is.'

She didn't have any mates in the way he meant it. She doubted that her sister Charlotte would deign to have a go, and Milly wasn't allowed to go to the fair on her own.

'You never know who you're going to meet there, and there could be some unsavoury types, so you must be careful,' Donald always warned his daughters, which only made Josie keener than ever to know what these unsavoury types were going to be like, and what was so dangerous about them.

Until then, all she had seen were hard-working chaps with their shirtsleeves rolled up to reveal strong brown arms and cheery voices as they called out to each other and to customers. They lived in caravans that travelled with them, along with huge painted fair wagons. There were women in gaudy clothes and ragged children running about the place as well, and it all conjured up a world that to Josie was excitingly exotic.

And then she had met Tony. He was older than herself, with a muscular figure, dark, bold eyes and curly black hair, and he was in charge of the Dodgem cars. She had accepted his offer of a free go and was thrilled when he sat down beside her to show her how to steer the car, his body pressing against hers as they swerved around the course with herself screaming with laughter. Then she had thrilled again at the sight of him leaping out of the car to swing on the rim before jumping from car to car to assist other paying customers.

Right from that first moment, Josie had fancied herself in love, but it was something she never dared to tell anyone, except her diary and, even then, it was mostly in a code that only she could understand. She had gone to the fair every day that it was here in Braydon last year, and finally a swarthy man with a heavy accent she couldn't understand began to tease her.

'Take no notice. That's just my dad,' Tony told her easily.

'Is he foreign?'

Tony laughed. 'He's Italian, like me. I'm really Antonio – you know, like in the song.'

Josie didn't know, but it intrigued her even more to think that Tony was part of a Italian family. Antonio ... his name was dreamy, and nothing like the boring names of the English boys she knew. On the last night before the fair moved on, she daringly asked him if he'd write to her and was rudely disappointed.

'Much better not, love. We're always on the move, and I don't have much time for letter writing. Besides, you're only a kid, and you should be mixing with kids your own age.'

'I'm over fourteen!' she had said, mortified that he should think her so far beneath him.

'And I'm eighteen. I'm damn sure your daddy wouldn't like you mixing with somebody so old – nor a fairground chap, either,' he added, a gleam in his eyes that reminded Josie of just what some of the townspeople thought of these rough chaps who came once a year – even if they did bring money and visitors to the town.

He saw the recognition on her face and nodded briefly. 'Never mind. Next year you'll be another year older, and who knows? See you around, kid.'

And now she was another year older, taller and rounder than the gawky kid she had been then, and in a month's time the fair wagons and caravans would be trundling towards the moorland field again, ready to set up hoop-la stalls and merry-go-rounds, and ice-cream and toffee-apple stalls, and Dodgem cars. And Josie would be there, wearing her best dress, looking out for Tony, and making sure he was looking out for her, too.

But right now she had better made tracks for home. She had left Clover and Milly far behind, knowing how Clover liked to dawdle to watch the antics of every dog, and to chat to its owner as if she knew them personally. She did know most of them, Josie thought, and they certainly knew her. Few of the dog-walking folk and everyone else could miss the colourful figure that Clover Elkins made.

She had to concede that at least Milly wasn't such a snob that she was embarrassed to accompany Clover on her walks, no matter how much of a token protest she habitually made. Milly loved her gran, as they all did, and Josie knew how much she really loved her daft old stories, too.

But now she had to help her mother and

Charlotte see to the midday meals for the regulars, even though Saturday's cold meat, salad and boiled potatoes was the easiest meal of the week to prepare. New guests never arrived until late afternoon. It was one of the rules of the hotel, to give the owners breathing-space and to get the bedrooms clean and ready.

The Retreat had its own set of rules, the way every hotel did. Guests were offered a cooked breakfast, plus toast and home-made preserves. Except for Saturdays, which was change-over day, there was a substantial hot meal at midday, which Donald insisted on calling lunch and not dinner; and high tea at six o'clock. Routine meant harmony, according to Donald and Ruth, and it never altered, but it was one of the things that the two older daughters of the house were starting to feel trapped by.

Milly wasn't bothered by it yet. She frequently confided grandly to Clover than when she was older, she had no intention of being a skivvy like Charlotte and Josie, which always resulted in a sharp rebuke from her grandmother.

'Working in a family-run hotel is an honourable profession, and a matter of pride, Milly,' Clover had said severely. 'Your parents can hold their heads up high in this town. Their names are well respected in Braydon.'

Milly always pouted at this. 'You didn't stay put in one place all your life, did you, Gran? Didn't my granddad have an honourable profession, then, and hold his head up high wherever you travelled?'

Clover laughed. 'You little minx. Don't put on that innocent air with me. We're talking about a very different kind of life, and a different age. Be thankful that because of men like my Tommy we live in a far safer world now. Your dad knows all about that, too. He did his bit in the Great War, don't forget. We should be thankful that such troubles are far behind us and enjoy the peaceful life.'

Mentally, she crossed her fingers as she spoke, knowing that to a ten-year-old, such things needed to be said; even though, in her heart of hearts, Clover had never been the type of woman to settle for the peaceful life. She had gloried in following Tommy wherever he was sent, sharing in the danger and the thrill of it all.

It wasn't the done thing to admit to this eager-eyed child that one of the pleasures of old age was that, in her heart and in her head, she could still go there.

Three

As preparation for her future career as a writer, Milly Elkins liked to weave stories about the hotel's prospective guests. The couple arriving that day, a Mr Kenneth and Mrs Elizabeth Parker, were no exception. She pictured them as young and fashionable, and never too busy to chat to somebody aged ten years and a bit. They would lead glamorous lives, probably in show business, and they might even offer her all sorts of openings as a child actress. At that point, her future ambitions might well change direction.

As Milly jotted down her thoughts in her exercise book, her fantasies ran away with themselves as usual, even though she knew that her own images of the new guests were destined to be totally wrong. Like most of them, they would probably be retired people, elderly and grey haired, and more inclined to chat with Clover and the Captain, and the Misses Green than to her. If they spoke to her at all, it would be as a pet more than a confidante, she thought, scowling.

The afternoon train pulled into the branch line of Braydon station at three forty-five precisely. Amongst the alighting passengers, the elegantly dressed couple in their late forties was immediately spotted by the porter, who took hold of their suitcases and ushered them outside to the station taxi.

'Where to, sir?' the porter asked, ready to give instructions to the driver.

'The Retreat Hotel,' the gentleman said. 'Do you know it?'

The driver smiled. 'Everybody knows The Retreat, sir and madam. 'Tis the best hotel on the sea front if that's what you're wanting, providing you don't get blown away by the winds and spray when the tide's up.'

'That's exactly what we do want,' Kenneth Parker said easily.

He gave the porter a nod and assisted his wife into the car. In a few minutes it was on its way through the town and down to the winding beach road where The Retreat was situated.

'Is this your first time in these parts, sir and madam?' the driver asked, eyeing them through his mirror and making his own assessment.

'It is,' Kenneth replied pleasantly, giving nothing away.

'You'll find it a mite quieter than where you're from, I daresay,' the man persisted. 'Have you come far?'

'Far enough to be glad of some time to relax after the journey,' Kenneth said, still telling him precisely nothing. With years of discretion behind him, a solicitor knew how to do that without seeming to be discourteous.

The skill with which he could outwit the most probing of questioners was a game he'd learnt long ago, and this man was no more than an amateur.

'Here we are, then,' the driver said reluctantly, finally realising he'd got nothing to report to his mates at the Dog and Whistle that evening.

The couple stepped out of the taxi, breathing in the very welcome sea air after the stuffiness of the train journey. Kenneth paid the driver his due and added a generous tip for his trouble, which satisfied the man.

'Thank goodness for that,' Elizabeth Parker murmured when the suitcases had been deposited outside the taxi and the man had driven away. 'I began to think we were in for the Spanish Inquisition.'

Kenneth laughed. 'You forget my training, my dear. Fending off unwanted questions is part of my business.'

'But not by appearing so mysterious that it makes people think there's something we have to hide,' she replied.

'If it pleases you, I'll unburden all our recent troubles on our fellow guests.'

'Please don't, Kenneth,' his wife said hurriedly, as a portly man came out of the hotel to greet them.

'Welcome, Mr and Mrs Parker,' Donald said with a smile. 'Come inside and I'll show you to your room. I hope you had a pleasant journey, and I daresay you'll want to freshen up first of all, and then my daughter will send up a complimentary tray of tea to your room.'

In the kitchen, Donald reported to his wife and daughters that the lady looked very frail and wan, and his guess was that she had been ill recently.

'Can I take up the tea tray?' Milly asked eagerly.

'No, you can't,' Charlotte told her at once. 'The last time you did it, you spilled it, and it didn't create a very good first impression.'

Milly snapped back. 'Oh, you're just as fuddy-duddy as most of the guests.'

'And you should learn to keep such remarks to yourself,' her sister said sharply, knowing that being fuddy-duddy was the last way that Melvin Philpott thought about her; and that the older this little madam got, the more she needed keeping in check.

If any of the guests had heard Milly, though, it would put the hotel in a very bad light and, even if she herself sometimes felt she wanted to do something different, she was always loyal to her family.

'Give it fifteen minutes, and then take up the tray, dear,' her mother told her, refusing to intervene in any squabbles between her daughters.

'What are they like, Dad?' Charlotte said, wishing that her mother would be a bit more assertive when Molly needed it.

'Well, I'd say he's a business person, maybe even a doctor.'

'That'll come in handy with the oldies, then,' Milly muttered.

'He won't be a doctor,' Ruth pointed out, ignoring her. 'He registered as Mr Parker, not Doctor Parker, remember.'

'How old then?' Charlotte went on.

'Good Lord, I don't know how to calculate people's ages. That's the kind of thing you females do. As long as they pay their bill, it makes no difference, does it?'

Clover had been sitting quietly in a window seat all this time, but from there she had had a clear view of the arrival of the taxi.

'They're about your mum and dad's ages, Charlotte,' she said now.

'Oh, ancient,' Milly said cheekily.

Ruth looked at her, finally exasperated. 'Don't you have something to do, Milly, instead of annoying everybody? Go and write something.'

Milly flounced out. 'I have to go for my piano lesson soon, and I *don't* want company,' she added, seeing Clover begin to move.

'Leave her, Mother,' Ruth advised. 'She's growing up, and we all have to make allowances.'

Charlotte bit her tongue with an effort until she saw that Josie was doing the same, and they burst out laughing together.

Charlotte paused outside the bedroom door and knocked gently. She couldn't be sure but she thought she could hear crying, and the last thing she wanted was to witness an embarrassing situation between their new guests. Kenneth Parker opened the door a crack and took the tray from Charlotte, even though it was one of her duties to take it inside and offer to pour for them.

She reported everything to her family in the kitchen, glad that Milly was no longer there, or she'd have had the man stabbing his wife and planning to throw her body into the sea. And if she didn't stop herself thinking such daft things, she'd end up as dippy as Milly – or as crazy as Clover, Charlotte thought uneasily.

'I'll collect the tray later,' Clover said at once. 'If the lady's of a nervous disposition, it may reassure her to see an older person. Going away from home for a spell can sometimes affect people in strange ways.'

'Well, she should know,' Josie said in an aside to her sister. 'She'll either reassure her or make her think she's come to a madhouse.'

'I might be daft, but I'm not deaf, Josie, dear,' Clover told her pleasantly.

'Sorry, Gran.'

'And it's *Clover*. How many more times do you need to be told?'

'I think it's time we made ourselves scarce as well,' Charlotte said hastily, seeing the sparks threatening to fly between the two of them. 'You don't need us for anything now, do you, Mum?'

'No, providing the dining-room's set up for high tea.'

The girls escaped to their bedroom. It was

one of their bugbears that, because of where they lived, the main part with the hotel's best rooms had to be kept for visitors, while the family used the extension to the original building. Clover and Milly had had a dividing partition erected in one of the larger bedrooms, so that they could have some privacy, but the two older girls were obliged to share. At least there were separate bathrooms for the guests and the family, to everyone's relief. (In more ways than one, Milly sometimes said daringly.)

'So how's the great romance?' Josie said, flopping down on her bed with her hands behind her head. 'Has old Melvin got frisky yet?'

'For goodness' sake, Josie, don't let Dad hear you saying such things!'

'Why not? He spends so much time with horses some of their antics are bound to rub off on him.'

Charlotte glared at her. 'Sometimes you can be as childish as Milly.'

'And you can be as pompous as Dad. So *has* he?'

Josie had sat up on her bed now, her long brown hair falling over her shoulders, her eyes eager to find out just how far Charlotte had gone with her glamorous blacksmith. Despite the question, Josie looked so young and so desperate to know *what went on* between lovers that Charlotte could only grin back at her. The thought of her and Melvin being *lovers,* too, was enough to make her blush, because of course they weren't. And, of course, they wouldn't be!

'You don't want to be thinking about such things, Josie—'

'And if you say *at your age*, I shall hit you! I bet he's kissed you, anyway, hasn't he? What was it like? Was it like the way they do it at the pictures?'

'Good Lord, of course not.'

'So he *has* done it, then!' Josie said, catching her out. 'You've got to tell me everything now.'

'No, I haven't,' Charlotte said crossly. 'And all right, he's kissed me once or twice, and it's nice, and quite different from the way Mum and Dad kiss us.'

'And Clover, too, I'll bet,' Josie said with a grimace. 'One of these days I swear she'll suck us right away with those gums of hers.'

Charlotte threw a pillow at her. 'Don't be so mean. She can't help it if she's only got a few teeth left, poor old love. So will you at her age.'

Josie shivered. 'I hope I never get to her age, then. I plan to die when I'm about forty, before I go to seed.'

'That's plain silly. You'd have Mum and Dad ready to pop their clogs now, then, would you? And that nice Parker couple, too.'

Josie's attention switched at once. 'What do you make of them, Charlie? Is she consumptive, do you think? She's thin enough.'

'I don't know, and it's none of our business.

But you can bet your life that if there's anything to discover about her, Clover will do it. I often think what a great spy she'd have made.'

The imagery of it made them start to giggle all over again, and then they were hurling pillows at one another, as madcap as Milly in those moments.

The new guests and the regulars made their passing acquaintance over high tea. By then Clover had reported that Mrs Parker had recently suffered a nervous breakdown, following a bereavement in the loss of her twin brother at sea.

'How do you do it, Clover?' Josie said admiringly, trying to avoid Charlotte's attempts to stifle her laughter at this unexpected piece of information.

Donald put in a stern word. 'She does it because she's nosey, and you girls should put such knowledge out of your minds. What goes on amongst the guests is none of our business. They come here for a holiday or a rest, and that's all we need to know about them.'

'Don't you ever get curious, though, Dad?' Charlotte asked. 'One of these days we could be harbouring a mass murderer for all we know, and you'd be glad enough then that Clover did her little bit of nosing.'

'Well said, dear,' Clover said, nodding.

'I think the pair of you have got a bit of Milly-itis to be saying such daft things,' he snapped. 'I might have expected such nonsense from Clover, but not from you, Charlotte.'

Charlotte felt herself flush, hating to be censured in this way in front of everybody, and she snapped back.

'Well, it's true, isn't it? We don't know what kind of people book into hotels. They don't have to tell us anything about themselves and, even if they did, how would we know if they were telling the truth?'

'That's enough, Charlotte. I thought we had only one teller of fairy tales in the family, but it seems we have two. Now please see if the guests have come down to the dining-room, and you girls start serving tea before I lose my patience.'

Charlotte strode off, none too pleased at the way this day was turning out. When she was married with a home of her own, she thought again, there would be none of this being at every stranger's beck and call. She would cook and clean for her husband, because that was what a good wife did, but that was all.

'You hit a nerve there, Charlie,' Josie whispered, close behind. 'I've overheard Clover say the very same thing in that weird way of hers, and Dad always gets furious with her when she does so. He'll start to think we're all going looney if you don't watch out – all except me, of course.'

'Well, Clover's getting old, and old people are entitled to say weird things, but I don't want to say anything more about it. They're all downstairs now, and it's time we made a start in the dining-room with the smoked haddock before Mum's ready with the apple pie, or that'll be wrong as well.'

She was definitely out of sorts that day, Charlotte decided, and for no really good reason. The fact that Melvin sometimes seemed more offhand than an ardent sweetheart was probably her own fault, because she didn't allow him to make more than a token assault on her body. Her face flamed as the unexpected words came into her mind, because she had no intention of doing any such thing, now or ever.

'Are you feeling quite well, Charlotte, dear?' Miss Hester Green said, peering at her through her thick spectacles. 'You do look rather hot.'

'It's a hot day, Miss Green,' she said, flashing her a quick smile. 'I'm surprised you didn't spend a little time in the garden this afternoon.'

It would be far healthier for the two elderly sisters than sitting in their stuffy bedroom, just watching other people taking the air on the beach promenade. How narrow their world was, she thought, since they seemed to do little else except to occupy their days endlessly knitting garments that never seemed to be finished.

She realised that the new people were watching her, and she smiled automatically at Mrs Parker, thinking what an attractive lady she was. No mass murderer there then ... and then she stumbled a little, wondering exactly what a mass murderer actually looked like.

'Careful, my dear,' the Captain boomed. 'Can't have you falling over your pretty little feet, can we?'

Charlotte kept her smile fixed. Sometimes she loathed his patronising manner; but in an hotel you couldn't have the luxury of doing such a thing, except in your head. And that was the one place where nobody else could go.

'Just a little fish for me, my dear – Charlotte, isn't it?' Mrs Parker murmured now. 'I have a very small appetite.'

The Elkinses were quite used to the regulars having small appetites, but it seemed a crying shame to see a pretty lady picking at her food, while her husband evidently had no such problems.

'She's got lovely eyes,' Charlotte reported to her mother back in the kitchen. 'They're a sort of violet colour, and her husband seems so attentive, as if he's afraid she'll break.'

Clover spoke matter-of-factly. 'He's probably anxious. Nervous breakdowns can make a person very unpredictable. She can be happy and smiling one minute, and throwing china about the next.'

'Well, I certainly hope she does no such thing here,' Ruth exclaimed. 'And don't you go putting those ideas into Milly's head, Clover, or she'll be watching every move the poor lady makes.'

Clover sniffed. 'I've offered to sit with her

while her husband has his business meetings. The reason they've booked in for two weeks, and may possibly stay longer, is because this is a sort of working holiday for him, and he'll be going to Bristol on the train several times during each week.'

Charlotte laughed. 'How on earth do you get all this information, Clover?'

'It's like Dad said; because she's so nosey,' Josie said in a loud stage whisper. 'Either that, or she's a witch, and she puts a spell on people to make them tell her their secrets.'

Clover considered it. 'I rather fancy being a witch. Then I could banish certain cheeky young girls out of my sight whenever I felt like it.'

Josie gave her a quick hug, wishing she'd never mentioned such a thing. 'You know I don't mean it, Gran. You know I love you really.'

'Well, I still rather fancy being a witch,' Clover went on airily. 'Think of all the good I could do. Or the bad, if I was so inclined! In fact, I think I probably was one in a previous life.'

Donald was exasperated. 'What nonsense you talk, Mother! If you aren't going to help, I suggest you get out of the kitchen and let us get on with things.'

'Do you think she was joking?' Josie's voice came out of the darkness.

It was very late, and the girls had been in bed for some time. Everyone in the hotel would be asleep by now, and Josie's voice made Charlotte jump.

'For goodness' sake, what are you talking about?' she said crossly.

'Clover. Being a witch.'

'Of course not. She was having us on, that's all. You're as bad as Milly if you take any notice of it. Forget it and go to sleep.'

Josie was quiet for all of two minutes.

'All the same, she did say she thought she probably was one in a previous life, didn't she? Do you believe in all that stuff, Charlotte? About having lived as somebody else in a previous life, I mean.'

'I don't know. I suppose I might. But there's no way anybody can know for certain, so what's the point in worrying about it?'

'Oh, you're always so *sensible*. I wonder who I was,' Josie mused

'A gypsy, I daresay, since you take such a fancy to the fairground people. Now, *shut up* and let me go to sleep!'

Charlotte banged her pillow and turned her back on her sister. But having been woken so abruptly, she now found it was impossible to sleep. If Clover had once been a witch, and Josie had once been a gypsy, then what would she have been? A Puritan, perhaps, since Josie seemed to think she was so sensible ... And that was a laugh, since there was nothing puritanical or sensible in the way she felt about Melvin Philpott. Quite the reverse, in fact. If it wasn't that she knew her duty to her family, and the respect in the town that her parents set such great store by, she knew very well she could abandon herself to love, the way those women on the silver screen did, and in the trashy novels Clover liked to read.

Charlotte found herself smiling, remembering how scandalised her mother had been when she had first discovered how Clover enjoyed reading about handsome, dashing sheikhs in the desert, capturing innocent young English girls and whisking them off to their tents to have their wicked ways with them.

Precisely how far those wicked ways went was never fully described in the novels, of course, but it was enough to stir the imagination and, in the few that Charlotte had sneaked to read, they had been quite a revelation. And it was about all the information in that department that any of the Elkins girls was likely to get, she thought ruefully.

Inevitably, her thoughts became centred on Melvin. He was handsome and dashing, too. She imagined him astride a great Arab stallion, dressed in flowing robes, his face half hidden to keep out the worst of a desert storm, scooping her up in his arms and riding off with her to his desert lair. She would be helpless to do anything but his bidding ... whatever that was going to be.

'Are you all right, Charlotte? You're breathing so heavily that I thought you were ill. I haven't upset you, have I?'

'No, you haven't upset me, and I'm not ill,' Charlotte croaked. 'I must have been dreaming, that's all.'

She wrapped her arms around her body and closed her eyes tightly, trying to slow down her breathing and telling herself not to be alarmed by the strange and wondrous sensations rushing through her at the thought of being a willing slave at Sheikh Melvin's mercy.

The sea air was evidently doing Elizabeth Parker a lot of good, and as Kenneth could conduct much of his business in Bristol, the two-week holiday was extended to a month, to the satisfaction of all concerned. The room was available until then, when it would be needed for the annual visit of the sales rep. There were two other rooms available, for which there were bookings for July and August.

It became clear that Clover was making it her mission to keep a watchful eye on Elizabeth Parker, especially on the days when her husband took the train to Bristol and didn't return until late in the afternoon. What was more remarkable was that the lady didn't seem to mind at all, and even appeared to welcome the times when Clover joined her in the garden of the hotel, which was well screened from the sea front and the road by shrubs and trees.

Josie thought it was weird but, since the fair was coming into town at the beginning of June, she had too many other things to think about than wondering why someone so elegant should want to spend time with a dotty old lady.

Sunday afternoon was more blustery than of late, and Charlotte had a job to hold down her skirt as she sauntered along the beach as if she had no special reason at all for being there. Instead of which every nerve in her body seemed to be on high alert, watching out for Melvin. She had brushed her long fair hair until it shone, but she might as well not have bothered trying to impress him, she thought mournfully, as the breeze whipped it around her face, and the sparse patches of coarse sand amongst the pebbly beach flew up and stung the eyes of all the promenade walkers.

She blinked rapidly, trying to wash it out with the sudden rush of tears, and then she heard a voice beside her.

'You'd better let me help,' said Melvin. 'You're much too pretty to have those eyes going all red and blotchy.'

She noted the first part of the comment and tried to ignore the second. Red and blotchy was not the way she wanted to appear to him. After a minute or two with what seemed to be a none-too-clean corner of a handkerchief she blinked again and found that the specks of sand had gone.

'Thanks,' she breathed. 'I hate having anything in my eyes.'

'So do I, unless it's you.'

She giggled. For all his rough-hewn ways,

he could be unexpectedly charming when he wanted to, and she was madly in love with him. She admitted it freely to herself, even if she never dared to do so to anybody else, not even him.

'So where shall we go? Do you want to march along the sea front with the rest of the old biddies, or shall we find somewhere out of the wind?'

'What do you suggest?' Charlotte said, with her nerves jumping now. 'The garden of the hotel's fairly sheltered if you don't mind my grandmother peering at us through her window and making sure I'm behaving myself.'

Melvin laughed, tucking her hand inside his arm and squeezing her to him. She felt a flutter of alarm mixed with delight, because the action made them look so very much an established couple. Almost an *engaged* couple, she thought, with another heart flutter.

'I wasn't thinking of the garden of your hotel, Charlie. Let's take a walk around the hill. There are plenty of hollows out of the wind up there.'

'You know that, do you?' Charlotte said, a stab of jealousy running through her now as she wondered just *how* he knew it.

'Oh, I've been around the hill a few times in my life. Haven't you?' he said, mildly mocking.

'Well, of course I have. I've lived here all my life, and I know just about every inch of the town, same as you. That's not what I meant.'

'I know what you meant, and you shouldn't

be so daft. Do you think I'm in the habit of walking out with anybody but my best girl?'

She relaxed against him. 'Am I your best girl?' she asked provocatively.

'My *only* one,' Melvin said, believing it.

She giggled again. Her hands were suddenly clammy, and she had the strangest feeling that she was heading for the unknown ... which was completely stupid, since they were merely heading for the hill beyond the beach, where older people as well as courting couples often went on Sunday afternoons. This was what she had longed for: to be assured that she was Melvin's only girl, and that there was no reason at all to be nervous at the thought of being alone with him in a secluded grassy hollow.

It made her realise just how naive she really was in matters of the heart. She was as bad as Josie, thinking that it was all going to be the way the Hollywood pictures made it out to be, and imagining that Melvin was like one of those fictitious sheikhs of the desert. But that was all make-believe, and she didn't really have the faintest idea how to behave with a boy; or just what her mother's awkward words had meant about a boy getting certain urges that couldn't always be controlled.

She knew she would never get anything more out of her mother. If she tried asking questions, her mother would immediately think the worst – that her daughter was getting into bad ways – and Melvin Philpott would be banned from making any more contact with Charlotte.

'Are we going to walk in silence for the rest of the day?' Melvin said. 'That's the second time I've asked if you want to go to the fair with me one night.'

'Yes, of course I would,' she said hastily, seeing him begin to frown.

'That's all right then. You've been so quiet for the last few minutes I thought you were going off me or something – or going peculiar like your gran.'

'She's not peculiar,' Charlotte said at once, defending her. 'She's just old.'

'Old, and peculiar,' Melvin said with a grin. 'Let's face it, Charlie, she does do some odd things sometimes. Would you walk along the sea front in the middle of the night in your nightdress? Mind you, I wouldn't mind being around if you did!'

He was teasing, but Charlotte felt a sudden rush of warmth for Clover and her eccentric ways. It was bad enough that half the town knew of them, but she didn't need her own young man mocking her.

The sky had darkened, and as a sudden squall of summer rain sent people running for shelter, Charlotte shook off his arm and snapped at him.

'I don't want to talk about my gran. And I don't want to get soaking wet walking around the hill with you, either. I'm going home.'

She turned and raced back the way she had come, with tears and rain stinging her eyes. She knew she was behaving like a childish idiot as his angry voice reached her ears, but she had the certain feeling that she might also have saved herself from doing something she might have regretted.

Four

Josie was bubbling with excitement at the thought that once the fair arrived, she would be seeing Tony again, and that she was no longer the gawky young girl she had been a year ago. She was well past fifteen now and he had to see her as a presentable young woman and not as a kid. On the first night the fair was here, she howled in protest when Donald insisted she should take Milly with her.

'I don't want her tagging along, Dad!'

'Why not? Is there any reason you don't want to be seen with your sister?'

Milly looked at her innocently, and Josie wasn't sure how much she had seen in her diary about Tony. She didn't think she had written much about him that wasn't in her special code, but Milly could soon put two and two together, and she wouldn't put it past the little wretch to blab to her father if Josie didn't take her to the fair. It was silent blackmail, and there was nothing she could do about it.

'Why can't Charlotte take her?'

Charlotte spoke at once. 'I don't want to go to the blessed fair, that's why. I don't like all those smelly engines and that crush of people.'

'No, you'd rather be crushed by just one,' Josie muttered.

Milly perked up at this little snippet, and her father decided to put a stop to the arguments once and for all.

'Let me put it this way, Josie. Either you take Milly to the fair on this one evening, or you don't go at all. It's your choice.'

As far as Josie was concerned, there was no choice at all, so that evening the two of them made their way to the field that was now transformed into the raucous and colourful fairground. Tinny music blared out, filling the air with noise, and the excitement of the crowds pouring along the streets and lanes towards it was almost tangible.

'I won't be a bother, Josie,' Milly said, ' as long as you let me have a go on the Dodgems.'

'I don't know about that. They're a bit dangerous.'

'Well, you like them, and I'll be all right in the same car as you, won't I?'

The too-innocent way she said it told Josie that Milly knew very well why she liked the Dodgem cars, and she fumed at her carelessness in mentioning the fact in her diary, which was now under lock and key and well out of the way of small, prying eyes.

They merged into the crowd. And even though her heart was thumping, Josie made her way as casually as possible to where the Dodgem cars were. And then she saw him, just as black haired and lithe of body as she remembered him. He was leaping from car to car as they whizzed around the oval track, sparks flying, and the smell of rubber as sharply pungent as she remembered it.

'Is that him?' Milly said, hopping from foot to foot in her excitement. 'Is he the one?'

As if becoming aware of being watched, Tony turned and looked their way. His wickedly dark eyes widened as he caught sight of Josie, as if he was seeing somebody new and yet familiar at the same time. Then he smiled and gave her a wave.

'He's the one,' Josie said softly.

Charlotte hadn't seen Melvin since the day she had made such a idiot of herself on the sea front. By now he must think her a silly little girl, and she was too mortified to make any move towards seeing him again. He hadn't come near the hotel, and she had moped around for a few days until her father reprimanded her for her gloomy face.

'You're not being a good advertisement for the hotel, Charlotte. I don't want the guests to see you drooping about like this. At least try to put on a cheerful face when you serve them their food or you'll put them off their dinner.'

She gave a half-smile, not sure if this was intended as a joke or not, since her father rarely joked about anything to do with the blessed hotel. He treated it as his life's work, she thought resentfully, which she supposed it was, but that didn't mean everybody else had to see it in the same way.

'She's in love,' Milly said triumphantly.

'Oh, go back to your school books and don't be so silly,' Charlotte told her, slapping pastry down on the cold slab and kneading it as if she had somebody's throat beneath her fingers. 'You don't know what you're talking about.'

'Yes I do! Josie's in love too, with a fair-ground chap!'

'What's this?' Donald said at once. 'Are you making up stories again, Milly?'

'No, I'm not. Ask her if you don't believe me.'

They hardly needed to ask. Josie's face had gone a dull, furious red by now and, without saying another word, Donald had grabbed his middle daughter by the arm and marched her out of the kitchen to a place where he could have private words with her. They all knew that those words would be harsh. He wasn't a violent man, but his words could be just as wounding and vicious.

'You're a little sneak, Milly,' Charlotte hissed at her. 'That was a really mean thing to do.'

Milly tossed her plaits but had the grace to look shamefaced before she slammed out of the kitchen.

'I hate you all,' she yelled back.

Her mother spoke shakily. 'That girl has got

to learn some self-control before she gets very much older.'

Then, seeing the way that Charlotte was still bashing the pastry as if her life depended on it, and that it would result in a pie that was as hard as rock, Ruth put a restraining hand on the girl's shoulder.

'What's wrong, darling? Surely Milly's thoughtless remarks didn't really upset you so much?'

There was such a wealth of sympathy in her mother's voice at that moment that it was very tempting for Charlotte to blurt out everything that was in her heart, all her frustrations and indecisions, all her uncertainties at growing up and being aware of her own body. But she knew that the moment she spoke about something so personal and intimate, her mother's face would get that closed, embarrassed look on it again, and she would get nowhere.

'I just wish she didn't say things that are hurtful to other people. She comes out with it with no thought for other people's feelings. She's upset Josie more than me, anyway.'

She didn't intentionally turn her mother's attention away from what might be troubling herself, but that was the way it happened. Ruth's mouth tightened at once.

'I hope Josie is learning a stern lesson from her father right now. She's little more than a child herself, and she has no business cavorting with those fairground people. It doesn't do for the townsfolk to see one of our girls in such dubious company.'

Charlotte bent her head over her task, trying hard not to make some sharp remark that would upset her mother further. They all knew Milly was in danger of being a snob if she passed her scholarship exam, but she hadn't realised the extent of her mother's snobbishness, too. It wasn't as if The Retreat was such a wonderful hotel, despite its good sea-front position. It didn't always pay its way unless they had a succession of summer visitors, either, as Charlotte had overheard her parents saying on more than one occasion. In reality, they were no better than other tradesfolk in Braydon, so what did they have to boast about?

She had to find out more about Josie and this fairground chap, though, and from Josie herself, not that little sneak Milly, with her ambitions to go to the grammar school and her fancy piano lessons that only resulted in the family having to listen to her tortuous scales on their old piano.

But more important than that, Charlotte had already decided who she could ask about the business of falling in love and what it really entailed. There was one person who wouldn't flinch away from telling her the truth, and that was her gran. Clover had had a flamboyant life with her Tommy, and she revelled in telling tales of that life to anybody who would listen. The Misses Green and Elizabeth Parker had probably got thoroughly tired of them by now, Charlotte thought with a grin but, this time, she would be seeking Clover out with a mission of her own.

Like most of the regulars, Clover usually had a rest after dinner, and Charlotte made sure that Milly was safely out of the way before she followed her up to her bedroom. She didn't want any eavesdroppers on this important conversation.

'Can we have a chat, Clover?' she asked. 'If you're too tired and you think I'm being a nuisance, just say so.'

Clover's eyes brightened. 'I'm not in the least tired, my love. I only come up to my bedroom to get out of your mother's way, and because they think I should. You can't always do as you please when you get old, you know, but I do most of my thinking lying on my bed after dinner.'

That was rich, coming from somebody who had always done pretty well exactly as she pleased, and still did, thought Charlotte.

She sat on the edge of Clover's bed, while her gran moved over on top of the covers to give her room.

'What's troubling you, Charlotte? I know there's been something for the last few days, and it's high time you gave it an airing instead of bottling it up. It's not just that business between Josie and Milly, is it?'

'It's not them, it's me, although I suppose it has some bearing on what happened downstairs as well.'

She fidgeted with a corner of the candlewick bed cover, not quite knowing how to begin now that the moment had come. How did you ask an elderly relative how it really felt to be in love and, more importantly, what you were supposed to do about it?

'It's your young man, I suppose,' Clover stated. 'Has he been getting fresh?'

'Gran! I didn't know you knew such modern words.'

Clover sniffed. 'I wasn't born yesterday, dear, as you very well know, and the ways of men and women are the same today as they always were. Young men with an ounce of spunk in them will always try to take advantage of pretty young girls, and pretty girls will always worry about how far to let them go. Am I right?'

Charlotte blushed. 'Well, yes.'

'So how far has young Melvin Philpott tried to go? Or is it that he hasn't yet tried to go far enough for your liking?'

Charlotte was startled until she saw how Clover's eyes were twinkling, and realised that as well as trying to shock her, she was also trying to defuse the tension in Charlotte's body. She laughed out loud.

'You're being wicked now, aren't you, Clover? I haven't encouraged him, if that's what you mean.'

'That's not what I mean at all. You'd be no granddaughter of mine if you didn't feel your passions aroused when a handsome young man kissed you and pressed his body against you.'

Charlotte gasped now, because it was so exactly how she did feel whenever Melvin's arms went around her.

'Your mother will have told you to save yourself for marriage, of course, if she's told you anything at all, that is,' Clover went on.

'Well, of course!'

'Oh, well, of course, but you don't have to live like a nun when you find the person you want to share your life with, providing you've really found that person.'

'I have. I know I have. I think I have, anyway. But how can you really tell?'

Clover laughed now, seeing how flustered Charlotte was becoming.

'Well, now you're asking the impossible, so let's think about it. How does he make you feel? Like you can't see anyone else in the world when he's around? Like you feel you could create blue murder towards any other girl who even looks at him? Like you think of him and dream about him all the time? Like you miss him the minute you're parted? Like his face is always as close to you as your own hand, even when he's not beside you, and his voice is still in your head, as clear as day?'

Charlotte was listening intently, until she realised that Clover's voice had imperceptibly changed. It had become dreamy, almost singsong. She wasn't even looking at Charlotte any more, and those bright eyes were gazing somewhere in the distance to a place that was private and hers alone, or shared with someone unseen, except to her. Charlotte stood up at once, feeling almost choked.

'You're tired, Gran, and I've got things to do,' she said hurriedly, knowing that she must be thinking about her Tommy now, and not about Charlotte's problems at all. As she reached the door, Clover's voice reached her again.

'I was never Gran where Tommy was concerned. I was always his darling Clover. His one and only. Remember that, Charlotte. Always Clover.'

Charlotte escaped with her heart beating uncomfortably fast, feeling as if she had witnessed something she shouldn't really have seen. And what had she really learnt that she didn't already know? Unless it was a lesson that true love never died, no matter how long and how permanent the parting.

She found Josie lying on her own bed, her face flushed and crumpled, and knew that she'd been crying.

'Did Dad give you a hard time?' she asked sympathetically.

'I could kill that little brat. What did she go and have to say that for? She always spoils everything. I wish I didn't have to live here. I wish I really *could* go and join the circus or the fairground people. But they don't want me, either. I thought it was all going to be all right this year, but Tony still sees me as a kid.'

Although Charlotte had heard very little about him, this Tony was presumably now thought of as the love of her life, and she was sorely tempted to tell her there were plenty of other young chaps in the town, without wasting her energies on this once-a-year Adonis. But who was she to talk, when Josie was looking so tragic?

'I'm sure he doesn't see you as a kid,' she began.

'Yes, he does. He told me so. He said he'd never go out with a girl under sixteen, and that he wasn't looking for that kind of trouble. He talks in riddles, but I know it's only to try to put me off.'

Charlotte had a little more insight than her sister on just what kind of trouble Tony was talking about. He was being responsible, she thought ... or he could just be implying that once a girl was sixteen he'd have no such inhibitions...

'You don't really know him at all, do you, Josie? You've only spoken to him a few times, haven't you?' she said carefully, knowing that Josie would be ready to fly at her in a minute if she thought she was being treated like a child.

'I like him,' she said. 'What more does anybody need to know? And since Dad will forbid me to go to the fair at all now, what chance do I have of ever getting to know him any better?!'

She sounded so doomed that Charlotte knew better than to smile.

'You need to know a great deal more about a person, I'd say. But maybe Dad will still let you go to the fair if we go together.'

Josie's face brightened so suddenly that Charlotte was startled by her sudden beauty. She admitted that she still thought of her as her kid sister, forever bleating that she wanted to do the things that Charlotte was allowed to do. But as if she was seeing her for the first time, Charlotte saw what Tony whoever-he-was must see. And she was even more glad that he didn't want the kind of trouble that could ensue from meddling with a young and impressionable girl.

'You're a real brick, Charlie,' Josie said, throwing her arms around her. 'I know he'll agree if you ask him.' She tried not to put too much emphasis on the fact that in her opinion Charlotte could do no wrong in her father's eyes, however mistaken that was.

'Yes, well, I may just have my own reasons for going there, anyway,' Charlotte felt bound to say. 'Melvin and me have had a ... a kind of falling out and, as we'd already planned to go to the fair, I hope he'll turn up and that everything will be all right again.'

'Gosh,' Josie said. 'What was it about, this falling out?'

She obviously saw this as something rather grand and grown up, and was eager to be her sister's confidante in love matters; but in view of the recent conversation Charlotte had had with Clover, and the hidden meaning behind the reluctance of Tony whoever-he-was to get too friendly with Josie, Charlotte had no intention of saying anything more. Some things were private.

'Oh, just a storm in a teacup, I daresay,' she replied, mentally crossing her fingers as she did so. And Josie had to be content with that.

After a lot of badgering on Charlotte's part, and pleading that was tantamount to grovelling on Josie's, they were finally allowed to go to the fair together.

Charlotte disliked the look of Tony on sight. He was too flashy, too slick, too greasy haired, too full of himself, and too everything she found repulsive. He was more like one of the cinema's villains than the hero and, even though she was making judgements on appearance only, she couldn't help it. In fact, whatever Josie saw in him that was so attractive, she couldn't think.

'You don't have to stay with me now that we're here,' Josie told her. 'Go and look for Melvin, and I'll see you in about an hour.'

'I'm not sure that's what Dad meant.'

'Well, he doesn't need to know, does he? I don't need a nursemaid, Charlie, and isn't that your blacksmith over by the hoop-la stall?'

By the time Charlotte had spun round to look for Melvin and realised she had been fooled, Josie had skipped away from her and was making her way back towards the Dodgem cars.

'Hello again,' Tony said with a wide smile. 'Can't keep away, can you?'

Charlotte gave a sigh. Josie was gone fifteen, and she couldn't expect to keep her by her side for ever. And nor did she want to be a nursemaid, either, she thought resentfully. She strolled around the fairground, watching the children on the rides and the adults winning goldfish or coconuts, pretending she was enjoying herself. But it wasn't much fun being on her own, and this was something else that was best done by two, she decided.

Finally, she caught sight of Melvin. He was chatting to a couple of girls she didn't know. For some reason the girls in the town seemed to think the Elkins girls were superior, or thought themselves so, and they had few real friends. But seeing Melvin with those two made her mad with jealousy and, if it didn't hurt so much, she would wash her hands of him. She turned away resolutely.

If he didn't want her, then she wouldn't want him.

'Are we friends again?' she heard him say, when she had been staring at the merry-go-round for so long she was starting to feel giddy.

'You seem to have found some new friends,' she said pointedly, even though the two girls had wandered off now.

'You mean the girls from one of the local farms? They bring their horses to us to be shod, so you wouldn't want me to be uncivil to them, would you?'

'Is that all they are to you? Girls from local farms?'

He put his head on one side, grinning down at her.

'Let's see now. Yes, they're girls and, yes, they live at local farms. Their dad asked me to keep an eye on them, so is there anything else your suspicious little mind wants to know, or do you want to have a ride on the merry-go-round?'

He was so darned cocksure of himself, Charlotte fumed. He knew very well she was jealous, and he wasn't letting her forget it.

'Don't you have to keep an eye on your charges?'

'Not all night. I'm not their nursemaid! So what are we waiting for?'

The fact that he'd used the same word that she'd used about Josie reminded Charlotte that she was meant to be in charge of her sister, too. But as Melvin said, it didn't need all night, and she wasn't anyone's nursemaid, either. Josie wouldn't thank her for treating her that way.

'All right,' she said, as the merry-go-round began slowing down, spilling people off the brightly coloured metal horses and mingling them with the crowds eager to get on. Minutes later, Charlotte was seated in front of Melvin as the machine began whirling around again, holding on to the head of the horse as his arms tightened around her waist and his chin nestled into her neck.

'This is a good excuse for a cuddle, isn't it, sweetheart?' he chuckled.

As the merry-go-round went faster and faster, so did her heartbeat, and then she was screaming and laughing with everybody else as the thrill of it all made her feel reckless. She turned and laughed into Melvin's face, and as she did so his mouth fastened on hers in a fiercely demanding kiss that she couldn't get away from even if she had wanted to. And she didn't ... she didn't ... she felt a great sense of freedom, more exhilarated than she had ever known, as though she was whirling into space with nobody but themselves in the universe. And she wanted this feeling to go on for ever, knowing it was the first time he had kissed her like that, and the first time she had responded so passionately.

It was only as the ride began to slow down and the rest of the world came into focus, with other people in the field waiting for the next ride, that she found herself looking into the open-mouthed face of her sister.

'Josie,' she croaked.

'What about her?' Melvin said easily, his arms still holding her tight and refusing to let her move until the ride had come to a complete stop as the owner instructed, and clearly aware of nothing but the close proximity of his girl that had turned out even better than he had hoped.

She struggled to free herself from his arms and slid off the horse, wondering just what Josie had thought about her sister behaving so outrageously in a public place. Making a public exhibition of themselves was the very thing their parents had always warned them about, and which was disapproved of so strongly.

And of all of them, she had been the one to do it. Not Josie, as they might have expected, but Charlotte, who could always be relied on to do the right thing. She smothered a sob in her throat as she looked around frantically for Josie but, in those split seconds, she seemed to have vanished into the crowd.

'Hey, where are you going?' she heard Melvin shout, as she twisted away from him and ran towards the Dodgem cars.

'I've got to find Josie,' she shouted back.

Melvin grabbed her. 'The kid's old enough and smart enough to look after herself, and you're acting like a lunatic.'

'Well, why wouldn't I? It runs in the family, doesn't it?' she flashed back.

She instantly wished she hadn't said the words, and she would have given her soul not to have done so. People thought her gran was odd, but she wasn't a lunatic or deranged, she was just eccentric. The family accepted that, so why couldn't everybody else?

'Don't be stupid, Charlotte. But they'll certainly think so if you don't stop racing around like a madwoman. I can see your sister at the toffee-apple stall, as calm as you like, so let's go over there and I'll buy us all one. Maybe it'll knock some sense into you.'

Maybe it would. And maybe it would just give her the jitters. Right now she felt as young and gauche as Milly, and all because Josie had witnessed her sharing a passionate kiss with her young man on the merry-go-round. Well, her sister and the rest of the townsfolk who were waiting for their rides.

But she couldn't stand there dithering all night, and she followed Melvin reluctantly to where the woman at the stall was handing Josie her toffee-apple.

'Put your money away, kid. We'll have two more of those, and I'm paying,' Melvin told the woman.

She grinned archly. 'Nice to have a champion, isn't it, girls?'

'Oh yes, very nice,' Josie muttered, with about as much grace as a flea.

But she knew, and Charlotte knew, that there wouldn't be any more objections to her hanging around the Dodgems that night. It was a small victory, and one that had been won in a way that neither of them had expected.

Five

There were two big social occasions in the Braydon calendar. One was the fair that arrived every June and the other was the town carnival at the end of September. It attracted people from roundabout as well as the townsfolk themselves and, with luck and a fair wind following, as Donald Elkins was wont to say, it would bring in a few casual visitors to the hotel when the main part of the season was over.

Donald hadn't inherited his parents' love of adventure, nor their optimism. He was a cautious man and very conscious of his position in the town. He was also a worrier, and kept the true state of affairs regarding the hotel from his family. He never revealed how much he prayed for those casual carnival visitors and others to call at The Retreat on the off-chance of a room. Thanks to the hospitality they received, those that came for a night frequently stayed for longer, full of praise for the hotel itself and the clean, bracing air of the Bristol Channel coast.

'It's not enough, Donald,' his accountant told him as usual on his half-yearly visit. 'For the hotel to pay its way, you should advertise far more than you do, and you should also put up the charges for your regulars. It's ridiculous to let them stay here for the same charges as when they first came. How long have they been here? Five, ten years?'

'Not that long, but I doubt that they could afford to pay more, and it would embarrass me to ask them,' Donald said, ignoring the length of time he knew the Captain and Misses Green had been with them. 'They're practically family now.'

'And that's another thing,' the accountant went on relentlessly. 'Your family. I'm not suggesting you throw them out on the street, but there are a lot of them for the hotel to support, Donald. Are you sure they're all needed? Couldn't one of the older girls get a secretarial or other job to bring in a little more money instead of being such a drain on you?'

Donald bridled at once. 'My girls are not a drain on me, Fellowes. Of course we need them to help with the cooking and waiting at tables. You can't expect my wife to do everything herself. Milly's got her education to think about, and I hope you're not going to suggest that my mother does any manual work at her age.'

Gilbert Fellowes gave a sigh, knowing he was beaten as usual. 'No, of course not. Well, I've given you the benefit of my advice and, if you won't act on it, that's up to you. But I've known you a long time, Donald, and I'd far rather see you swim than sink.'

'I'll keep it all in mind,' Donald said tightly, knowing he would do no such thing. Ruth relied on the older girls' help, and the thought of their youngest girl going to the grammar school was a matter of pride to them both, even though he chose not to dwell too much on the cost of uniforms and shoes and all the other paraphernalia such an event would entail.

As far as the hotel was concerned, it was a matter of pride too that he did only a small, discreet amount of advertising, and that their reputation was won in a large part by word of mouth. The same people came back year after year, and newcomers such as the Parkers promised to return again and to recommend them.

They had gone home now, and the jovial hardware sales rep had made his annual visit, filling Josie's head with all kinds of nonsense about what he called his territory, which merely meant the area he covered in his ramshackle motor car to demonstrate his supplies of kitchen goods, to replenish orders and take new ones. One of his ports of call was Hallam's Food Supplies, and as a gesture of goodwill he never failed to leave some new gadget for Ruth.

The females were all charmed by the man, of course, Donald thought with faint derision, but that was part of his stock-in-trade. He had the gift of the gab, as it was called. And if Donald didn't stop thinking in these well-worn terms, he thought to himself, he'd be letting himself down and spouting rubbish in front of his guests.

The fair only spent five days in Braydon before moving on, and now it was over. After all the excitement it generated, its departure left many people with a slightly deflated feeling, not least Josie Elkins. Although she had had the satisfaction, on the last night, of being around when Tony had leapt off the Dodgems for a half-hour break and come to join her at one of the amusement stalls.

'Want me to win you something? What do you want, a goldfish or a soft toy?' he said with a grin, already holding the three darts in his hand and ready to aim.

She was about to retort that she was too old for soft toys, when she noticed a black-and-white-spotted china dog amongst the rubbishy prizes piled up at the back of the stall. He was supposedly sitting up and begging, but was so badly made that it looked as though he was about to fall over at any minute. He was also so ugly that she fell for him instantly.

'How about that?' she said, pointing to it. 'My gran would love that. She likes anything that's a bit peculiar. Like her, really,' she said, without meaning to do so.

'She's not that old lady who's often bundled up in a long coat with a scarf wound around her neck as if it's mid-winter, is she? I've seen her a couple of times walking along the sea front and talking to herself. She sometimes has a hat rammed on her head, too, all colours of the rainbow. You can't miss her.'

'That's her,' Josie muttered, not sure if he was mocking Clover or not, and not sure whether to be embarrassed at his description, or rushing to her defence.

'Don't worry, kid. We've all got one,' Tony said easily.

She wasn't about to ask if he meant a grandmother or a lunatic relative.

'So are you going to win me the dog or not?' she snapped.

He did so quite easily and, as he handed it to her in triumph, their hands brushed. For a moment his fingers lingered over hers, and Josie found her heart thumping twice as fast as usual.

'See you next year, kid,' he said softly.

'And make sure you call me Josie then,' she said, choked.

He laughed and melted into the crowd to go back to his work. And she clutched the ugly little china dog, knowing she wouldn't be giving it to anybody, because it was the first gift a boy had ever given her. She knew it was hardly a love token but, if she chose to think of it that way, who was to stop her?

'Where did you get *that* awful thing?' Milly hooted when Josie took it home. 'It's really ugly and it's boss-eyed!'

Josie felt protective of her dog and decided he was worth a little white lie. 'I won him at the fair, if you must know, and he's not ugly.

He's got character. And since he's going to sit on my bedroom window sill and you can keep out, you don't ever need to see him.'

'He's sweet,' Clover said. 'I like him, Josie.'

'Thank you, Clover,' she said, guilty at once at having told Tony the dog was for her grandmother. But she couldn't part with him now. Not when she remembered that moment when he had given the dog to her, and their hands had touched so briefly. If Clover knew about that, Josie was sure she'd understand, but it wasn't something she was about to tell her or anyone else.

She might have known Charlotte would object to seeing the china dog in the window sill every day, though. Charlotte thought china animals were a poor substitute for the real thing, such as the horses that Melvin Philpott and his father shoed at the smithy. Charlotte had watched them on more than one occasion, marvelling at the men's skill and admiring the patience of the horses as they were shod.

'Doesn't it hurt?' she had ventured to say, watching as the nails were hammered through the made-to-measure shoe into the horse's foot.

'It might if it went into flesh,' Melvin told her. 'But the hooves are as thick and as hard as nails and, if they didn't have the shoes on them, they would wear away and give the animal considerable pain. They know we're doing them a favour.'

She also liked the way he really seemed to

care about the animals. Having seen a couple of mangy dogs around the fairground caravans, she wasn't so sure that the owners thought the same way about any of theirs.

'The dog's precious because Tony won him for me, if you must know,' she heard Josie say defiantly, when she protested again at the monstrosity on their window sill. 'I'm calling him Spotty. And when did Melvin ever give you anything?'

Charlotte couldn't answer that. Melvin was not the most generous of young men. He usually paid for her when they went to the pictures, depending on how much money he had. Apart from that, they went for walks or sat in the hotel garden, and that cost him nothing.

'I don't go out with Melvin because of what he gives me,' she said shortly, wishing such material things hadn't come into her head.

'Well, not money or presents, anyway,' Josie said, her face breaking into a grin. 'Is he a good kisser?'

Charlotte had to laugh at her eager face. It was extraordinary how the likeness between her two younger sisters was so evident at times, especially when either of them got that mischievous, animated look on their faces.

'Mind your own business,' she said.

'What's it like, Charlie? Being kissed properly, I mean. It can't be the same as when Dad kisses us, at least, I hope it's not. When he needs a shave it's like being kissed by a bristly nail brush.'

'Good Lord, I should just think it's not the same! You don't expect your father to be passionate about kissing his daughters, do you? It wouldn't be nice.'

'Well, go on, then. What's it like to be kissed passionately by a boy?' Josie said, sulking now.

The two years between them suddenly seemed to open up like a gulf. It had never seemed so wide before, and Charlotte was acutely conscious of just how curious Josie really was, how eager for this so-personal knowledge that couldn't be given by someone else, and had to be experienced for yourself. But she knew she had to say something.

'It's very nice,' she said lamely. 'It makes me feel all warm inside, and excited too. If his chin is bristly that only makes it more exciting, but it's hard to explain, Josie, and not really the sort of thing anyone should be talking about. Anyway, he hasn't kissed me all that many times.'

'Why not?'

'For pity's sake, stop going on about it. He respects me, that's why.'

Josie gave a snort that was worthy of Clover. 'Oh, I shan't be satisfied with the occasional kiss from a boy because he *respects* me. I want to be irresistible and swept off my feet and drive him wild with passion for me.'

'You'll find yourself heading for a whole load of trouble if you do,' Charlotte said, choking with laughter at her dramatics. 'Anyway, keep that Spotty dog under control. I don't want his boss-eyes looking at me all night.'

The conversation with Josie had made Charlotte think, though. It was a little white lie to say that Melvin hadn't kissed her very often, and if it had rarely gone to passionate lengths it was partly due to her and not to him. He was an earthy young man, and she knew he was restraining himself. She respected him for that.

And there was that wretched word *respect* again, she thought crossly. It was a good word and one of which her parents would strongly approve, but what was the matter with her if she couldn't feel the need to be as uninhibited as Josie obviously did? Maybe Melvin would eventually tire of her and find some more willing girl for his affections. Maybe she wasn't even cut out for marriage.

She shivered, and for some reason her thoughts went to the Misses Green, each of them the epitome of every fictional ageing spinster: a little withered, a little faded, far too dependent on one another, and with the narrowest outlook on life. She certainly didn't want to end up like them.

Then there was her grandmother, still full of energy in her eighties, still living a fulfilled life with a family who adored her, still wickedly remembering days with her dashing Tommy, still madly eccentric. Would she have been so marvellously bright now, if it hadn't been for the memories of that full and adventurous marriage?

Charlotte was still thinking about Clover when she fell asleep that night, trying to imagine what it must have been like to follow Tommy wherever the army sent him, even into certain danger. You had to really love a man to do that...

She awoke with a start, conscious that somebody was looking at her. There was a small figure at the end of her bed, wreathed in white in the light from the window. Her heart pounded with fear until the figure moved, and she realised it was no ghostly apparition at all.

'*Milly*,' she hissed. 'What do you think you're playing at, scaring me half to death like that?'

'It's Gran. Clover. She's gone,' Milly croaked.

'What do you mean, she's gone?'

'I had to go to the lav, and when I got back to my room I looked out of my window and saw somebody walking along the sea front, waving their arms about. I thought it was a ghost. I went to look for Gran but her bed's empty. Has she been kidnapped, do you think?'

Charlotte was already out of bed and pulling on a dressing-gown and slippers. This was no more than one of Clover's usual jaunts, but then she realised how Milly was shaking, and saw that she was really scared.

'Of course nobody's kidnapped her,' she

said quickly. She looked across at Josie, who was sound asleep. Nothing was going to waken her by the looks of it.

'Milly, get into my bed, then you'll have company.'

'What are you going to do?' Milly was already halfway in the bed, anyway, ready to pull the covers over her head.

'I'm going to wake up Dad and then we're going to go and look for Clover. Don't worry, she'll only be taking a little walk the way she sometimes does. You know that.'

By now, Milly was recovering and ready to snap. 'Well, I think she's loony, and I hope none of the girls at my new school next year get to hear about me having a loony gran who goes off walking in the middle of the night!'

'Oh, *Milly*.' But Charlotte didn't have time to stop to tell her that was about the most snobbish thing she'd heard yet. She sped quietly along to her parents' room and, after a small tap on the door that produced no reply, she went in and shook her father's arm.

'What is it? What the blazes is going on?' he said, awake at once.

'Dad, Clover's gone out,' she said simply. She didn't have to say any more.

'Go and get dressed and we'll fetch her back. No need to wake your mother.'

'I'm awake,' Ruth said sleepily. 'Should I come with you?'

'It doesn't need an army of us, my dear, and we don't want to waken the regulars or the other guests by too much activity. Go back to sleep and don't worry.'

There was never any need to worry, except that it was hardly the sanest thing for an elderly lady to be wandering about in her night clothes in the middle of the night. Now, it was a warm and balmy night in midsummer, but there had been winter occasions when Clover had been wandering about in the rain and wind, and once in the snow, when they had found her throwing snowballs at an imaginary foe and laughing crazily. This was not the action of a sane woman. She was lucky in having a family who loved her and was fiercely protective of her, otherwise who knew where she would have ended up.

'Ready?' Donald asked his daughter, when they met downstairs, both dressed in outdoor clothes.

Charlotte nodded. She really didn't like this. There was no knowing what mood Clover was going to be in. She was always living in the past, as if it was an extension of a dream she had been having. Sometimes she was very excitable, babbling about going to a party or a social occasion with officers and their wives, exclaiming about gowns and jewellery and the thrills of recent military expeditions.

At other times she would be in the depths of depression, weeping uncontrollably and asking why Tommy had left her to live so many years without him. At such times she wasn't averse to coming out with blasphemies and the sort of choice language that was more suited to an army barracks, and Charlotte always tried to close her ears to such things, trying to believe that this was not really her gran at all, but some strange and angry being who was taking possession of her.

Charlotte didn't care to think of her like that but, as she and Donald struck out along the sea front, she couldn't help wondering which Clover they were going to find tonight. Milly had said she was waving her arms about. That could mean she was imagining herself dancing, floating in Tommy's arms, in which case she would be loving and docile.

The night was cooler after the heat of the day, and a sea mist hung about the shore. It hovered above the sea and seemed to float in wisps along the sea front, changing the day-time appearance of a familiar place into a kind of eerie wonderland. The moonlight that penetrated the mist still had enough power to sparkle on the water rippling on to the sandy coves and pebbles.

Then they saw her. She was sitting on a rock in one of the coves, right near the water's edge. From this distance she was a tiny figure in her nightgown, sitting erect with her hands clasped around her knees. She was singing softly.

'Dear God, what have we got now?' Donald muttered. 'She'll be telling us she's been seeing mermaids next.'

'Please be gentle, Dad. Don't alarm her.'

'I do know how to handle my own mother, Charlotte. She's been going this way for years, and it's time it stopped.'

Charlotte felt a stab of alarm. 'You wouldn't send her away, would you? Dad, you couldn't be so cruel. This is her home, and the only place she really ever knew as home when she and Tommy weren't travelling the world. It would kill her if you sent her away to be shut up in one of those awful asylums.'

'For pity's sake, girl, I'm not sending her away anywhere. I'm just saying it's got to stop. I shall ask the family doctor if he can give her some sedatives so that she sleeps all night and doesn't waken the rest of the hotel. It doesn't do much for our business reputation for outsiders to get wind of it, either, and too many probably know of it already.'

Charlotte could hardly believe what he was saying. She wasn't sure whether his own mother's health or the reputation of his precious hotel was more important to him, and she burst out at him at once.

'That's so unkind! Gran can't help it, any more than Milly can help being such a beastly little snob.' She just managed not to add that in him, her sister had a darn good example to follow.

But before they could get into a proper argument, Clover had caught the sound of their voices and turned her head. The singing had stopped, and she waved to them, just as if this was an ordinary day and not the middle of the night, when all good folk should be in bed and asleep. They scrambled down the slope of the cove towards her. She spoke eagerly, her face animated.

'Did you see them?'

'Who, Clover?' Charlotte said cautiously.

'Out there. The dolphins. They say if you sing to them, they'll come in closer to shore, but I daresay they weren't in the mood for company tonight.'

'There aren't any blessed dolphins in the Bristol Channel,' Donald snapped. 'For heaven's sake, Mother, come back to the hotel before you catch your death.'

'Don't be so stuffy, Donald. I won't catch my death. It's not my time.'

Charlotte caught at her hand. 'Please come back with us now, Clover. Milly woke up and discovered you'd gone missing. She thought you'd been kidnapped. I think you should come back and let her know you're all right.'

'Oh, well, if the little one's worried about me, I'll come. But kidnapped?!' She gave a great hooting laugh. 'Who'd want to kidnap an old biddy like me?!'

'I can think of one or two,' Donald muttered beneath his breath.

As Clover allowed them to help her off the rock and climb back up the slope of the cove, she looked sorrowfully at her son.

'How did me and Tommy ever produce such a fusspot as you, I wonder? I doubt that you ever did a spontaneous thing in the whole of your life. Not like my Tommy. If I said I wanted to go off on a spree tomorrow, he'd have said yes, and off we'd go! He was a real man.'

'Yes, well, I'm sure he was,' Donald said, nettled at these slights in front of his eldest daughter. 'But there are more ways of being a man than going off to war.'

'You'd fight for your country again if you had to, though, wouldn't you, Dad?' Charlotte said, as they walked along the sea front with Clover held firmly between them now and wearing Donald's coat over her nightdress.

'Thankfully, such a thought doesn't arise,' he replied. 'Please God that we never have another war. If we did it wouldn't be the likes of me that had to go. It would be your blacksmith, and then see what you thought about him being a hero, or being sent over the top as those poor devils were in the Great War.'

'You shouldn't talk about such things,' Clover said in a shrill voice. 'It's bad luck to speculate like that. Cross your fingers and take the thoughts back.'

'For God's sake, Mother,' Donald groaned.

'I know what we'll do,' Clover went on brightly, as if the last awkward exchanges had never happened. 'We'll have a midnight feast in the kitchen, just the three of us. I shall bake some cakes and Charlotte will make us all some cocoa.'

'You will do no such thing,' Donald thundered now. 'You will go straight to bed and put Milly's mind at rest that you're not completely mad, and I don't want to see you again until the morning. Is that clear?'

'Well, if those are your orders, Captain, it's perfectly clear!'

By the time they got back to the hotel Milly was fast asleep so, rather than disturb her, Charlotte decided to sleep in her bed, with the partition wall between herself and Clover. She tried not to dwell on the events of the night, even though her nerves were still jumping, but, just as she was finally falling asleep, she heard a small, plaintive voice from the other side of the partition.

'I'm not really mad, you know, Charlotte, whatever they say.'

'I know, Gran.'

'But there will be another war one day. Tommy's told me so more than once, even though he doesn't know when it will be, but I'll pray that your blacksmith will be too old to be sent for as a soldier when that day comes. Goodnight, Charlotte, dear, and sweet dreams.'

'Good night, Clover.'

And after hearing that little lot, a fat chance she had of getting to sleep and having sweet dreams now!

Six

The whole of Braydon was preparing for the end-of-September carnival. It was always led by the town's brass band, followed by local tradesmen who decorated their vans and lorries with bunting and glitter. It was as good as an advertising display for the tradesmen and they made the most of it. The fire engine came next, always cheered on by local people thronging the streets, and then individuals dressed up in costumes ranging from the sweet to the bizarre.

The farm next to the smithy always provided a couple of shire horses, brushed to shining perfection and dressed in gleaming horse brasses, and each bearing a placard announcing that they were shod by Philpott's Smithy. The shire horses hadn't appeared yet, but Charlotte waited eagerly for the first sight of her beloved astride one of them.

'I don't know why they bother to announce who they are, when there's no other smithy for miles,' Josie said as she stood outside The Retreat with the rest of the Elkins family on that late September morning, watching the procession pass by. All except Clover, who was in the thick of it as usual.

'It's good for business,' Donald told her, trying to ignore the sight of his mother, prancing about like a two-year-old as she waved her bucket towards anybody willing to spare a few coppers for charity. Ordering them to do so, more like, Donald thought with a scowl, and making a spectacle of herself as usual in her colourful get-up, a bright yellow knitted hat on her head, and a floor-length scarf trailing around her feet. One of these days she was going to trip herself up and break her neck, he thought.

His wife looked at him archly. 'You don't think it's a bit lowering to advertise on the side of a horse then, do you? For somebody who doesn't care to advertise anywhere if he can help it, that's a bit rich, Donald.'

'Hotels are in a different class of business from a smithy, Ruth.'

'Thank you for that, Dad,' Charlotte put in, nettled at the inference that a blacksmith's business was farther down the social scale than their own.

'Now don't get that huffy look on your face, Charlotte. We usually leave that to Milly.'

His youngest daughter's reply was lost in the sudden roar from the crowd as the float from Hallam's Food Supplies came into sight, decked out with a variety of household goods and appliances, clanking together with every movement of the van.

'Remind me not to buy any new saucepans in the near future,' Ruth breathed into Donald's ear. 'By the time the carnival's over, they'll be dented to high heaven, to say nothing of the stupid man's van.'

By now his daughters were studying the group of excited small girls coming towards them. They belonged to Veronica Wadeley's Dance Class and, dressed in matching gaudy costumes, were meant to resemble wood nymphs. They practised their floating arm movements with as much finesse as possible for their doting families. Watching them, Josie was finding it hard to contain her mirth.

'Just look at the idiots. They're more like baby elephants than wood nymphs,' she said, choking with laughter.

'Don't be mean, Josie,' Charlotte said, hiding a grin. 'I was just thinking that Milly could do better with her time by joining the Dance Class than trying to play the piano and torturing our ears every day.'

'Well, now *you're* being mean,' Milly howled. 'I don't torture anybody's ears, and I wouldn't want to mince about looking stupid in those costumes, either.'

'That's because she doesn't have the legs for it,' Josie whispered in an aside, glancing at Milly's sturdy limbs.

The girl lifted her head up high and stalked away from the family to stand beside the regulars. The Misses Green tucked their arms through hers, instantly making her feel as though she was stuck in the middle of them like a trophy.

'Never mind, dear,' Hester Green said sympathetically. 'Our mother always said that whatever else she had, a person with a good set of pins always had a strong base to work from.'

Milly extricated herself at once. Sometimes she thought these two were as batty as her gran – and that was saying something. She cringed ever time she saw her in the carnival procession, wishing she'd stop doing it, but they all knew she'd continue until she dropped. One of the highlights of Clover's year was to be wearing her brash, normal clothes and not be out of place amongst the rest of them!

Milly knew she wouldn't want to join Veronica Wadeley's Dance Class, anyway. They were all silly, soppy girls, always giggling together, and without a brain in their heads. None of them would ever pass their scholarship and get to the grammar school. And she didn't care a hoot if they thought her stuck-up and didn't bother to speak to her at school. She didn't need them.

She caught sight of her sister Charlotte at that moment, looking nearly as soppy as the wood nymphs now. She knew the reason for it, of course. Melvin Philpott was sitting astride one of the shire horses, looking for all the world like a Viking or a Greek God or the king of the world...

Josie giggled again. 'It's a wonder he doesn't split his difference, having his legs so far apart like that,' she whispered to Charlotte.

'What would you know about that?' Charlotte said, annoyed with her for ruining the moment.

'Not much, but I bet you do.'

Charlotte felt her face flame, just at the moment when Melvin drew close to where she stood, and gave a silly kind of salute to her, pressing his hand to his heart, followed by a wink and a blown kiss. If it didn't make it obvious that Melvin Philpott and Charlotte Elkins were sweet on one another, she didn't know what did. She also knew what her father would think about such a gesture.

He didn't mention it until the carnival procession had passed. By then, people were starting to disperse, and the members of the Elkins family were going back inside the hotel to serve their guests with afternoon tea, including Clover, exhausted now by her antics of the afternoon, but well pleased with her bucket collection, which had been duly handed over to the organisers.

Donald caught at his daughter's arm. 'Charlotte, you know I don't object to your seeing the Philpott boy. He belongs to an honourable profession and is well respected for the work that he does. But I don't approve of his making your association so obvious in public.'

Before Charlotte could think of a suitable rely, Clover had spoken up.

'Oh, for goodness' sake, Donald, stop being such a killjoy over a bit of harmless fun. I swear I don't know how me and my Tommy ever came to spawn such a one as you.'

'Thank you, Mother,' Donald said tightly,

'and I swear I don't know why you find pleasure in using such crude expressions. *Frogs* spawn and they produce tadpoles, not people.'

He became aware that all his womenfolk were finding it hard to stifle their laughter now, and he marched back into the hotel ahead of them, hoping that none of the guests had heard the ridiculous little exchange, and wishing he hadn't been stupid enough to be drawn into it.

Melvin had promised to come back to the hotel that evening, once the carnival was over and the town had returned to something nearing normality. The end of September was still balmy, the nights soft and warm, as if the summer was loath to go away that year, and, as usual, people would still be talking about the carnival procession for days and weeks to come. The buckets that had been passed around the crowds would have been filled with pennies and threepenny bits and sixpences, to be put to good use for local charities, and the organisers would be congratulating themselves on another successful year. There was always an air of well-being at the end of carnival day, and this one was no exception, especially for Charlotte Elkins, awaiting the arrival of her sweetheart.

She felt almost feverishly excited as she helped her parents finish her allotted tasks for the day.

'Meeting your young man later, are you, my

dear?' the Captain asked her.

'That's right. Did you see him today, Captain?' she said eagerly, wanting him to say how splendid Melvin looked on the back of the shire horse.

'Oh, yes, I saw him. Couldn't miss him, could I? A fine figure of a fellow he was, too. Reminded me of the time I was in India, when the cavalry rode through the cities in their dress uniforms and their finery. The only thing missing in your young blacksmith was the regalia they wore.'

Charlotte laughed. 'Well, you couldn't expect Melvin to dress up like a soldier when he didn't have the right, could you?'

'Certainly not,' he agreed.

Josie was hovering nearby and couldn't resist putting in her twopennyworth.

'I don't see why he couldn't have dressed up. Everybody else was in fancy dress or weird costumes, so why wasn't he?'

'Because he wasn't representing anyone else but himself and his profession, you ninny,' Charlotte told her sharply, refusing to let the thrill of seeing Melvin so handsome on the shire horse be diminished in any way. 'I dare-say your fairground chap would have turned up in the carnival with one of those checked scarves around his neck and those awful baggy trousers they wear.'

Josie flushed darkly. 'You don't have to be bitchy about him,' she hissed.

'And you don't have to waste your time dreaming about a chap that you only see once a year and may never see again. Who's to say if he'll come back next year – or if he'll even remember you?'

'Who's to say he won't!' Josie said, flouncing away.

The Captain chuckled. 'You've touched a raw spot there, my dear,' he told Charlotte. 'But she's young, and she'll get over it. In a week or two she'll probably be dreaming over some other young chap.'

'If Dad has his way, he'll make sure she's not dreaming about any young chap for a couple of years yet,' Charlotte said, wishing she had never got into this conversation, and as usual saying a little more than she intended.

But the regulars had a strange knack of winkling things out of them. They weren't family, but they were far from being strangers, and she guessed that when they got together they formed a busy trio of gossips. She found herself smiling at the thought of their three grey old heads nodding together at some spicy bit of news. They didn't have much else to do to occupy their time, though, nor any other excitement in their lives, so who could blame them?

But she wasn't going to think about them any more. She was going to put on a pretty dress and wait for Melvin to arrive. That evening they were going to cycle up to the ruins of the old priory overlooking the town, which was a favourite place for courting couples, and she knew he would be in a very good mood after the carnival. He should have been on the stage, she thought. He had the good looks and all the self-confidence to go with them. Her nerves tingled at the thought.

She admitted that in a funny way he scared her sometimes. But it was also a good, honest, exciting kind of fear that made her heart beat faster and her whole body feel alive when she was with him. She knew he had a healthy appetite as far as pleasure was concerned, and she knew he wanted more than she was ready to give; and on a heady night like this, who knew where passion might lead them?

It was something that held her in check every time she thought about it. It wasn't that she didn't want to know more about where that passion could lead, because she did. The stumbling words of her mother, advising her to keep herself clean and to respect herself at all times, did nothing to assuage her curiosity about this wonderful thing that drew men and women together – this thing called love. And besides, she was a woman now. She was seventeen, and fully grown, and she had a boy who loved her.

She caught sight of her grandmother watching her, and felt her face go red. Sometimes it was as though Clover had a sixth sense for knowing just what was going on in somebody else's mind.

'Have I got a smut on my nose or something?' she asked her lightly, turning away and pretending to look in the hall mirror.

'I think you've got more than that on your mind, darling. Take it slowly, that's all, and be very sure it's what you really want.'

Charlotte laughed shakily. She would swear that the old girl was halfway to being a witch, even if a very nice one, and if she didn't actually see too much, she surmised it. It probably came from living too long. But for all that, Charlotte still hoped she would go on for ever. She gave her an impulsive hug.

'Don't know what you're talking about, Gran, but I'll keep it in mind.'

And there was one thing for sure. Whatever happened between her and Melvin, she was glad she'd never taken to writing everything down in a diary, the way Josie did. With a kid sister like Milly around, it was simply asking for trouble.

She heard Melvin before she saw him. She was still inspecting her chin in the mirror, and praying that the tiny red mark wasn't going to turn into a huge tomato of a spot, when she heard him whistle approvingly. She groaned, knowing how her dad hated what he called something so common. But before turning around, she caught sight of the way Melvin was looking at her face in the mirror, and she caught her breath.

It was such a perfect moment. The reflection of the two of them was captured together, like an oil painting framed by the gilt mirror surround, and she wished she could hold it and keep it there for ever.

And then the moment was broken as Melvin laughed.

'What's up? Cat got your tongue?'

'Oh – *you!*' she said, frowning.

'What have I done now? I've just come to take my lady out, like I promised, so if you're ready, let's go. There's no point in hanging about here and wasting this gorgeous evening. Besides,' he said, dropping his voice, 'I want you all to myself, not sharing you with a household of kids and old codgers.'

Charlotte giggled, thankful that Clover had gone to her room, and everybody else was occupied. Her dad was only just tolerant of Melvin, but he wouldn't stand for him sneering at the clientele who meant so much for him. The hotel was full at present and it was the way Donald liked it to be.

'Well, I'm ready, so what are we waiting for?' she said.

She was shivery with excitement now. They didn't get too many chances to be alone together and on this night, when the whole town was alive and happy with the success of the day, it was a marvellous feeling to be so wanted by someone who was so special to her. Poets tried their best to put into words how it felt to be in love, but sometimes there were no words. There was just *being*.

'You've got that soppy look on your face again,' Melvin told her as they went outside to fetch their bicycles.

'What look is that? she said with a grin, too besotted to take offence.

He laughed. 'The one that tells me we're going to enjoy this evening, sweetheart, without having anyone breathing down our necks and reminding us of the time or anything else. The one that tells me you're *my girl*.'

It was an exhilarating thought, but she felt an odd sliver of nervousness again as they cycled through the still-busy streets of the town, as if people were still reluctant to call an end to this lovely day.

'I won't have to be too late though, Melvin.'

'Don't worry. I'll get Cinderella back long before the clock strikes midnight.'

He reached out his hand to squeeze hers, and she wobbled on her cycle, telling him laughingly to behave himself if he wanted them to reach the old priory hill in one piece. Then her thoughts unexpectedly jolted, wondering just exactly what those words meant to her, and to him.

As she wobbled again, he advised her to keep her mind on the road, but it was impossible to think of anything else now but what he might have in mind for this tryst on the wooded hillside of the priory, the traditional place for courting couples. It wasn't as if they hadn't been there before. They had, many times, but tonight was different. She didn't know how and she didn't know why. She just knew that it was.

'It's no good, I'll have to walk the last bit, Melvin,' she said finally, puffing as the slope towards the hillside became steeper. She slid off her cycle and leant on the handlebars for a moment.

'Come on, girl. Where's your stamina?' he yelled back, bending over his own machine and pedalling faster.

Well, it wasn't spent in wrestling with horses who didn't want to be shod, or dealing with the heat and dangers of the smithy, she thought, mildly resentful. He had more than one burn scar on his arms to remind her of the daily risks his craft demanded. But he was the sort who thrived on danger, while she only had to deal with carrying plates of food from the kitchen to the dining-room for the hotel guests, and making up their rooms for the next guests when they left. It seemed pretty feeble compared with his job.

He had stopped now, smiling at her as she almost trudged towards him.

'You're out of condition, my girl. You should take more exercise.'

'Thanks,' she muttered, feeling more like seventy than seventeen at such a remark. 'Anyway, I can normally rival you any day – just not today.'

'That's all right. I like my ladies docile.'

Her eyes sparkled. 'Really? How many have you got then?'

His arm went around her at once, ignoring the cumbersome cycles between them, and his kiss was ardent on her cheek.

'Only one, my sweet, and once we get to the top of this perishing hill, I'll show you how much I think of you.'

'Melvin,' she began uneasily.

'Stop talking, Charlotte, and save your breath for more interesting things,' he called back, already moving away from her. 'If we don't get up to the top soon, it'll be time to come down again.'

She followed, as she always did, asking herself what she was being so nervous about. She had longed for this evening to come, ever since she had seen him looking so marvellous on the back of the shire horse that afternoon. She had been so proud of him, and so full of a special glow at knowing that he was hers. She still was.

As expected, they weren't the only ones spending time on Priory Hill that evening. It gave Charlotte an odd sense of belonging and an inexplicable sense of relief too. Far below them the town resembled toytown, bathed now in a rosy aura from the lingering sunlight that hadn't yet dipped down to the horizon over the Bristol Channel. She caught her breath, knowing it was the perfect setting for romance.

They had thrown down their bicycles now, and found a hollow of their own, the way that other couples were undoubtedly doing. It was a favourite pastime to watch the sun go down as it turned the sea into ever-changing colours. Across the Channel was the coast of Wales, and Charlotte sometimes mused about whether there were young Welsh lovers finding a special place of their own and if they were doing the very same thing across the water.

'Come here, wench,' Melvin said roughly, and at the gleam in his eyes she knew his thoughts were nowhere near as poetic as her own, and just as quickly she abandoned all of them.

She gloried in the fact that he loved her and wanted her, and that she was his girl. She made no demur when his body half covered hers and his kisses were more passionate than usual, feeling her arms wind about his neck and pulling him ever closer into her. He was her sweetheart, her lover...

'Melvin, no,' she stuttered suddenly, realising that his hand was creeping slowly upwards and pushing her skirt aside. 'You promised me—'

'What the hell did I ever promise except to be true to you, sweetheart?' he said, his voice hoarser than usual. 'And you know I have been just that for months, even though you've kept me at arms' length for far too long.'

'But that's what we always intended, didn't we? We mustn't go to far, Melvin. It's madness, and it's wrong.'

His hand paused in its upward movement, and he gazed down at her flushed face in the soft, dying daylight.

'It's not wrong, Charlotte. When two people love each other, nothing's wrong between them. And you do love me, don't you?'

'Yes,' she whispered. 'You know I do.'

'So what's more natural between lovers than for us to know one another completely? You do know what I'm talking about, don't you, darling? You're not that naive.'

The small barb made her sharp. 'Of course not. But I'm also well aware that giving in to temptation can result in far more than people bargain for.'

She groaned inside, for didn't she want to do exactly as he did? Didn't she want to know the feel of him inside her, and to be carried away by passion and love? But one of them had to be sensible, even if she had voiced her fears of falling for a baby so grandly and obscurely.

His voice softened and his hand was stroking her thigh now, so gently and so seductively that she had to bite her lips to stop from crying out in pleasure.

'Charlotte, darling, don't you know that I'd never let anything bad happen to you? There are ways and means of preventing little accidents, you know.'

If her face had been flushed before, she felt it burn now. He may have been trying to reassure her, but she found it the most humiliating and coarse thing she had ever heard. She pushed his hand away and heard him curse.

'Well, now see what you've done to me,' he said angrily, grabbing her hand and thrusting it on the bulge in his trousers. 'Do you know how badly a chap can suffer if he's encouraged and then let down?'

She wanted to pull away her hand, but he kept it trapped there with his own. She could feel small movements from the thing inside and she didn't know whether to be excited or alarmed. But she was ultimately just too curious not to know.

'Does it hurt?' she said awkwardly.

'It does but, Charlotte, if you're not ready to go all the way just yet, at least let's go a little way,' he pleaded. 'We owe that much to each other.'

'Do we? I'm not sure what you mean.'

'I mean we don't have to go *all* the way,' he repeated. 'Just let me touch you, and you can do the same for me. If we're going to be more to each other in the future, we should at least have this knowledge of one another, shouldn't we? It's what all lovers do, sweetheart.'

He made it sound so logical, so normal, and she had no guidance to tell her whether or not he was telling the truth. But she did love him, and she wanted to be with him for always, and so she gave the slightest nod and lay back as his hand resumed its journey. She gasped when it reached its goal and then felt the most enormous surge of pleasure as he stroked and caressed her and made no attempt to go any further.

She was hardly aware of how her own hand had somehow reached inside his trousers and for the first time in her life she knew the feel of a man's private parts. He didn't allow it for very long, and she was grateful for his consideration as he left her for a few moments so she could rearrange her clothes. When he returned he covered her face with tender kisses and he was once again all the lover she could ever want.

'We've reached a milestone tonight, Charlotte,' he murmured against her mouth. 'We're almost part of one another now.'

'I know,' she said dreamily, still caught up in the enchantment of the evening, and hardly noticing the implication in his words that being part of one another was still unfinished.

Seven

'So what did you and old Melvin get up to tonight?' came Josie's sleepy voice in the darkness of their bedroom. She didn't really care and she didn't really want to know. It was simply something to say.

Charlotte snapped back. 'None of your business.'

The sharp reply was so unexpected that Josie was wide awake at once. She turned her head quickly to see Charlotte's profile in the other bed.

'Did he try something on? I bet he did.'

'Honestly, Josie, what kind of talk is that? No wonder Dad doesn't like you going anywhere near those fairground people if that's the kind of rubbish you talk.'

'You always have to turn everything around so that you can get in a snide remark about

Tony, don't you? Anyway, *he's* never tried anything on. He's very sweet, if you must know.' Although 'sweet' wasn't exactly the word that came to mind whenever she thought about his smouldering dark eyes and Latin looks.

'Well, I'm glad. I hope he stays that way,' Charlotte muttered. 'Now let's go to sleep, for goodness' sake. I'm exhausted after all the excitement of today.'

She wasn't so much exhausted as overcome with guilt and shame now. She knew very well that keeping herself clean for marriage didn't include letting a young man she was almost sure was going to propose one day touch her in intimate places. It definitely didn't mean letting passion run away with her to the extent of finding her own inexperienced fingers somewhere she had never expected them to go.

Even now, she couldn't think how it had happened. Everything had happened so swiftly, and her heart had been beating so fast, her breath so tight in her chest because they were entering unknown territory. And amid all the heightened passion of the moment, it had been Melvin who had thrust her hand down inside his trousers and gasped at the sensation of her fingers closing around him. She shut her eyes tightly and bit her lips, not with a delicious memory of what had happened, but with the thought that this mustn't happen again. If it did, she knew he wouldn't want to leave it there. He would want more.

Her breath was ragged in her throat again. Wanting more meant becoming a bad girl, and bad girls usually ended up being sent away to stay with some mythical aunt for months on end. Nobody ever believed the story, of course. Everyone knew why a girl had been sent away and why she eventually came back, subdued and miserable, and changed for ever from the way she was before.

Charlotte didn't want that to happen to her. She couldn't bear it for herself, nor for the shame it would bring to her family. Her dad might be over-pompous in the importance of The Retreat and his position in the town, but he had immense pride in his hotel and his family, and she would never let him down.

She didn't realise she had been holding her breath for so long until it came out in a sort of gasping groan.

'Are you all right, Charlotte?' came Josie's cautious voice. 'I didn't mean to upset you.'

'You didn't, and of course I'm all right. Go to sleep, there's a love.'

In any case, it was the most bizarre thing to be imagining about herself. She was the sensible oldest sister and, if anyone was likely to go off the rails, it would be Josie. It was one more reason why she had to set a good example and let Melvin be sure that what happened tonight was not going to happen again. Not until and unless they were engaged and on the brink of marriage, anyway, she amended silently ... because she wasn't so sensible that she couldn't admit that that brief taste of intimacy on Priory Hill had been exciting, and daring, filling her with sensations she had never known before.

She turned over restlessly in her bed and tried to put it all out of her mind, telling herself that it was enough that such delights, and more, were still to come.

As if to put paid to any hope for a long and lingering autumn, October was wet and blustery. November followed suit, with cold winds that stripped every leaf from the trees and curtailed folk from going outside except when it was absolutely necessary. Few visitors came to seaside resorts now, and owners were glad of their regulars, who huddled together in the guests' sitting-room to gossip and play cards, with elderly ladies like the Misses Green doing their interminable knitting.

At least they had a pleasant outlook from there, whatever the weather. The sitting-room had a big open fireplace that was warmed by a cosy wood fire for the benefit of old bones now, and the floor-length French windows looked straight out on to the Bristol Channel. When the tide was in, the wind churned the sea into a pewter inferno. Far from being afraid of its force, the regulars, often with Clover joining them, always relished watching the way the spume was flung up on to the shore and hearing the waves crashing on to the rocks farther along the bay.

'The force of nature should never be underestimated, and mountainous seas have been known to destroy the mightiest of ships,' the Captain said one evening after supper. He stood at the window, arms folded across his chest, legs astride and clearly fancying himself as a Colossus bracing himself from a storm.

'It's hardly the Atlantic Ocean out there, Captain,' Clover said mildly. 'And if you remember the disaster that befell all those poor people on the *Titanic* was on the calmest of seas. It was an iceberg that caused the damage, and a flaw in the ship's construction that finished it off.'

'Yes, dear lady,' the Captain said, prepared to indulge her. 'But if the ship hadn't been at sea in the first place, such a disaster could never have happened, could it? And if it had been equipped with enough lifeboats, and the night watch had been more alert to see the danger ahead, so many of those poor wretches could have been saved.'

Miss Hester Green chuckled, her knitting needles clacking ever more industriously at hearing the usual little banter between the two.

'You'll never get the better of him, dear. He always likes to have the last word, don't you, Captain?'

'If a person has the last sensible word, I believe it's up to him to voice it.'

'Lord grant me patience,' Clover muttered beneath her breath, but loudly enough for the two ladies to hear it and to giggle with their heads bent as they continued clacking their needles.

They were timid souls and rarely entered into an argument themselves, but they always enjoyed hearing other people's.

'Who's for a game of cards then?' the Captain suddenly barked. 'Do you want to make up a four at whist, dear lady?' he asked Clover.

She agreed that she would, if only to relieve the boredom of the day. It hadn't stopped raining from the moment she awoke, and young Milly had come home from school soaked to the skin and grumbling at everybody.

In fact, the whole family was in a similar mood, thought Clover. Donald was fretting about the finances of the hotel, even though she wasn't supposed to know it; Josie was fed up with waiting at tables and playing with the idea of getting an outside job, if only for the winter months; and Charlotte was despondent at not seeing her young man as often as she would like now. It wasn't Melvin Philpott's idea of spending an evening with his girl to have to spend it in a hotel sitting-room with a lot of older people. But Clover sometimes thought she detected a hint of relief in Charlotte's voice when she said they couldn't even go for walks to Priory Hill or anywhere else now that the ground was so sodden. Having been a passionate young woman in her own youth, Clover had her own private opinions about why that should be, but she wasn't going to pry if the girl didn't want to confide in her.

A little drop of rain shouldn't stop anybody going for walks though, Clover thought stoically. It had never stopped her. There was nothing so exhilarating as striding, body half bent against the force of the wind, along a stormy sea front. She had done it more times in her lifetime than the girls had had breakfasts. People were puny these days, she reflected. At least the Captain still had some spunk about him, even if he was living on past glories.

Her Tommy now ... her eyes softened. Now there was a man...

Charlotte wasn't the only Elkins girl with a secret. To her own unease Milly realised she was slowly changing her mind about going to the grammar school. She hadn't dared to mention such a thing at home yet, but she was getting so much scoffing and back-biting from her classmates at school, that she wasn't sure if she could bear to be thought such a show-off any longer.

It had made her head swell at first, being a teacher's pet because of her marks at school, but now she didn't like the way the other girls and boys were so stand-offish. She'd known them all since they were infants, and they'd all been friends, of sorts, and she was honest enough to admit that she'd been the one to stick her nose in the air and preen herself because she was always top of the class. Now, they seemed to see her as a bit of a freak, and she didn't like it. She didn't like it one bit. She wanted to be liked, and being so clever had made her feel that she always would be. Now, she was learning that it wasn't as clever as she had thought to stick her nose in the air and brag about her future.

That day had been the worst. It had been pouring with rain all morning but, when it eased a little, their teacher had insisted the children should get out of their stuffy classroom for ten minutes. They were instructed to wrap themselves up in coats and hats and run around the playground to get some fresh air into their lungs.

Milly had slipped in the playground and scraped her knee badly. It stung like billy-oh and she had a job to hold back the tears. What was worse, though, was that nobody had come to help her up until a stupid boy they all thought of as the dummy in the class asked if she was all right.

'Of course I'm all right,' she had snapped. 'It's only a little graze.'

'That's blood,' he'd announced, and she stared down at her leg then. The long socks she wore barely reached her knees, and now there was a fine trickle of red running down the left one.

To her horror a small group of children crowded around her, chanting and jeering until their teacher came to see what all the fuss was about and took her away to clean her up. But the whole episode had unnerved her and made her realise how isolated she really was, just because she was clever.

But she knew it was more than that. It had also told her something else. If you wanted friends, you had to be a friend, and not a snob. The trouble was, she didn't know how to go about it. She wouldn't ask Charlotte or Josie, because they wouldn't believe she wanted to change. They'd think she had some ulterior motive in mind. She'd just learnt that expression, and she chewed it over in her head, liking the sound of it ... and then she began feeling miserable all over again, because it just seemed to show how she was attaching far too much importance to how clever she was. If anyone could tell her what to do, it would be Clover, she thought. Clover wouldn't think she was being stupid, or losing face in wanting people to like her, and not having the faintest idea how to go about it.

If she felt daring enough, she might even sound out Clover about what her parents might say if she told them she may not really want to go to the grammar school after all. In fact, the more she said the words in her head, the more she knew it was the way she really felt. But she shivered, knowing that it would cause such ructions that, for now, it was a thought that was best kept to herself.

There was something about the wildness and the vagaries of nature that had always touched Clover's adventurous soul. Not that she and Tommy had ever done anything as fantastic as big-game hunting in Africa, or deep-sea diving to explore the depths of the ocean, but the thought of living a humdrum life had never been for them. She had always counted herself the most fortunate of women in meeting and marrying a man whose ideas so closely matched her own. A man after her own heart, in every respect, she often thought dreamily. She still missed him more than words could ever say, but she was perfectly sure that he was still with her in spirit, so that she had never really lost him.

It wasn't something the young ones would understand, certainly not her staid son and his obedient wife, much as she loved them. The girls were too young to appreciate how love could go on, even after death ... Charlotte was the most perceptive of them in that respect, but it wasn't something you brought up in ordinary conversation. Besides which, there was an undoubted touch of jealousy in her heart, in keeping the close connection between herself and Tommy, which she still felt so strongly, all to herself.

He often spoke to her in the night. Spoke, and whispered, and came to her, as clearly as if she could reach out and touch him. There was nothing in the least spooky in feeling that way, but that was something else that the others could never understand. The regulars might have done if they weren't such devoted spinster ladies who had never known a man between them, she wouldn't wonder ... and as for the Captain, he was a crusty old bachelor, too, so none of them could ever be a real confidant. Anyway, she didn't need them. She had her Tommy, and he was all and everything to her.

On a night like this, so wild and wonderful in its awesome power, she could almost hear him laughing in her ear, telling her that they should go walking in the hills and the rain and supplicate themselves to nature ... he had such enthusiasm for whatever he did, her Tommy, like no other man she had ever known or ever wanted to know. If she said she wanted to go to Timbuktu or climb a mountain, he'd say why not, and never raise a hint of an objection. They'd done it, too.

Unfortunately the old bones didn't allow for such extravagancies these days, she thought ruefully. She was restricted to dreaming and, if those dreams sometimes took on the night-time excursions her family disapproved of so strongly, it was no business of theirs, just hers and Tommy's.

Hearing the wind soughing through the trees outside the hotel, sighing and whispering and calling to her with Tommy's voice, made this such a splendid night for a caper, she thought exuberantly...

'Where's Mother this morning?' Donald said irritably. 'It's not like her not to be downstairs for breakfast, and Milly makes so much noise in the morning it's enough to waken the dead.'

'I'll go and call her,' Charlotte said at once. 'There's no reason for her to get up so early, though, and you always say she gets under your feet in the morning.'

'I already called her,' Milly said resentfully, having been silently practising how to be friendly to the other schoolchildren in her class and not too bothered that her grandmother hadn't yet got out of bed. 'She made a kind of mumbling sound and said she was going back to sleep and told me to go away.'

'Well, that's not like her at all,' Ruth exclaimed. 'Go and see if she's feeling all right, Charlotte.'

They were all still scratchy with one another. The weather was having a bad effect on them all, and the rain hadn't eased at all during the night. It was so cold outside now that all the windows inside the hotel were steamed up, making the whole place seem even more clammy and claustrophobic.

Charlotte went up to the partitioned bedroom that Clover shared with Milly and tapped on her door. There was no reply so, after tapping slightly louder and still hearing nothing, she opened the door quietly and stepped inside. The figure bundled up beneath the bedclothes looked pathetically small, and Charlotte felt suddenly anxious. But having already seen the discarded outer garments scattered about the floor, their dampness seeping into the rugs, Charlotte knew.

'Gran, were you out in that awful weather

last night?' she hissed at her.

Clover didn't answer, but a feeble lift of her hand above the bedclothes gave Charlotte all the acknowledgement she needed. Charlotte moved towards her swiftly, wrinkling her nose at the combined smells of dampness and stale air.

Clover raised her head a fraction and then dropped it down on the pillow again. 'No need to fuss, my love. But if you fancy bringing me a hot cup of tea, I wouldn't say no.'

'You look as if you need more than a hot cup of tea,' Charlotte exclaimed. 'You look terrible!'

She put her hand on Clover's burning forehead. She was no nurse, but it was obvious to anyone that her gran was running a fever, and a woman of her years was not always able to combat such a thing.

'That's not very flattering, Charlotte,' Clover said feebly.

'It's not meant to be. I'm going to fetch Mum, and once she sees you I'm sure she'll want to send for the doctor.'

'I don't want the doctor. A drop of rain never hurt anybody.'

'It was more than a drop of rain. It was *pouring* last night. And I'd better pick up these sodden cloths before Mum sees them, too.'

Clover spoke a little more tetchily. 'Charlotte, I'll thank you not to treat me like an infant. It's no matter to me whether your mother sees my clothes or not. Now go away and let me rest.'

Charlotte stared at her. She was acting so very unlike herself, and she looked truly awful, so blotchy faced and wild eyed. They *had* to get the doctor.

She turned and ran down the stairs, unable to stay in that stuffy room a minute longer. She went straight to the kitchen, glad that Milly had gone to school by now and that Josie had been sent for groceries. The regulars would still be in the dining-room, lingering over breakfast as usual, and there were only her mother and father in the kitchen. She burst out the words.

'Mum, Gran's ill, and she looks so awful I think she should see the doctor right away. Will you come up and see what you think? She wants a hot cup of tea and she feels terribly hot but she seems to be shivering at the same time.'

Ruth looked startled for a moment, and then she and Donald were bounding for the stairs together, with Charlotte close behind them. It was almost unheard of for Clover to stay in bed and ask for tea, and it was even more unheard of for her to admit to being ill.

When they reached the bedroom, Clover was half sitting up and looking annoyed at the invasion that burst in on her.

'What's all this? Can't a woman of my age have a little privacy now, then?'

She sounded so normal that Charlotte thought she might have imagined the feebleness of minutes before. But at the same time, she looked anything but normal. Her eyes were too bright, her face too flushed, her limbs too trembling.

'Mother, you're ill,' Donald stated. 'I'm sending Charlotte for the doctor.'

'I've already told her I don't want him. You can't *make* me talk to him,' she replied in a childish sulk.

Ruth took charge, going to her bedside and urging her gently back down beneath the bedclothes. 'Clover, darling, we all want to see you back to your old self again, so please do as Donald says. I'll get you that tea you wanted, and some hot porridge as well.'

'I never said I wanted tea. I hate tea. I want hot milk.'

Charlotte felt the tears welling up in her throat. This was not the normal Clover talking at all. This was not her darling gran. This was some cantankerous old woman who resembled her gran but who seemed to have aged considerably since last night. Charlotte turned and went back downstairs to prepare a tray with hot tea, hot milk and hot porridge, her own hands shaking.

'Leave that to me, Charlotte, and go and fetch the doctor,' she heard Ruth's quiet voice say a few minutes later.

'Is she very ill, do you think, Mum?'

Donald's temper was set to fly. 'She's no worse than any damn silly woman of her age would be after tramping about half the night in the rain. And don't try to deny it or to defend her, Charlotte. We both saw the pile of clothes you'd picked up off the floor.'

'It's probably no more than a heavy chill,' Ruth said soothingly to her daughter, ignoring him. 'But at her age we can't be too careful.'

Charlotte was glad to escape on her bicycle to fetch the doctor. She was shamefully aware of thinking that, as it had been so wretched last night, at least none of the local people would have seen Clover wandering along the sea front in the middle of the night like a lunatic. Her dad would have been relieved about that, if nothing else. Her breath caught on a sob as she leant over the handlebars. As if it mattered. Nothing mattered but the fact that Clover looked so ill, and she wanted so desperately for her to be well, and as eccentrically endearing to them all as she always was.

Josie came back from the grocery store, not unduly alarmed to see the doctor's ancient car outside the hotel. One or other of the regulars was often sending for him, which always made Clover scoff that they had no backbone. Josie glanced into the dining-room, glad to have got out of the breakfast chores that day, and then went into the guests' sitting-room, where three excited faces turned towards her. Her heart gave a sudden jolt.

'Who's ill?' she said in a hoarse voice.

The Misses Green rose from their armchairs as if they were joined by an invisible cord and rushed towards her, their arms reaching out as if to envelop her. Josie took an involuntary step backward, warding them off by her action. They trilled in unison.

'Oh, Josie dear, it's your poor gran. She must have taken ill in the night, and Charlotte had to go rushing off to fetch the doctor. He's been with her a long time, and your parents are upstairs with her, too.'

'Where's Charlotte now?' Josie said harshly, hearing the Captain continually clearing his throat as if not sure how to handle this situation. He could deal with a regiment of soldiers but not a couple of twittering elderly women, constantly wringing their hands and expecting the worst.

'I don't know,' Hester said vaguely.

'Never mind. I'll find her,' Josie said, twisting away from their dismal faces. They had Clover already dead and buried, she thought savagely, and she was sure it was nothing as dire as that. Not Clover, who was as tough as nails and had gone through a couple of wars with her Tommy and never faltered.

She found Charlotte busily putting washing into the big tub in the scullery and stabbing it for all she was worth with the boiler stick. Her eyes were as blotchy as Clover's, and for the first time Josie felt really scared.

'She's not really ill, is she?' she said huskily. 'She's not ill enough to – to *die* – is she?'

Charlotte couldn't speak, and then Josie had twisted away from her sister, unable to face an answer, whatever that answer might be. She rushed upstairs to her own room and slammed the door behind her, as if to shut out every unpleasant thing that might be ahead of her. She didn't want to be morbid, but she had never seen a dead person before, and the sudden thought that it might be happening to Clover was something she couldn't bear to consider. She buried her head in her pillow like an ostrich, and was still there when she found it yanked from under her.

'A fat lot of use you're going to be if you fall to pieces before we even know what's wrong,' Charlotte snapped.

'I'm scared, Charlie,' Josie answered, her voice wobbling.

Charlotte put her arms around her at once. 'I'm scared, too, but we mustn't show it. She wouldn't want us to, would she? And we've got to be strong for Milly's sake. Besides, we haven't even heard what the doctor has to say yet.'

'But she's never ill, so it must be something bad!'

Charlotte took hold of Josie's hands and held them tightly. 'Now you just listen to me. Gran's tough, and whatever it is, she'll get over it. We've got to keep on thinking that way, and we mustn't let Mum and Dad see us with gloomy faces either. You know they'll say it's bad for the hotel.'

That was enough to produce a watery smile from Josie.

'All right, I'll try. It was those frumpies in the sitting-room who made me feel so bad when I went in there, not knowing what was going on.'

'Well, until we do know, let's go and do something useful to keep ourselves occupied. You can help me with the weekly wash to save Mum a job. That'll cheer you up, won't it?'

The scowl that followed said more than words about that.

Eight

They were told that Clover had a severe chill, brought about by wandering along the sea front on that terrible November night. She refused to answer any questions about it, and simply turned her face to the wall if anyone started quizzing her or remonstrating with her.

Doctor Jacobs spoke sternly to Donald and Ruth after he had made his diagnosis and didn't mince his words. 'By rights she should be in a proper nursing home with people who can deal with this kind of ailment. It's not just her age, it's this inability to keep her thoughts in the present. Once she had insisted that you both left the bedroom, she kept asking me if I had seen Tommy, when we all know he died many years ago. She seems to think he is still alive, and I fear that it is her mind, as much as her body, that is wearing out. By the time she was drifting off to sleep again after the sedative I gave her, she was garbling something about dancing in the moonlight with him.'

'She's not going into any nursing home,' Donald said at once, ignoring the rest of the doctor's words and knowing the kind of place he was thinking about. 'We've never had anything of this kind in our family, and she can have all the care she needs right here.'

'My dear Mr Elkins, noble as it sounds, you are not qualified in the psychiatric field of medicine, and neither am I. Once the mind begins to lose control there is little that anyone without specialist knowledge can do for it.'

'I'm not having my mother shut away,' Donald shouted. 'She merely has a severe chill, and once she has recovered she'll be back to her normal self again.'

'Yes, and I'm afraid the whole town is only too well aware of what her normal self is like,' the doctor said bluntly, not bothering to restrict his words. 'If you won't heed my advice and let me seek further help for your mother, I'll leave you a prescription for some medicine that will calm her and help to lessen the symptoms of the chill. You will, of course, send for me at any time if you think I am needed. And now I shall bid you good day.'

He went out of the hotel stiffly, leaving Donald cursing behind him.

'Bloody doctors think they're God Almighty. As if we can't care for our own as well as anybody. But we'd best send one of the girls for his medicine, and just hope that it'll do the trick.'

'We'll *pray* that it does, too,' Ruth reminded him.

'That too.'

He looked at his wife silently. 'And if it doesn't, then we'll see about having a nurse companion living in the hotel to look after her permanently, no matter how much it costs. I'll not send her away.'

Ruth's eyes softened and she put her hand on his arm. 'I know you'd do anything for your mother, Donald, and of course I would back you in whatever you decide, but I dread to think how such a move would stretch our resources.'

'Do you think I care about such a thing now?' he said angrily, pushing her away. In his heart, though, he knew that if the time came, he would have to care, and that Ruth was absolutely right.

The entire hotel was in a state of chaos for a few hours, with the regulars agog to know what was happening and only being given the bare bones of it. It was impossible to keep them completely uninformed. They weren't part of the family, but they had formed a unique bond with the Elkins family after all these years, and with Clover in particular, being of comparable ages. The only person who still didn't know what had happened was Milly.

She came skipping home from school that

afternoon, jumping and splashing her boots in the rain puddles. She was feeling chirpier than she had been for days, since she had discovered that offering the hand of friendship wasn't just a silly phrase that was used in a school textbook to demonstrate the use of metaphor.

It really worked, especially when that hand held a few sweets for a chosen companion at playtime. If it was construed as bribery she didn't care. She now had a sort of friend in Dorothy Yard. Dorothy wasn't brainy enough to pass the scholarship exam, but she wasn't a dunce either. She was pleasantly plump and cheerful, and she didn't mind when Milly put her right in her sums or her spelling.

The rain had finally eased to a fine drizzle, but it skittered coldly about the sea front, aided by the wind that was roaring steadily up the Channel. Milly shivered as she burst into the hotel like a little tornado, shouting to everyone that she was home and near to freezing. She was shushed at once by the four people inside the kitchen.

'Keep your voice down, Milly,' her father said sharply.

She stared at him. 'Why? What's wrong?'

Without answering, her mother scolded her, finding a brief solace in domestic matters. 'Milly, take off those boots at once. Look at the state they're in.'

Milly glanced warily at her sisters. They looked funny. Not funny ha ha, but more like funny peculiar. There was definitely something wrong and she didn't know what it was, but it made her heart thump all the same.

Nobody was dead, because they were all here. All except...

'Where's Gran?' she said in a quavering voice.

After a small silence, everybody spoke at once.

'It's nothing to worry about—'

'It's just a little chill, that's all—'

'She'll be all right in a few days' time—'

'The doctor's given her some medicine, but she'll have to stay in bed for the time being until she gets her strength back—'

Milly's heart beat faster. 'She's never ill in bed. I don't have to sleep right next to her, do I?' Her voice rose. 'She might die!'

Donald spoke angrily. 'Don't be ridiculous, Milly. Nobody dies from a little chill, and your grandmother is tougher than that.'

Charlotte noted how suddenly nobody was referring to her as Clover any more. She was being given the dignity of age. Old age, she thought, shivering as hard as Milly now. But she could see the alarm in her young sister's eyes. She moved towards her and gave her a hug, regardless of her damp outer clothes that she hadn't yet removed.

'Of course you don't have to sleep in your own room, Milly. We wouldn't want to risk you catching it as well, and I'm sure Gran would prefer to be on her own, without hearing you clumping about all the time. You can have a camp-bed in our room for the time being, can't she, Josie?'

She glared at Josie, willing her to agree to the indignity of having a ten-year-old infiltrating their bedroom but, for once, Josie didn't have the heart to argue.

'Should I go and see her then?' Milly said uneasily.

It was painfully obvious to all of them that Milly was scared of what she would see. They were a particularly robust family, and rarely ill, so this was a new occurrence and an unwelcome one.

'Of course you can and I'll come with you,' Charlotte said at once. 'But we must be quiet because she's probably asleep.'

She hardly knew why she was taking charge like this, but her parents had done all that was necessary and were trying to get the hotel back to normal. Josie was behaving as if she didn't know how to deal with an unusually inactive Clover, and didn't want to know, either. Charlotte hadn't fully realised before how much Josie hated the thought of illness of any kind.

Five minutes later she and Milly had tiptoed into the bedroom where Clover lay on her back, her eyes closed. The curtains were drawn across to allow her to sleep and the room smelled stuffy with the indefinable smell of old age.

'She doesn't look too bad,' Milly whispered uneasily.

'She's not deaf either,' Clover murmured.

As Charlotte gave her a little push, Milly

moved nearer to the bed and Clover opened her eyes and spoke weakly.

'Don't worry, chick, I'm not about to turn up my toes just yet, whatever they told you.'

'They said you had a chill.'

'Well, that's what I've got then,' Clover said complacently.

'Is it all right if I sleep in Charlotte and Josie's room until you get better? So you can get some proper sleep,' Milly added.

''Course it is. Best thing for both of us.'

Milly stared down at her, not too sure about this easy acceptance. There was something different about her gran, but Milly couldn't think what it was. Whatever it was, she wasn't sure that she liked it. She liked it when Clover was up and about, marching about the place and dressed to the nines in her gaudy outfits as she put the world to rights. She liked to hear tales of where Clover had been during the night, whether it had happened for real or in her vivid imagination, which they all knew it so often had.

Milly was sure she had never in her life before seen Clover lying ill in bed. Other people's grandmothers got ill and then died, but not hers. When you were ten years old you never expected it to happen. You expected the people you loved to live for ever, and to be surrounded by a family group that never changed. She gulped, and Clover patted her hand.

'Go along and get your stuff moved into Charlotte's room, love. I'm weary and I want to go back to sleep.'

On an impulse Milly leant over and kissed Clover's cheek. It was normally dry and papery, like those of the regulars, but now it was clammy and she tried not to flinch as she drew away, leaving Clover with a slight smile on her lips.

'Come on, Milly, let's get on with it,' Charlotte said swiftly, realising that despite all the reassurances it was slowly dawning on her young sister that this might be no ordinary chill after all, but something far more serious. It was dawning on Charlotte too.

It was never going to be an easy situation with the three girls all in the same bedroom. Milly's jitters didn't abate, and she found it hard to go to sleep in the unfamiliar surroundings. She always seemed to be awake, wanting to talk, when the others came to bed, and after a week of it the older ones began to tire of hearing about this wonderful new friend called Dorothy, who wasn't likely to be going to the grammar school next year, and how much Milly was going to miss her when she went.

'Considering she's the first girl at that school you've really bothered about, I suppose we shouldn't be surprised that you've found yourself a little lap-dog at last,' Josie said sarcastically.

'Dorothy's not a little lap-dog. She's nice, and her dad has a tackle shop where they sell bags and suitcases as well, and it smells lovely when you go inside, like new shoes that have just been polished.'

'You don't mean that tackle and leather goods shop in Taylor's Yard?' Charlotte said.

'That's the one.'

'No wonder you come home smelling horsey sometimes, even worse than Charlie does when she's been to the smithy,' Josie sniggered.

Charlotte threw a pillow at her and the next minute the three of them were hurling pillows at one another until they were stopped by the sound of the door opening and their mother entering the bedroom.

'For the love of heaven, what do you all think you're doing?' Ruth said, appalled. 'Have you forgotten that your grandmother is ill and needs her rest? You're behaving like a lot of hooligans, and if this nonsense continues Milly's camp-bed will be moved into our room until Clover gets better.'

'Sorry, we didn't think,' Charlotte muttered.

'Well, you should have, Charlotte, even if I might have expected the other two to behave without concern for other people's feelings. Now go to sleep, all of you, and don't let me hear from you again until morning.'

Charlotte smarted after her mother had gone, finding it totally unfair that she should come off worst. But nobody dared to speak again for a long while, and it was only when she heard Milly's deeper breathing and was sure she was asleep, that Josie whispered wickedly in the darkness.

'I bet Dad won't agree to having the infant in their bedroom. It would put a stop to any cuddles and stuff, wouldn't it? That is, if they still do any of that lovey-dovey stuff at their age. What do you think, Charlie?'

Charlotte muttered something unintelligible beneath the bedclothes. It was ludicrous to think that parents *didn't* do any of the lovey-dovey stuff, but somehow you never thought that they did, nor wanted to imagine it, either. She particularly *didn't* want to think about it, especially now that she had had that personal knowledge of a man's body in the nether regions. She couldn't imagine that Josie had any idea of that, either. She had better not, she thought fiercely.

But inevitably, her thoughts moved towards Melvin and how little she had seen of him recently. He didn't even know of her gran's illness, which was being kept a private matter, because so much of her time, and that of all of them, had been taken up in catering to Clover's every need. But he could have called to see her any time, Charlotte thought resentfully. He could have sent her a note saying he missed her and hoped they could get together soon.

Just because they couldn't go walking out on the beach or up in the hills the way they liked to do ... just because they couldn't repeat what had happened on Priory Hill until the weather improved ... her heart lurched. Maybe this was what happened when you gave in to a boy's demands. Maybe this was what older people meant when they said you should keep yourself clean and pure for marriage, because once a boy had taken what he wanted, what else was there for him to take?

The horrible sinking feeling in her stomach wouldn't go away until she told herself not to be so stupid. She *hadn't* given him everything, and nor would she, no matter how much he pleaded about it being bad for a young man's health to be denied. She wasn't that gullible, even if she was only seventeen. She knew right from wrong and, if she had to keep away from him to avoid temptation, well, wasn't there an old saying that absence made the heart grow fonder?

It was about the only thing that calmed her jittering nerves before she finally managed to fall asleep.

She was jerked into wakefulness, either by some sixth sense that told her something was wrong, or by shuffling sounds that she couldn't identify. She tried to tell herself it was Milly being restless in her sleep, and at least she was sure it couldn't be Clover on the move, because she was simply too weak. All the same, she found herself slipping out of bed and silently crossing over to the window to pull back the curtains an inch or two and peer outside.

'Can you see anything?' came Josie's whispered voice behind her a moment later, making her jump so much her heart stopped beating before racing on.

'You nearly gave me a heart attack,' she hissed. 'And there's nothing to see, so go back to bed.'

'What's that, then?' Josie said, her arm reaching out beyond Charlotte to point to something moving along the sea front.

The rain had stopped at last and faint moonlight shone intermittently behind the scudding clouds. A small lone figure in what looked like a long white gown and bare feet was dancing along the promenade, arms held out as if she was in the embrace of an unseen partner.

'Oh God, what's she doing?' Josie breathed.

'She's dancing with Tommy, that's what she's doing,' Charlotte said, her voice breaking harshly. 'It's absolute madness for her to be out there after being so ill, and she should be brought back in the warm. Lord knows how she had the strength to go outside, anyway.'

'Should we go and get her back?'

'There's no need,' Charlotte said, drawing back into the room as she caught sight of her parents running along the sea front to capture Clover between them and throw a coat around her shoulders before hurrying her back to the hotel.

The noises that had woken her had obviously been her parents preparing to bring Clover back. Hopefully, she would be docile and ready for as dreamless a sleep as Milly was having now.

'I'm going downstairs to put the kettle on for a hot-water bottle to put in her bed, and to see what I can do to help.'

'I can help too—'

'No, it's best if we don't all crowd her or alarm her. She might be very excitable, and I really think it's best if you stay here, Josie.'

Josie didn't need much persuading, and moments later Charlotte had put on her dressing-gown and was running silently downstairs, her hands shaking so much that the water spilled over her as she filled the kettle. No matter how calm she had tried to be, she was really afraid for Clover now. A woman of her age and in her poor state of health had done the worst possible thing she could in being outside in the cold night air. She prayed that no one else had witnessed the mad dancing and thought her gran completely crazy.

Her hopes of that were dashed as soon as her father came indoors, telling Ruth to get Clover straight up to bed before she expired on the spot.

'I'm making her a hot-water bottle,' Charlotte said at once.

'A tot of brandy is probably a better idea,' Donald snapped. 'She's done it good and proper this time, with some late-night revellers standing about and laughing at her antics. Take that bottle upstairs and I'll fetch the brandy. I could do with some myself. It's bitter out there tonight.'

Charlotte moved away from him as soon as she had fastened the stopper on the rubber hot-water bottle. Her father was in a foul mood, and she couldn't blame him. But she couldn't blame Clover, either. Short of locking her in at night, how could they stop her doing what she thought was right? But even that might become a necessity, Charlotte thought sadly.

Ruth was tiptoeing out of the bedroom now.

'She's exhausted, and no wonder. What on earth was she thinking about?'

'I don't know, Mum. I've got her hot-water bottle, and Dad's bringing her up a tot of brandy.'

'I'll tell him not to bother. She's asleep already. Just see that she's warmly tucked up and get to bed yourself, dear.'

Charlotte crept over to the bed and put the hot-water bottle next to Clover's frozen feet, pulling her nightgown down over her as far as possible and tucking the bedclothes in around her tightly. She heard her parents muttering quietly, and then their bedroom door closed behind them. She looked down at her grandmother, so small in the bed, as she had thought once before, and still with the heightened flush of the chill in her cheeks, yet with an oddly peaceful look around her mouth.

'He was calling to me, Charlotte, so I had to go to him, didn't I?' Clover suddenly whispered in a dreamy, conspiratorial voice that held more than a hint of excitement even while it wavered. 'It was so wonderful to be dancing in his arms again the way we used to.'

'You were dreaming, Gran.'

Clover's eyes opened wide, burning bright now as she shook her head.

'Oh no, darling. It was more than a dream. You don't understand yet, but someday you will. Tommy came for me, calling to me to meet him in the moonlight. He said our time had come, and I believed him, as I always did. Did you see me in my lovely white gown? It was just like the one I used to wear in the Officers' Mess on special occasions when we danced the night away.'

'Oh, Gran,' Charlotte whispered as Clover's eyes became clouded again as if she was seeing something very far away from this cloying bedroom.

'I'm going to sleep now, Charlotte. Dancing tires me nowadays, but I'll be better in the morning. Come and see me then, sweet girl.'

As Clover's voice became thinner and weaker, Charlotte leant forward and kissed her, aware of a horrible presentiment as she saw that strange smile curve Clover's lips again. One instinct was to stay beside her while she slept, keeping a silent vigil, and another was to flee from what she sensed was inevitable. Clover had already gone so far away from them that there was surely no turning back. The only comfort was that it was to a place her grandmother so dearly wanted to go.

'I'm very sorry to tell you that my mother

passed over during the night,' Donald told the shocked group of regulars the following morning. 'She simply fell asleep and never woke up.'

'Oh dear, Mr Elkins, we're all so very sorry,' Miss Hester Green said, sniffing back the tears and echoed by her sister as usual. 'We thought we heard some disturbance in the night, but we were clearly mistaken. But as long as the dear lady didn't suffer, it's all any of us could wish for in our passing.'

Josie was less than charitable as she heard the trite words coming from the dining-room after she had taken in their morning tea.

'Just listen to them being so pious in there,' she raged. 'And Dad, too. Gran hasn't passed over anywhere. She's dead, and no amount of soapy words are going to bring her back.'

'Josie, be quiet,' Ruth said angrily. 'This is not the time to be airing your opinions, and you should show some respect for Clover.'

'I *do* respect her. I just don't see why we should dress things up in stupid language. It doesn't make things any easier. She's still dead, whatever you call it.'

She rushed past Milly, who was coming downstairs to get ready for school, still ignorant of what had happened since the older girls had got up early, and who grumbled at being pushed out of the way. Charlotte was just coming indoors from informing the doctor of what had happened.

'What have I done?' Milly asked suspiciously, when her mother and sister looked at her dumbly for a moment.

Charlotte took control, since her mother suddenly looked so inadequate. And why shouldn't she? She'd never had to explain to a child that a well-loved grandmother was dead. Neither had Charlotte, but she had always been a stronger person than her mother, and she needed that strength now.

'Darling, come into the sitting-room for a minute, so that we can have a chat.'

'Why is everybody being so strange?' Milly said shrilly as Charlotte closed the door of the sitting-room behind them. 'And why are you calling me darling? I don't want to have a chat and I'll be late for school.'

'I don't think you'll be going to school today, Milly.'

The next ten minutes were the hardest Charlotte had ever faced. Milly was sobbing in her arms, wanting to know so many details she simply couldn't answer. Where was Clover now? Was she with the angels, and had they come for her in the night? Did Charlotte think she knew she was dying? Did it hurt? Was she frightened? Did she want to leave them? And finally, fearfully, was Clover's dead body still upstairs in the partitioned bedroom next to Milly's?

'Yes, but it's all right, love, you don't have to go back in there until you're ready,' Charlotte said gently. 'I think she'll be taken away from here quite soon, though.'

Because, of course, they couldn't keep a dead person, even a beloved one, in an hotel where there were paying guests. The mundane thoughts flitted in and out of Charlotte's head, even while she tried to pacify her bereft youngest sister.

It was odd how differently it was taking them all, she thought. She was the oldest of the sisters, and she was relatively calm, which perhaps came from knowing that Clover was reunited with her beloved Tommy at last. Josie was simply angry, refusing to think about death at all, and Milly was the submissive, enquiring child she had always been before she got above herself, as Clover would say.

Charlotte stifled a sob in her throat at the memory, knowing there would be many moments like this, when one of Clover's old sayings would come surging into her head.

None of them would stay the way they were now, of course. Josie's rage would subside and she would mourn for her gran as they all would. Milly wouldn't stay submissive for ever, and she would soon be back to her old form, while Charlotte herself ... without warning, she found herself rocking Milly back and forth in her arms, both weeping as if their hearts would break.

Nine

The news of Clover Elkins' death soon got around the town. Unfortunately it was also accompanied by gossip from the revellers who had witnessed her late-night dancing, boasting that they were probably the last people to see her alive apart from her family. It diluted some of the town's sympathy and stamped Clover for ever as that madwoman who scared decent God-fearing folk to death by her night-time activities, especially when there was a full moon, as the revellers exaggerated.

'Is it true that your gran was a witch?' Dorothy Yard asked Milly Elkins in a hushed, excited voice when she returned to school a few days later and they were walking around the playground arm in arm before lessons began.

Milly lashed out at once, swinging her school satchel around and giving Dorothy a hefty clout on the side of her head.

'Of course she wasn't a witch,' Milly shouted as Dorothy howled in pain. 'Anybody who says so is wicked, and I don't want to be friends with you any more.'

'It wasn't me who said it,' Dorothy yelled

back. 'I heard it from some other kids, and my mum heard it too, and she don't want me to be friends with you no more, so there! She says you're probably all tarred with the same brush.'

Milly stared at her. Dorothy was still rubbing her head and Miss Brown, their teacher, was rushing across to see what all the rumpus was about.

'What's going on here?'

'She says my gran was a witch, and she *wasn't* a witch. She was just my gran,' Milly bawled, her mouth starting to wobble as other kids were starting to crowd around them now.

'Well, of course Mrs Elkins wasn't a witch,' Miss Brown said briskly. 'She may have been a little eccentric, but that's not such a terrible thing to be, and old people do sometimes have odd ideas.'

An older boy joined in excitedly. 'My dad says she used to go out at midnight howling at the moon, and if that ain't being a witch, he don't know what is!'

'Shut *up*, you pig!' Milly shouted, near to sobbing now. 'My gran never did such a thing, and if she was a witch she'd have put a spell on your stupid dad for saying such wicked things about her.'

She could hear herself gabbling now, making things worse with every word she said, putting thoughts into people's heads without meaning to.

'Milly, dear, I think you've come back to

school too soon,' Miss Brown was saying gently. 'I think it's best if you go home again and come back in a week or so after your gran's funeral. You'll feel calmer then.'

'She might if the old duck don't come back to haunt us,' the boy with the know-all dad sniggered uneasily, at which he was hauled off by another teacher to sit in a corner in the classroom and write a hundred lines regretting his bad manners.

'Shall I go home with her, Miss?' Dorothy said in a small voice, as if conscious that all this fuss had been started by her one remark. 'I'll still be her friend, if she wants me to be, whatever my mum says.'

'That's very kind of you, dear,' Miss Brown began doubtfully.

Milly gave them both a watery grimace in lieu of a smile. 'No, thanks. I'd rather go on my own, but I daresay Dorothy can still be my friend at school.'

'That's all right, then,' Miss Brown said, glad to get the troublesome matter settled. 'You go on home, Milly, and tell your parents why I think it's best for you. And please give them my condolences.' As the morning bell sounded for lessons, she seemed to encompass the small group of children in front of her as she shooed them inside the school, leaving Milly feeling more alone and isolated than ever.

But by the time she reached home she was also furious to think that anyone could think such bad things about her gran, and she stormed into the kitchen to tell her mother what had happened.

By now, Clover's body had been removed to the Chapel of Rest and the hotel had resumed an uneasy sort of peace. The funeral would take place in three days' time, and as Milly burst out with all that had gone on, Ruth did her best to calm her.

'Milly, love, it's all nonsense, and you must believe that. Clover *was* an eccentric old lady and we all knew of her odd little ways, but we loved her and cared for her as well, didn't we?'

'People are saying she was a witch,' Milly said, wishing she didn't even have to say the words at all, but desperate to hear her mother's reassurance.

'Well, now that *is* nonsense. If that were true, the vicar wouldn't allow her to be buried in consecrated ground. It's very sad when a perfectly harmless old lady has such unpleasant things said about her, especially after her death, but we must all keep our dignity and not let such things upset us. Does that make you feel any better?'

Milly wasn't sure. The bit about the vicar did, she supposed, but it was hard to keep your dignity and not let things upset you when you were only ten years old.

She sought out Charlotte for comfort, finding her dusting furniture in the regulars' bedrooms. Such an ordinary, everyday task, as if their whole lives hadn't been overturned in the last few days.

'Who's upset you?' Charlotte said, straightening up at once and seeing the tension in her sister's young body.

'Kids at school,' Milly muttered. 'Even Dorothy. They were saying nasty things about Gran – Clover. I've been sent home until after – after – well, you know.'

Charlotte knew she had to be careful in her response. She wasn't a psychiatrist or someone who was clever with words, but Milly's normally sunny face was so troubled and bewildered now, and Charlotte knew she would be grieving in her own way. The last thing she needed was to have the other children at school mocking her.

'It's a funeral, darling. It's what happens when people die. It's a way of putting them to rest and allowing us to say our proper goodbyes to them. It's nothing to be afraid of. It happens to everybody eventually, and it's as natural as being born. Gran knew that and she wasn't afraid. In fact, I think she secretly welcomed it, because she was going to be with her Tommy again.'

'Did she really believe that?' Milly asked.

'Well, of course she did. I believed it, too. Didn't you?'

'Yes. No. I don't know. I suppose so. But you can't really *know*, can you?'

Charlotte put her arms around the tense little body.

'That's part of the mystery of it all. Believing that we'll see our loved ones again is what our parents and grandparents pass down to us, and it's important that we don't lose faith every time something goes against us.'

Embarrassed at somehow being drawn into a pompous and philosophical conversation that was beyond her, too, Charlotte wished she could get out of it before Milly started asking about the meaning of life and all that high-falutin' stuff. But to her relief, she suddenly heard Milly giggle, and then the girl shook herself away from her, the colour returning to her cheeks.

'Do you think they're all up there in heaven, sitting on their clouds, looking down at us and all arguing the way we do?'

'Probably, especially Clover, setting heaven to rights,' Charlotte said dryly. 'Now, since you're not at school, why don't you help me with the dusting and then you can come with me to the smithy, if you like. I'm going to see Melvin today.'

Milly wrinkled her nose. 'No, thanks. I don't want to be a gooseberry. I might go and do some drawing, or I'll go and annoy the regulars,' she added with a grin.

As Milly skipped out of the room, Charlotte let out her breath with a sigh of relief. Milly would recover and, once the funeral was over, so would they all, even though the memory of Clover was one they would always hold dear. She was sure they all shed their tears in their private times, even Josie, who put on a hard front whenever she could. But this wasn't the best of times, and she bent to finish whisking the duster around the

Captain's tallboy before she got maudlin.

Melvin hadn't been to the hotel since Clover's death, although he had sent a note to Charlotte, saying he was sorry to hear the news. The awkwardness he felt oozed out of every word. He had never been good at expressing emotion, and she knew he preferred to keep his distance from the grieving family.

They couldn't keep their distance from the emotions that overcame them from time to time, though, Charlotte thought with a swift stab of resentment, even though the everyday business of the hotel had to go on. But the summer seemed a long time ago now, and that night on Priory Hill was the farthest from her mind as she cycled to the smithy on that blustery November morning.

Melvin looked up from his work as she approached, pushing back from his forehead the helmet he wore to shield his eyes, giving him the illusion of a sometime warrior. It usually impressed her, but she was feeling less than impressed now.

'How is it going, then?' he asked warily.

'How is what going?' she asked, giving him no help.

'Well, uh, the arrangements and all that.'

She folded her arms, leaning on her bicycle and pursing her lips. She had missed him, and wanted to see him. She hadn't come here to pick a fight, but she was almost certain it was going to happen. Milly wasn't the only one feeling over-sensitive at this time, she realised.

'If you mean the arrangements for my grandmother's funeral, why don't you say so?'

His face darkened. 'For God's sake, Charlotte, I was trying to save your feelings. Of course that's what I meant. What else would you be thinking about?'

'Well, not you, that's for sure.'

They glared at one another and then he spoke shortly.

'What are you doing here, then?'

Her legs seemed to buckle and she released her folded arms and clung on to her handlebars, her voice jerky. 'I don't know. I wanted to see you. To know that we're still all right, I suppose, and that not everything's changed.'

'Well, not on my account, it hasn't.'

He glanced around swiftly and saw that no one else was in sight before he moved forward and caught her in his arms with some difficulty, considering that the bicycle was a barrier between them.

'I wanted to see you too, Charlie, but you know how useless I am at saying what I feel at times like this. Of course we're still all right. I proved that to you after the carnival, didn't I?'

She heard the smile in his voice. He was trying to cheer her up, and she knew that, but it was the wrong time to be remembering such things, and her nerves were so on edge that she flew at him in a rage.

'Oh, you would reduce everything to *that*, wouldn't you? Clover was right when she said that all men were only after one thing.'

Clover's name trembled on her lips and then to her horror she was sobbing again. Melvin stayed where he was with his arms around her until she had calmed down to a quiet snuffling.

'Well, Clover was a wise old bird, and she was right about that,' she heard him say. 'If she wasn't, the whole damn human race would die out, wouldn't it? Besides, if her old man hadn't been after *one thing*, your dad wouldn't have been born, and neither would you. So don't knock it, girl.'

For a moment she was speechless that he could be so brutal and so nonchalant about the love between Clover and Tommy. And just as quickly, she knew that, even if he never managed to say things with any finesse, of course he was right. Clover was right, and she was being an idiot.

She felt his chin nuzzle against hers, and she couldn't deny the frisson of a thrill as his mouth moved upwards to touch hers in a brief kiss. Life went on, and they had to go on with it.

'Better now?' Melvin said, and she nodded.

'I know I over-reacted but, once we get the funeral over and Milly recovers from the taunts at school, and Josie gets back to her normal self, I'll be able to see things more clearly.'

'God Almighty, let's hope so,' he said, as she

listed everything that was on her mind. 'Let your folks bear the brunt of it, Charlotte. It's not all down to you.'

Well, she knew that, and she felt a mite less fraught as she cycled home. She was being foolish and short-sighted to think that it was all down to her. Even finding Ruth sorting out the clothes and personal belongings in Clover's bedroom when she returned could not flatten her mood, especially as they began to laugh and cry together over some of Clover's more outrageous outfits.

'I was going to send most of this to a jumble sale,' Ruth gasped, wiping her eyes, 'but I can't imagine another woman in the town wanting to look like Clover!'

'That's because *nobody* could ever look like Clover, or be like her,' Charlotte said fiercely. 'She was a very special lady.'

'So she was,' Ruth said, unable to resist a smile as she took out of the drawer the several yards of a bright yellow and blue woollen scarf, and the tea-cosy hat that went with it. She glanced at Charlotte. 'This can give us a few laughs, but there are also some letters and papers for your father to go through. Clover always said she didn't believe in wills, they were too gruesome. But there's a little jewellery that is of no great value, but I'm sure Clover would have wanted you girls to take your pick of it. I think it's better if we leave all that until after the funeral, though.'

Much better, thought Charlotte. Otherwise it would feel as if they were picking over

Clover's personal belongings before she was in her grave. She looked at her mother, the tears not far away.

'We'll miss her, won't we, Mum?'

If there was one thing they were all learning, it was that nobody could remain in a high state of grief for ever. The funeral was attended by family and townspeople, though there had been no reply from Clover's one sister, living somewhere on Exmoor. Not that they had been close, nor kept in touch, but she could have acknowledged the fact, Donald thought angrily.

Milly returned to school in a better humour when she discovered her classmates had been given a good talking-to on her account, and by now she was taking bets on which of the hotel regulars would be next to turn up their toes. She used Clover's description to make them laugh, until Miss Brown found there were sweets being distributed in a clandestine betting circle, and that was the end of that.

Dorothy's mother had reluctantly said she could be Milly's friend again, and Dorothy said she had never thought Milly's gran was a witch, anyway.

'I'd have had to see her riding a broomstick before I believed *that*,' she said scornfully.

'Well, she didn't, so don't keep going on about it.'

Dorothy perked up. 'My dad said I can start having horse-riding lessons next year. Why don't you come as well? It's on the farm next to the smithy where my dad supplies tackle and stuff like that.'

'You on the back of a horse? You'd make the poor thing collapse,' Milly said, hooting with laughter.

'No, I wouldn't. Anyway, you could see what goes on between your sister and that blacksmith, couldn't you?' Dorothy said slyly. 'Do you think they've kissed yet?'

'Ugh, how do I know! I don't expect so. We don't see him much now, but I bet Josie kissed her fairground chap. I read stuff in her diary once,' she confided.

'What stuff?'

Milly suddenly discovered she had Clover's imagination as she elaborated on the few things she had learnt from Josie's diary. 'She was going to run away with him one time, but the fair left town before she could get her things packed.'

Dorothy hooted again. 'You're making that up, Milly Elkins. Your Josie wouldn't do anything like that, not with your dad around!'

'Well, perhaps not, but I'm not going to talk about it any more,' Milly said crossly, thinking that Dorothy would do well on the back of a horse. She already honked like one.

There were only occasional visitors to the hotel at the end of the year. If they got any bookings at all, it would usually be from elderly couples with no family, who wanted to spend Christmas in the company of other people. The Elkins family were thankful when two such couples arrived that year to make up the hotel's consignment of guests, not only for the welcome financial support, but because it also kept them busy and prevented them dwelling too much on the fact that this was the first Christmas without Clover.

'It's always the first of anything that hits hard,' Miss Hester Green ruminated, watching Charlotte and Josie hanging up some of the usual Christmas decorations to make the guests' sitting-room look festive. 'The first Christmas without a loved one, the first anniversary of their birthday and, of course, the first anniversary of the day they died. After that it somehow becomes a little easier to bear.'

Even so, hearing Hester's voice become gloomier, Charlotte climbed down from the small steps in the sitting-room and spoke firmly before Josie had time to launch into her own tirade, as her older sister guessed she was about to do.

'We know all that, Miss Green, and of course we'll never forget Gran. But we're all determined not to let what happened spoil Christmas for everyone else. We have to remember that this is a hotel and the other guests have come here for a cheerful time, so it's best not to go about with sad faces, isn't it? And I'm perfectly sure Gran wouldn't have wanted us to be sad at Christmas, either.'

'Oh, of course she wouldn't, and you're always so sensible, dear.'

Charlotte heard her sister snort, and

hustled her out of the room now that they had finished their task. She didn't feel sensible at all. She had a lump in her throat, remembering how very much Clover had loved this season, and she was smarting too, because it seemed that Melvin was still keeping his distance, and she was sure his passion had waned after all. But she knew Josie would have something to say about the elderly spinster's gushing words.

'You're always so sensible, dear!' Josie mimicked as soon as they were out of earshot. 'And you're such a favourite, aren't you? Just like you were with Clover.'

'Don't be stupid, Josie.'

'Well, it's true, and why you keep toadying up to them I don't know.'

'I do not toady up to them. What a ridiculous thing to say. But I don't see any reason not to be pleasant to them. It's what we're paid to do, isn't it?'

As they went upstairs to fetch the change of sheets and towels out of the linen cupboard, Josie went off on a different tack.

'Is this what you want to do for the rest of your life, Charlie? Wait on tables and change smelly old folks' bed linen once a week? Can you see yourself doing this when you're old and doddery? Because I can't!'

'What's your plan, then?' Charlotte said, starting to laugh at the image of it. 'Are you going off to join the circus; or more likely, the fairground people? I can't exactly see you living in a caravan.'

'I might. You'll probably end up getting married to Melvin Philpott and having a parcel of kids.'

'I might do that if he ever got around to asking me,' Charlotte said, suddenly drooping. 'And don't even think about anything so daft as going off like that, Josie. I was only joking, and you couldn't leave Dad in the lurch.'

Josie scowled. 'Well, I don't think this tin-pot hotel is so darned wonderful, even if he does. There are much bigger ones in Bristol.'

'But they don't have the sea on their doorstep like we do and such lovely sunsets across the Channel. They're hot and impersonal, and because we're smaller we can give our guests the personal touch. Oh, come, Josie, cheer up. It's nearly Christmas, remember?'

She leant over the bed, gathering up the soiled sheets and trying not to remember other Christmases when Clover had been the life and soul of any party, filling it with colour in her own special way. This one would be so different.

By now, the family rooms had been re-organised since Milly had flatly refused to sleep by herself in the adjoining one to Clover's. Charlotte had no such qualms, and when her parents had decided to throw out her gran's old bed, she had offered to have her own bed moved into Clover's old room herself, finding a strange and piquant sense of continuity in doing so.

The arrangement also suited Josie admirably, since she now had a room to herself. She could write whatever she chose in her diary and lock it away in the small bureau she had inherited from Clover's room with no fear of Milly's prying eyes. She could dream impossible dreams and make impossible plans that were nothing like as mundane and ordinary as her sister Charlie had, which all ended up with marrying her dreary blacksmith.

At The Retreat no one was allowed to be miserable at Christmas. The hotel prided itself on providing good Christmas fare for guests and family alike, and the regulars were in fine form, regaling the other guests with tales of Christmases past at home and abroad, and hearing their stories in return.

They formed small card parties amongst themselves, and wrapped themselves up in coats and scarves and boots on fine days, despite the cold winds, and strode along the sea front like so many others were doing to off-set the Christmas excesses.

The family drank a small toast to the memory of Clover Elkins, and each in their own way they remembered her with love. And they all acknowledged that it had been good to be busy and to be cheerful for the sake of their guests. They didn't forget Clover at this time, and she was too strong and vivid a personality for them ever to do so, but by silent admission they each determined not to descend into misery at her passing for ever.

The Captain in particular was always jovial

at the approach of a new year and, since the temporary guests were about to leave soon afterwards, he entertained them on their last evening with a lantern show of his army days. The Misses Green had seen it all before but were dutifully attentive and admitted that he had a way with words and made each commentary and anecdote amusing.

But all too soon, it seemed, the festivities were over, the trimmings were taken down for another year, and the hotel returned to normality. All except for Charlotte, who was smarting even more because Melvin hadn't even turned up to wish her a happy Christmas. She wouldn't make the first move, since it wasn't a girl's place to do so, but if he no longer wanted her, then she wouldn't want him.

Except that she did ... oh, she *did*...

And then she heard from Mr Hallam at Hallam's Food Supplies that the blacksmith's wife – meaning Melvin's mother – had been taken quite ill with pneumonia just before Christmas and had only just been sent home from hospital. Even while she was concerned to hear it, Charlotte's face cleared, for of course Melvin and his father would have been too worried to think about anything but Melvin's mother, and she could hardly have expected him to bother about herself. Charlotte readily excused him for not being able to see her and blamed herself for not trusting him more.

'He could still have sent you a card,' Josie

pointed out. 'He'd have to pass a post office on the way to see his mother in hospital. It wouldn't have been too much trouble, and you forgive him too easily, Charlie. You always do.'

'Well, that's because I care about him, and I know he cares about me, even if he doesn't come around too often. But now that I know what's happened, I shall take Mrs Philpott a get-well card and some flowers.'

It was the ideal reason for going to the smithy, and it didn't even occur to her to wonder why she felt she needed such an excuse.

Ten

If the end of the previous year had been fairly mellow apart from the high winds, January roared in like a lion. The Channel had some spectacular tides, and there were dire warnings that the sea defences might not hold against the onslaught.

'They've been saying such things for years,' Donald Elkins said. 'And every year we sit tight and nothing ever happens. Besides, if it brings a few unexpected visitors to the town to watch the antics of the wind and waves, I'm not going to grumble, for one.'

It was never likely that casual visitors in

January would want overnight accommodation, but there was a sign outside the hotel now advertising light lunches and afternoon teas, and there was a certain amount of custom, even amongst the locals, taking advantage of coming in from the cold for an hour or so.

'Clover would have loved this,' Charlotte commented to the regulars, as they watched those who were hardy enough to brave the elements along the sea front, heads bent, barely able to stand up straight, but determined to make the most of the bracing air.

'I think they're all mad,' Miss Hester Green said mildly. 'They'll all be next for the hospital with pneumonia like that dear Mrs Philpott. I take it that she's quite recovered, Charlotte, dear?'

'Oh, yes, thank you, though she has to rest every afternoon. She always had a delicate chest, I believe.'

'And her with such a strapping husband and son, too.'

Charlotte hid a smile. She didn't need any confirmation of Mrs Philpott's strapping son. As if to make up for his lack of attention lately, Melvin had started coming to the hotel at the weekends, and twice recently they had been to the cinema, sitting in the back row with Melvin's arm around her shoulders, until the light from the usherette's torch had shone on them, and made him drop it hastily.

She certainly had no desire to go for walks along the sea front in this furious wind like those idiots were doing now, nor anywhere else until the warmer weather came again. Watching the sea surge over the breakwater and seeing the walkers scamper back, screaming with shock and excitement as they were soaked to the skin, only made them look more idiotic than ever.

She had to admit that she and Josie had done it a few times but, once they had returned home to change out of their sodden clothes and dried out, both had wondered what the attraction was. Oddly enough, it was mostly middle-aged or elderly folk who were out there, the ones who should have more sense. Unless they saw it as a last chance for a bit of excitement and adventure, of course. And almost certainly, Clover would have been amongst them – and probably still was, in some form or another, Charlotte thought wryly.

She often thought about Clover, especially when she was curled up in bed at night in the room that had once been Clover's. There was still so much of her here; though she knew better than to say as much to anyone, especially Milly, who would be scared stiff at the thought of some ghostly presence, even a loveable one, as Clover's would surely be.

Charlotte often wondered about the life she had led with Tommy. It had always sounded so glamorous and exciting, but it must have been dangerous at times, too, and apparently neither of them would have baulked at that. She wondered why Clover had never left a will, but it had been no surprise when none had been found, since she had always said airily that she had nothing to leave but her memory and whatever bits and pieces of her belongings they chose as keepsakes. And her memory was always unreliable. She frequently forgot the things she had said minutes before, let alone half a century ago.

As February approached, the winter winds and high seas hadn't abated, though by now the intrepid sea-front walkers had given up their expeditions, preferring to huddle indoors in front of roaring fires that sparked up chimneys and sometimes sent flurries of smoke and smuts into living-rooms.

'I don't like it,' the Captain said one early evening when the sky had gone as dark as if it was midnight, and the howl of the wind was starting to be unnerving. 'There's a bad feeling in the air tonight, you mark my words.'

'For goodness' sake, Captain, you're scaring my sister,' Miss Hester Green said crossly, putting the onus on her sister when she was jittery herself. 'It's only a storm and we've weathered bad storms before.'

'It's not only the wind howling,' he said. 'Did you hear the dogs earlier?'

'There aren't any dogs here, only the usual strays that have always roamed about the beach and they're surely not out on a night like this.'

'Well, there were dogs howling somewhere and that's a sure sign that something's afoot. Animals know what's coming before we do.'

Ruth Elkins came into the guests' sitting-room to tell them supper was ready, just in time to hear this last remark, as the Misses Green were gathering up their knitting in a fluster.

'Thank goodness, Mrs Elkins. Now perhaps this scare-monger will stop filling our heads with nonsense and let us have our supper in peace.'

Ruth smiled, but when later she related the Captain's remark to the family, Donald frowned.

'There's usually more than a grain of substance in what he says, and it's true that animals have a sixth sense about any sort of trouble. We'll just make sure that all the doors and windows are firmly fastened tonight, and remind the regulars to do the same in their rooms. We don't want to risk any windows being smashed.'

'We don't want to alarm the old people, either,' Ruth said anxiously.

'It's better for them to be forewarned than scared to death by having a shower of glass blown in on them during the night. I'll tell them myself, and you girls remember to shut your own windows tightly as well.'

'It's a bit like a siege,' Milly said importantly, having just begun the history of the Middle Ages at school now and airing her knowledge.

'Yes, well, perhaps it is,' Ruth said, 'but at least we've got plenty of food and water to last us through the night, so none of us need worry about being starved.'

'Does that mean we can come downstairs if we can't sleep and have a midnight feast?' Milly asked hopefully.

'It does not,' Donald told her. 'It means you can bury your head beneath the bedclothes if need be and stop talking such nonsense, Milly.'

'Or she can jump in with me if she's really scared,' Charlotte added.

'I'm not scared. It's exciting.'

None of them was thinking that way as the storm intensified during the night. Windows rattled and shook as if the hotel was in the throes of an earthquake. Loud splintering sounds outside spoke of trees falling down or driftwood being thrown up by the boiling tide and being smashed against the hotel in the shrieking winds.

In the early hours of the morning, unable to sleep, Donald went downstairs with a flashlight to check if there had been any structural damage. So far he couldn't see any, but he knew the tide hadn't reached its height yet, and that the Bristol Channel experienced some of the highest tides in the world. For the first time, he felt real fear at what could happen to The Retreat and its vulnerability to this onslaught.

'Come back to bed, Donald,' he heard Ruth say quietly, when he had been prowling about for more than half an hour. 'Everything's been made secure, so we'll just have to ride it out, the same as everyone else in the town.'

'Not everyone else's property is on the edge of the sea,' he muttered. 'But I daresay you're right, and we'll assess if any damage has been done in daylight.'

They were on their way back upstairs when a ferocious crack, louder than all the rest, made Ruth gasp and clutch his arm in fright.

'What was that?' she whispered.

'God knows, but I'm going to find out. It sounded to me as if the sea wall has gone, and if that's happened—'

He didn't need to say more. Theirs was the only property so close to the sea defences. Even a normal high tide could send waves crashing over the top and into the lower-lying grounds of the hotel. If once that sea wall was breached, there was no knowing what might happen.

Donald turned around on the stairs, his heart pounding, intent on going outside to see for himself what damage had occurred, despite the wind and lashing rain. But before he had a chance to do so, a second crack like thunder burst open the doors at the rear of the hotel, and what seemed like a tidal wave of water hurtled inside, flooding the kitchen and all the lower rooms at once, and swilling down through all available crevices into the disused cellars below.

As he heard terrified screams, Donald glanced back to the top of the stairs and saw that Ruth had been joined by his daughters and the Captain. The girls clung together, while their father stared futilely at the surging waters below. Even as he looked, kitchen utensils and crockery began falling, together with pictures and ornaments in the sitting-rooms, rocked by the force of the tidal invasion. He knew in an instant that he was facing ruin, but he had too much pride to put such thoughts into words yet.

'You might as well all get back to bed,' he said hoarsely. 'There's not much any of us can do until morning, except take whatever furniture we can upstairs, and then we'll start the cleaning-up process in daylight and see what else can be salvaged. Once we can find our way out of the place, we'll see about getting the guests into another hotel for the time being, until we start the clearing-up process and see if anything can be salvaged here.'

'We'll not desert you, sir,' the Captain boomed.

'You may have to,' Donald muttered beneath his breath.

He couldn't bear to look at the way the filthy water was taking control of the entire ground floor now, greedily seeking every corner like an alien force. It wasn't manly to cry but, by God, he had never felt more like doing so.

It was a long while later before the storm had done its worst but, after urging everyone to go back to bed, Donald sat for a long time on the top of the stairs, his head in his hands.

He had never felt so alone. This beautiful little hotel that he had cared for, for so long, was virtually under water now, at least the ground floor and whatever was below it. He could only hope and pray that some of the water would have seeped away by the time morning came, so that at least they could inspect the damage properly and see what could be salvaged. He doubted that anyone slept properly for the rest of that terrible night but by daybreak, when all was quiet at last, he couldn't lie in bed any longer. He dressed in warm clothes and went out of the bedroom, leaving Ruth restlessly tossing and turning. At the head of the stairs he stopped abruptly.

It was as though his worst nightmares had come true. Below him was a sea of water where rugs and linoleum had been. Furniture that had been chosen with loving care over the years now floated about like so much flotsam as the water surged gently in rippling waves, as if to remind him that the sea still held command.

He tried to subdue the choking sobs in his throat, knowing he had to be strong. He heard a noise behind him, and then came the Captain's voice again, roughened with shock.

'Good God, man, the whole place is like a scene of wartime devastation.'

'You don't need to tell me, Captain,' Donald said harshly, swallowing hard. 'I'm looking ruin in the face.'

The Captain's hand gripped his shoulder. 'A lot of good men faced worse than this in the trenches, man, and never came back to tell of the horrors they saw. At least your wife and children are safe. Material things are of little consequence compared with people. A man does well to remember that.'

'I know you're right but, since the hotel is the livelihood of us all, I find it hard to find comfort in such philosophies right now, Captain.'

He didn't need them, either. And the Captain had yet to realise that there would be no question that he and the other regulars could stay here now. They would have to leave. Hotel guests could hardly be expected to exist on the top floor of the hotel – and neither could the family. The enormity of it all was almost too much...

The sound of a fire engine penetrated his senses. There were other noises too; the sounds of vehicles and men shouting, and almost before he had time to register it, men wearing wet-weather clothes and long waders were appearing below, in what had once been the entrance hall of The Retreat. For a moment, it seemed as though they were all frozen in time, as the two men at the top of the stairs and the group of rescuers below stared in disbelief at each other.

'Is everyone all right, Mr Elkins?' one of the man shouted. 'It was assumed the hotel would have been evacuated before the storm got so bad. The tide's well on the turn now, and the firemen are going to start pumping out here, while the local workmen begin making repairs to the sea defences. It will be a temporary measure until they can bring in larger equipment, but it should be enough to hold in case of another storm like last night.'

Donald was unable to speak as the man prattled on, and then he saw that the firemen were already bringing in their equipment to pump out the ground floor of the hotel. From being quiet a few moments ago, they were bombarded with noise and activity all around, and Ruth and the girls had reappeared on the top landing to see what was happening. The Misses Green normally took sleeping pills each night, and had presumably slept through it all, but surely not for much longer.

'Oh, Donald,' Ruth whispered, her voice breaking, her hand clapped over her mouth at the scene below.

The spokesman glanced up and spoke cheerfully.

'Don't you worry, ma'am. It looks bad now but, once the water's been pumped out, you'll soon be able to get things ship-shape again.'

The three girls were still wearing their dressing-gowns, and Josie snapped into Charlotte's ear as Milly whimpered, wide-eyed and frightened.

'How are we supposed to get any breakfast when all the food and everything else downstairs is under water?'

'Breakfast is the least of our worries, you idiot. The only thing Dad needs to do now is to find out how much damage has been caused by the storm.'

They had already looked out of their bedroom windows and seen the way the pleasant sea-front promenade and the green beyond it had been turned into a gigantic lake by the incoming tide. Even though that tide was receding fast now, and the heavy winds had eased, the water would take time to soak into the ground, and some of it might never recover.

Milly turned and ran back to her bedroom. 'I'm staying in bed,' she shouted. 'I'm not going to school today and nobody's going to make me!'

'Well, as there's about two feet of water down below, she'd be up to her neck in it, anyway,' Josie muttered. 'We're all trapped now. Until they can pump this water out, we're stuck up here like convicts in a jail.'

'Oh, stop being so dramatic, Josie,' Charlotte said, quickly losing patience with her. 'If you can't think of anything sensible to say, why don't you just keep quiet?'

'Why don't you all do the same?' Ruth put in shakily. 'We won't help matters by snapping at one another, and let's hope this operation won't take too long. You girls go and get dressed and make yourselves respectable with all these workmen about. Once we can get through the water, you can go to the shops and get some bread and butter and marmalade and some cheese for later. If we can gather up some cutlery and plates and make sure they're clean, at least we can offer our guests a cold breakfast in their rooms, and a bit of a snack at midday.'

'That's the spirit, ma'am,' the Captain said. 'Practical as ever. The good old British spirit never fails in times of trouble.'

Ruth clasped Donald's hand tightly, knowing, as he did, that it was going to take more than the good old British spirit to help them recover from this disaster.

A couple of hours later, by the time the firemen had done their job, the family were able to make their tentative way downstairs. All of them had a job not to weep. It wasn't only water that had flooded the hotel. There was mud and sludge and debris everywhere, all covered in a thick brown, evil-smelling slime. Even the heaviest of the upturned furniture looked as if it had been tossed about and smashed by a giant's hand.

The Misses Green had awoken now and were fully aware of the horror below them. While the family squelched their way through the downstairs rooms in bedroom slippers that were destined for the dustbin, the older ladies were quietly keening on the upstairs landing, being comforted in his gruff way by the Captain. Finally, Donald went back to the trio, knowing what he had to do.

'It pains me to say it, but it will be obvious to you all that we can no longer cater for your needs until we can assess what's to be done here. In the meantime, I will be making alternative arrangements for you all just as soon as I can contact another hotel.'

Although they made a few feeble remonstrations about not wanting to leave, they all realised they had no choice. It was also urgent. The regulars were elderly and needed proper comfort.

Once the older girls had found their inelegant wellington boots they usually scorned, which were kept on a high enough shelf not to have succumbed to the water, they abandoned the feel of the damp, cold interiors that made them squirm. Then Josie was sent to buy provisions, and Charlotte was despatched with a letter to the manager of the Seaview Hotel to request ongoing accommodation for the three people in these unusual circumstances. She also had to contact the gas office, since the only serviceable things in the hotel now were candles and flashlights.

By the middle of the afternoon everyone had had a scrappy meal of bread and cheese, prepared ignominiously in Donald and Ruth's bedroom, and the regulars had packed up all their belongings. Each of them had been lifted across the ruined ground floor of the hotel by the obliging workmen and others who had turned up to lend a hand, and had said a tearful farewell to the home they had known for so long. It was a wrench for all of them, and being assured that they felt as though they were deserting a sinking ship did nothing to help the feelings of the family left with the results of the storm.

All day long there was a cacophony of noise from the lorries and workmen desperately repairing what they could of the sea defences before the next tide, with the noise adding to the misery of those left behind in the hotel.

Milly had been persuaded to go to school in the afternoon, wearing her wellington boots with a pair of shoes in her satchel, full of excited importance now at the stories she had to tell of how the sea had flooded their hotel.

Working inside The Retreat, everyone wore boots and outer clothes now, for although the weather had eased it was still the coldest part of the year. Together with several volunteers, Donald and Ruth had begun the heartbreaking task of sweeping out the mud and sludge as best they could, knowing that nothing could be saved of the furniture they had cherished for so long. A good deal of kitchen equipment had been battered and smashed or rendered useless, and it was becoming more and more obvious that it would take a miracle to restore the hotel, and far more money than they possessed to replace all that had been lost.

'The insurance company doesn't allow compensation for Acts of God, which is what this is considered to be,' Donald said bitterly, pausing for a rest on the stairs as they surveyed what little they seemed to have accomplished all this while. 'And we're supposed to thank God for His mercy! He had little mercy as far as we were concerned.'

'Hush, Donald, you'll do no good by thinking that way,' Ruth said.

'Oh, no? Well, I'll tell you something else.

The only thing I'm thanking God for right now is that my mother wasn't up to her old tricks last night as well, or we'd all have been washed away while we were out looking for her.'

The volunteers looked at one another uneasily as his voice rose angrily, not keen on hearing what was almost blasphemy from a respected hotel owner's mouth. Nor did any of them care to be reminded of the mad-woman who had lived here until such a short time ago.

'I reckon we've done about all we can in the kitchen and entrance hall, Mr Elkins. Shouldn't we start on the sitting-rooms now?' one of them said.

Donald grunted. 'I'm coming, Jack. There's no point in just thinking about it, I suppose.'

Even though that was exactly what he had been doing for the last ten minutes.

He stumped out of the entrance hall, his boots heavy with sludge now, like all of them. He followed the two men into the guests' sitting-room, wondering fleetingly if it would ever be used for such a genteel purpose again. The men were already shovelling the worst of the muck towards what was left of the French windows, which had long since been blown in, shedding glass everywhere, when they heard a sudden loud crack and the sound of splintering wood. In seconds the water-softened linoleum split open as a gaping hole appeared in the flooring, and much of the muck went slithering through to the disused cellars below.

'Christ Almighty,' the man called Jack gasped out, leaping backwards to save himself from falling through, and staggering against the sitting-room wall, already showing ominous cracks. 'I reckon you've got more trouble here than you bargained for, Elkins. This flooring's probably been rotten for years, and it only took last night's deluge to finish it off.'

'Are you all right?' Donald said harshly, realising how near the man had come to go plunging through the hole himself. He'd have been liable for far more than a ruined hotel then. His heart banged against his ribs, and he felt physically sick at the thought.

'Don't worry about me,' Jack muttered. 'We've had experience of this kind of thing before, but we'd best get the rest of this lino up so we can see what's what. You and the missus keep out of the way while me and Ted get on with it.'

'Are you sure? We don't want to risk any accidents.' Nor any personal insurance claims, he thought. They had enough to worry about without that. He was finding it difficult to think sensibly at all. He had always prided himself on being a level-headed businessman, but for the first time in his life he simply didn't know what to do. The future seemed to stretch away from him like the vast empty hollow below their feet, he thought with a shudder, and he could no longer visualise it.

Minutes later he heard Jack speak in a strange monotone, and he realised the two men had been momentarily silent.

'Mr Elkins, I think you'd better come in here, and bring your flashlight with you.'

With a feeling of dread that he couldn't explain, Donald grabbed his flashlight and went into the guests' ruined sitting-room to stare at the ashen faces of the two volunteers, who were now peering down into the gaping hole in the floor. He shone the light downwards, on to some objects that were hard and white, sticking out of the mud that had been carried down with the broken floorboards.

'What is it?' he said uneasily.

As if by one accord the two workmen straightened up and backed away.

Ted spoke hoarsely. 'It looks very much like old bones to us, and we're not going any further. You'd best get somebody to come and take a proper look, and I reckon the police will want to take an interest, too.'

Eleven

Donald began to feel as if he was living through a never-ending nightmare. Unwilling to send his wife or one of his daughters for the police, and not wanting to leave the hotel himself until he knew exactly what was down in the cellars, he enlisted the help of the reluctant workmen. He could understand their nervousness. God alone knew what those bones were, how long they had been down there, or how they got there.

Knowing by now of the disaster that had befallen the seaside hotel, a number of people had turned up offering help, and one of them agreed at once to go and inform the police and also Doctor Jacobs. What a doctor could do in the circumstances, Donald didn't know, but it seemed the right and decent thing to do, if they were indeed bones in the cellar. Someone had arrived with a camping stove and some crockery and, with the provisions that Josie had brought back from Hallam's Food Supplies, they were able to make pots of tea to steady their nerves and try hard not to speculate on the outcome of the discovery. It was supposed to help to be doing something practical, though he could see Ruth's hands shaking as she handed round tea and biscuits.

And why shouldn't she be shaking? he thought, taking refuge in anger. This wasn't a bloody garden party. He wasn't often given to cursing but, if there was ever a time when he felt justified in doing so, it was now.

'There's no use any of us making wild suggestions until we know for sure what it is,' Donald said harshly, seeing Jack and Ted in a huddle with some of the other helpers now.

'Still, there's no hiding the fact that it's got to be the remains of a body of some sort,' Ted pointed out. 'You don't get bones unless there's been a body covering 'em before it rotted away. There's probably a skull down there somewhere as well, and I daresay the police will want to be looking for records of any missing persons that have stayed in the hotel.'

Donald saw his womenfolk shudder at his graphic words. The thought that there might have been – *must* have been – a body in the cellars beneath their feet for Lord knew how many months or years was enough to turn all their stomachs. There was also a sinister and criminal implication in Ted's words that he didn't care to think about too closely.

He was thankful that Milly had gone to school after all that afternoon and wasn't here to witness the first shock of discovery. More people seemed to have appeared from nowhere now, and he suspected that word was quickly circulating that something unidentifiable had been found in the cellars of The Retreat. All kinds of rumours would be spreading, he thought savagely, and any hope he had of hushing this up was gone for ever.

Not that he had anything to hide, but people talked, and the hotel hadn't been without incident all these years, even if it had all been harmless nonsense on account of Clover's nocturnal activities and her loud style of dressing. He knew some people didn't see it as being merely eccentric, though, and it grieved as well as angered him that people could think ill of his mother.

The police turned up a short while later and asked everyone except the family to clear out of the building until they could see what was happening.

'Presumably there's a door down to the cellars, Mr Elkins?' the officer in charge asked. 'I'm not expecting my men to go down through this hole in the floorboards.'

'Of course there is,' Donald said testily. 'Not that it's been used in living memory, and I've certainly never been through it, nor had any reason to do so.'

He wished he didn't sound so defensive, when he knew there was no need to be. He vaguely remembered the previous owners telling him they were always worried about rats being down there, and that they had had an occasional bit of flooding from the sea. The only precaution they had taken was to keep the cellar door firmly boarded up, saying it would be too damp in any case to use the space as a storeroom, and Donald had simply never taken down the boards to do any kind of inspection. He knew how stupidly short-sighted that had been now.

If a crime had been committed all those years ago and anything bad was to be found down there, he didn't want to imagine what the outcome might be. Even the fact that the door had been boarded up for years could have implications that he didn't want to think about. It was obvious from Ruth's frightened eyes and the way his two older daughters clung together now that they had similar feelings.

A commotion at the outer door made him turn his head sharply. One of the police constables was on what he called 'door patrol', keeping out the curious while the investigation went on.

'There's somebody here wants to know if he can have a few words with you, Mr Elkins. It's probably all right for you to talk to him about the hotel damage, but he'll have to wait until my officer gives the say-so before he can have an official statement about the findings.'

Donald glared at the newcomer. He was young and sharp-looking, wearing a tidy suit and hat. Beside him, Donald felt dishevelled and weary, and it was not the way a normally immaculate hotel owner cared to appear. Then he felt his shoulders sag. When was he ever going to look the way he had always prided himself? At that moment, he felt as if those days had gone for ever.

'Who are you?' he snapped.

The man held out a business card. 'I'm Steve Bailey from the *Evening Chronicle*, Mr Elkins. And may I say how very sorry I am to see the damage your hotel has suffered, and to offer the newspaper's sympathy to you and your family.'

He took in Ruth and the girls at a glance, and gave Charlotte a slight smile. Seeing it, Donald frowned.

'You can say what you like, but you'll get no story from me for your wretched rag.'

'I understand your feelings, Mr Elkins, but people will be interested, and I've already interviewed your three elderly guests who have been moved to the Seaview Hotel. They all say how distressed they are to leave such a warm and comfortable environment and they hope to return as soon as it has been restored to the way it was before.'

'Do they indeed!' Donald almost exploded at the man's smooth manner, and the way he was consulting his notebook now to relate exactly what the regulars had said. 'Well, I'd say that from the looks of things, they'll see hell freeze before that happens!'

'Donald,' Ruth began warningly, but he brushed her aside.

'I can't waste time talking to newspaper ghouls. My hotel's falling apart and that's the only important thing to me right now.'

He strode away and Ruth took charge, speaking nervously.

'You must forgive my husband, Mr Bailey.

As you can imagine, we've had a terribly stressful time.'

'Would you like a cup of tea?' Charlotte said, for the only reason that it was probably better to give the man something to do than for him to be standing around like the rest of them, awaiting developments.

'That's very civil of you, Miss Elkins. Charlotte, isn't it? Captain Bellamy mentioned your names,' he said, in explanation. 'And I'm Steve.'

It was the most bizarre way to spend an afternoon, to be offering tea to a stranger while the police were probing the contents of the hotel cellars to see if a crime had been committed. By now the doctor and another officious-looking man had appeared and been allowed access. Other than that, the guests' sitting-room was sealed off to all comers.

'What are you doing?' Josie hissed as Charlotte went to find another cup and saucer. 'He could be saying anything about us in his newspaper. Just because he's good-looking and fancies you, there's no need to make him feel welcome.'

'Don't be silly. Of course he doesn't fancy me. He doesn't even know me.'

All the same, she didn't miss the spark of interest in the reporter's eyes when she handed him his cup of tea. He had a friendly smile, but she glared back at him, tilting her head as she moved as far from him as possible in the entrance hall. She already had a young man and she didn't want another one. She was also suspicious about what could be written in newspapers through a careless word or two.

'So, Charlotte, what can you tell me about this last dreadful night?' Steve said coolly. 'It must have been very frightening for you young ladies.'

She continued to stare at him, saying nothing. What kind of a fool was he if he needed to ask such stupid questions? Then he spoke more apologetically, just as if he could see right into her thoughts.

'Sorry, that was an idiotic thing to ask, wasn't it? Sometimes I wonder why I do this job, having to probe into people's feelings at the worst possible times. It's no wonder people think all reporters are insensitive oafs.'

'I'm sure they don't,' Charlotte found herself muttering, hearing Josie give a snort of agreement behind her.

'Let him say what he thinks, Charlie, then perhaps he'll stop hounding us.'

Steve looked at her in amusement. 'I've hardly started yet, love, but everyone in Braydon will be interested to know what happened here last night, and they'll be sympathetic too, providing they get an accurate report.'

It was obvious what he meant. If he wasn't given the facts, he'd probably invent them, and that could put the family and the hotel in an even worse light, considering whatever was going on in the cellars now. But neither of the girls wanted to be the one to give him any information, nor thought that they should, and they looked around in relief when Ruth came back to join them.

'You'll have to ask my mother,' Charlotte said shortly.

It was obvious, too, that he wasn't going to go away until something had been resolved about the find in the cellars. Ruth had spoken to Donald and agreed that they could reveal the events of the night as far as the hotel flooding was concerned, but details of the discovery in the cellars was not to be disclosed for the present. The police were insisting on discretion. Ruth's voice shook as she carefully skirted around the fact of why they were here, for as yet none of them had any idea who or what had been disposed of in a previous time, or by what manner, and Steve had to be satisfied with what sketchy information he was given.

Arnie Hallam arrived in his van during the afternoon while they were still standing around awkwardly. By now the atmosphere was becoming more tense. Donald had whispered that the bones had been lifted out of the cellar and were being examined in a corner of the sitting-room. The entire central floor area of the room was now in a precarious state, and it was forbidden for anyone else to enter.

Donald snapped at the shopkeeper as soon as he saw him.

'There's nothing for you to gawp at here, Hallam.'

'Calm down, man, I'm not here for gawping. I've brought some meat pies for you and the family. I doubt that your missus will be doing much cooking here tonight. Take them as a gesture of sympathy in your plight,' he went on piously.

'That's very kind of you, Mr Hallam,' Ruth put in before Donald could explode at what he would consider just a ploy to see what was going on.

'Is there anything else I can do while I'm here?'

'No, there isn't,' Donald said. 'Thank you, anyway.'

There was movement inside the sitting-room now, and he couldn't get the shop-keeper out of the hotel soon enough. Gossip was part of the man's stock-in-trade, and many a customer spent more time than money in his shop, while avidly gleaning the latest local tittle-tattle.

A short while later the doctor and his companion, both wearing rubber gloves, came through to the entrance hall where the family was gathered, along with the reporter, who was refusing to budge. They carried something wrapped in a cloth, which was presumably the collection of old bones, and Charlotte felt Josie's hand grip hers as they both looked at it in horror. The other man spoke up.

'We need to take these bones away for further examination, Mr Elkins, but it's fairly certain that they are not human bones, and

I'm sure that whatever it is can be quickly established.'

'Not human?' Ruth said faintly.

Doctor Jacobs intervened. 'The bones are almost certainly that of an animal, probably a dog, but, until we can be certain what is involved here, and to eliminate all suggestion of foul play, the police will be making a through investigation of the cellars. This will take some time, considering the state of the place, but you are at liberty to continue your normal lives as best you can in the circumstances.'

Charlotte put her hand on her father's arm, seeing the veins on his forehead standing out with fury now. He shook her off angrily.

'Normal lives, man? What kind of a bloody normal life do you think we're going to have here now, with the ground floor of the hotel virtually wrecked? And as for any suggestion of foul play, whose damn fool idea is that?'

'Mr Elkins, I advise you to keep calm for your own sake,' the doctor went on. 'I'm sure it's merely a matter of procedure, but the police have their job to do, the same as Mr Leaver and I have ours. As soon as possible, we will let you know the results of our findings. Now good day to you.'

There was silence for a moment when they had gone, and then the sound of Ruth's hysterical laughter broke through the tension.

'The bones of a *dog*! Is that what's been frightening us out of our wits all this time? The bones of a wretched *dog*, which was probably one of those awful strays!'

'The question is,' Steve Bailey put in thoughtfully, 'if it was a dog, it might well have been a stray. But if it wasn't, who did it belong to? How did it get there, and was it deliberately left there to die?'

Ruth stopped laughing, and the whole family turned to glower at him at the suggestion of animal cruelty. At the same moment, Milly returned from school, her face a furious red with a mixture of excitement and outrage.

'It's not fair! The kids at school are saying our hotel is bewitched,' she shouted. 'They're saying Gran put a spell on it before she died, and that's why bad things are happening to us. They wouldn't stop going on about it, and Miss Brown told me I'd better go home early because I wouldn't stop screaming back at them. And why was the doctor and that other man here, and what was that parcel they were taking away with them?'

She paused for breath, looking from one to another with huge round eyes. Nobody answered for a moment and then Ruth put her arms around her youngest daughter.

'Darling, you know Gran would never do such a wicked thing, even if she could! Those children are just being silly and you mustn't take any notice of them.'

'I wouldn't, but now Dorothy agrees with them too,' Milly said with a gulp. 'It's not *fair*, is it?'

'No, it's not,' Ruth said sadly. 'But once everything has been sorted out, I'm sure they'll realise how foolish they're being.'

Steve Bailey cleared his throat. 'Mr Elkins, could I have a word with you?'

'I don't think I have anything more to say to you, Mr Bailey.'

'Please.' He glanced at Charlotte, as if seeking some approval.

A sixth sense told her what he was about, and she whispered to her mother.

'Mum, do you think we should let the newspaper readers know how unhappy all this silly talk is making Milly?' Even so, she didn't speak quietly enough for Steve Bailey's acute hearing. Donald overheard, too, and took umbrage at once.

'I certainly don't intend to make public what those idiotic children are saying. Do you want Milly to be made so conspicuous? It could end up with her being bullied or held up to ridicule. The less people know of our business the better.'

Steve spoke quickly. 'I fear it's not possible to suppress rumours easily in a close-knit little town like ours, Mr Elkins. Sometimes it's far better to come out in the open with such rumours and give them a proper airing. Once they're squashed, they usually die.'

'And sometimes they don't. But I'll not have my daughter subjected to this nonsense. I shall go to the school myself and confront the teachers to ask why they can't control their pupils.'

'Don't do that, Dad,' Milly wailed. 'You'll only make things worse.'

'Anyway,' Josie put in mischievously, 'I reckon Clover would be tickled pink to know people were still talking about her. She's probably up there now, looking down on us and smiling, knowing she was still making her mark.'

'Who's Clover?' Steve Bailey asked.

The policemen were finally satisfied that there was nothing else to be found in the cellars below the floors of The Retreat. With a comment that was no less a warning, it was suggested that the Elkins family could now continue repairing as much as they could of the hotel, and that the gas people could now be allowed in to connect them to the essential service again.

'Thank heavens for that,' Ruth said feelingly. 'The thought of spending tonight in darkness and still worrying about the sea defences would be just too much. And of course there's no way we intend leaving here.'

'Absolutely not,' Donald echoed, brushing aside the uneasy thought that leaving the hotel – even leaving Braydon – was what they might yet have to do.

He conceded that they were fortunate in one respect. All the guest bedrooms were above the original part of the hotel. Years ago an extension had been built to include the smarter entrance hall and stairs, kitchen and service rooms, with the family rooms above. The rotting floorboards in the guests' sitting-room and the danger of crumbling foundations didn't affect this extension so, while they could no longer accommodate guests safely, their own living quarters were intact.

Beyond the sea-front promenade that was still awash with water, the breached sea wall had now been closed with sandbags and blocks of stone that would hold until they could be fully repaired. Work would be started immediately, and whatever else they had to endure, the drone and rasp of heavy machinery would continue for weeks to come. Even if it were possible to have guests staying at the hotel, who would want to come here now?

They were finally left alone. All the rugs and linoleum in the downstairs rooms had been taken up and thrown outside for burning, along with chairs and tables. The smell on them was indescribable, and everyone had been on their hands and knees scrubbing the bare floorboards in their own quarters. The gaping hole in the middle of the guests' sitting-room had been covered by boards for now, if only to smother the evil smell from the drowned cellars that was making everyone nauseous.

The garden chairs for the use of guests in summer weather had been brought inside the kitchen and dried sufficiently for the family to have somewhere to sit while they ate their supper of cold meat pies and boiled potatoes. It was hard for any of them to speak now. In the aftermath of last night's storm, it was difficult to believe the damage that had been done in a few short hours.

Melvin Philpott arrived during the early evening, by which time Milly had gone to bed, exhausted, and Charlotte and Josie were helping their mother clear away the supper things, finding a minuscule sense of normality in domesticity. Donald had gone out to inspect the initial work on the sea wall.

'My God, this is terrible,' Melvin said in an awed voice. 'We heard you'd been badly hit by the storm, but I had no idea it would be like this. I would have come sooner, Charlie, but Dad and I have been helping the farmer next to us. One of his stable doors was battered in the storm, and a couple of his horses got loose and they were pretty crazed by the time we rounded them up again.'

Charlotte was suddenly aware of the bruises and scratches on his face and hands, and guessed that he had had a bad time of it, too. But nothing like they had had here. Nothing could compare with that...

Without warning her hands shook and the plate she had been holding slipped through her fingers, slid to the floor and smashed. She burst into uncontrollable tears and, the next moment, regardless of her mother and Josie's astonished eyes, Melvin had crossed the kitchen floor and was holding her tightly in his arms.

'Come on, sweetheart, it was only a plate. The worst is over now. You're all here, and I'm sure the damage to the hotel can be put right. You'll all bounce back.'

But his voice trailed away uneasily as Ruth said nothing and Josie began muttering that he was more stupid than he looked if he thought that.

'Well, I never said Rome was built in a day, did I?' he lashed out at her.

'My God, he's educated, too,' Josie sneered.

'That's quite enough of that kind of talk, young lady,' Ruth said sharply. 'Charlotte, you and Melvin go into the family sitting-room for a few minutes' privacy while Josie and I clear up here.'

'She smashed the plate,' Josie howled.

'And you will clear it up,' her mother told her.

Melvin didn't wait to hear any more. Still holding Charlotte, he steered her out of the kitchen and into the small family sitting-room. Like everywhere else it was bare of floor covering now and sparsely furnished, with a couple of chairs stacked on top of the sideboard. Melvin lifted one down and pulled Charlotte onto his lap. He had expected a token resistance, if not more, considering her father could appear at any moment, but she simply allowed herself to be manoeuvred wherever he chose. She seemed numb to whatever was happening now, and he began to feel more and more alarmed.

'We had it bad over at the stables, too, Charlie,' he said roughly. 'At one time, Farmer Miles thought one of his horses would have to be put down, and you can imagine what a blow that would have been to his livelihood.'

He knew it was a mistake as soon as he'd said it. He felt Charlotte tense in his arms, and she tried to pull away from him even as he tried to hold her tight. Although they hadn't turned on the popping gas-light, there was still enough daylight for him to see how her eyes seemed to burn.

'If you think the loss of one horse can be compared to what's happened here, then you really are stupid!' she snapped shrilly.

'I'm not stupid,' he said angrily. 'I was just trying to remind you that you're not the only people to have been affected by the storm. Other people suffered as well as the precious Elkins family.'

She was still trying to wrestle out of his arms, but he held her fast.

'You're a hateful pig,' she panted, 'and you've got no idea of what all this will mean to my family.'

'Of course I do, and you know I'll do anything I can to help, Charlie.'

As she became aware of the rough concern in his voice now, she gave a small whimpering cry and went limp against him. The last thing she wanted to do was fight with him, when she was so glad he was here. When she wanted him so much.

His cheek was warm against hers, and she had felt so cold for so long that it was like manna from heaven to feel him so close now. His lips gently brushed her mouth and then fastened on them more firmly, and she was kissing him back with more passion than she had believed she'd be capable of feeling again. It was as though the storm had wiped away all her capacity for loving feelings, but it was all rushing back now as she clung to him as though she would never let him go.

'What the devil's going on in here?' her father's voice roared as the door abruptly opened and the twilight was split by the glare of a flashlight.

Melvin let her go so fast she almost fell off his lap and on to the floor. If she hadn't clutched at his shoulders, she would certainly have done so, and she felt the blood rush to her face at her father's ominous tone.

'I felt faint, Dad,' she stammered, and at the same time Melvin blustered.

'It wasn't how it looked, Mr Elkins!'

'I know exactly how it looked, boy, and I'll thank you not to molest my daughter or take advantage of this miserable situation. We still have a position in this town to uphold, whatever fate throws at us.'

'Dad, he wasn't taking advantage of me!' Charlotte exclaimed, humiliated.

'I would never do such a thing,' Melvin snarled, even though they both knew he wouldn't normally have baulked at such a chance.

'Charlotte, get upstairs to your room and I'll talk to you later when I've had a few words with this young man.'

She was furious at being treated like a child

and near to tears. 'But it's barely seven o'clock! You can't send me to bed as if I'm Milly's age!'

'You're not too old for me to get my strap to you, girl, and if you want to have this fellow here witness it, you can stand there and defy me for exactly one minute longer and no more.'

She turned and fled, aware that Melvin had no intention of intervening now. She couldn't blame him. When Donald really saw red his anger was explosive and, although he had never taken a strap to any of his daughters in his life, the threat of it was always enough.

She flew through the entrance hall, not daring to go to the kitchen and tell her mother what was happening. She flung herself onto her bed and sobbed her heart out, uncaring whether or not Milly was still awake in the next room. It was all too much. Too much had happened in so short a time. This time yesterday, from the warmth and comfort of the hotel, they and the regulars had been watching how the wind had whipped up the waves out in the Channel, never dreaming that in so short a time the hotel was in imminent threat of ruin.

The whole world had since gone topsy-turvy, and the one constant thought in her mind had been that of seeing Melvin again, and to be reassured of his feelings for her. Now, on top of everything else, she thought bitterly, her father was at this very moment intent on ruining any chance they ever had of walking out again.

Melvin was far too arrogant to want to see her again now, having felt the wrath of her father at his most bombastic. Donald Elkins had always thought himself a cut above everybody else, especially a blacksmith's son.

Charlotte buried her face in her pillow. She was seventeen years old and she wished that she was dead.

Twelve

A few days later, the *Evening Chronicle* had published an account of the disaster with many photographs of the sea front and surroundings that had temporarily turned into a lake; the broken and battered sea defences; and the hotel that had taken the brunt of the flooding. By then Donald had been horrified by the estimates and costs of building work that would be necessary to make the hotel a viable proposition again.

Once he had obtained some early figures, he had a lengthy meeting with Gilbert Fellowes, his accountant, who gave him the sombre news that unless a miracle was forthcoming, he would be in debt for years to pay off any loan that would be required to put the hotel back on its feet.

'And that's providing the bank would be

willing to give you such funds,' the accountant warned. 'The last thing you want to do is go to any loan sharks who will charge extortionate fees for the privilege.'

'We've always had good relations with the bank, and the manager is an old friend, so it may not be the problem you suggest.'

Fellowes sniffed. 'Bank managers are always friends to those with money to invest. Once a business goes down, you'll find the friendly smiles have a habit of ceasing. There's a huge amount of work to be done here, Donald, and apart from the financial aspect you'll be unable to carry on with any kind of business for some months until it's all finished. You don't only have yourself to consider, either. You have a family.'

'Do you think I don't know that?! So what are you saying? That the whole idea is hopeless, and that I should sell up and try to get what I can for the land the hotel stands on, and move elsewhere? That's providing anyone would want to buy it, of course, considering its history. And what would I do then? I don't know anything but the hotel business, and I'm too old to start anything new.'

'For pity's sake, man, you're not Methuselah. You're not fifty yet, and you have a good business head on your shoulders. Plenty of other hotels would be glad to have your expertise as manager if not as owner. As for your daughters, they'll have no trouble finding work elsewhere.'

'I dare say they won't, but we've always

been a family business, and that's how we want to stay,' he said stubbornly. 'Sending my girls out to work would be to admit failure.'

The accountant began to put his papers back in his briefcase. 'Then I fear you're putting your head in the sand, Donald. I grant you, there's sufficient money to refurnish all that you've lost on the ground floor, and thank heavens your own family extension is sound. But the problem is with the foundations of the original part of the hotel, which have obviously lacked inspection for years. It's the structural work that's going to cost the money, and you simply don't have it.'

'Then I'll just have to find it, won't I?'

He sat in the small sitting-room alone for a long time after the accountant had left, not wanting to relate everything to Ruth yet. The bare floorboards in the extension that had all borne the onslaught of the flood had now been covered by a few rugs. As a temporary measure they had bought a cheap lot of chairs and tables from the local auction rooms so that the family at least had somewhere to sit and eat their food. The kitchen was more or less in working order, but none of it was up to the elegance of what The Retreat had once known, and the large sitting-room for the guests was still in a state of chaos. Donald dreaded to think how their lovely bedrooms would fare if the whole lot came tumbling down, and it had taken a lot of persuasion on his part to make the inspectors allow everything from the guest bedrooms to be carefully removed into their own quarters and storeroom, all now overloaded with extra furniture. But his pride would never allow him to admit to outsiders how far he had fallen. Even though it was through no fault of his own, Donald felt acutely bitter at his fate.

The door opened, and Ruth came into the sitting-room where he sat so dejectedly. He still didn't feel able to explain things to her. The longer he could keep the drastic state of their affairs to himself, the less real they became. Then he realised there was someone else with her.

'The Captain's here to see you, Donald. I'll bring you both some tea as soon as you're settled.'

It was too late to say he wasn't in the mood for receiving visitors. Captain Bellamy was inside the room and pumping his hand almost before he stood up. 'No need to stand on ceremony, Elkins,' the man said brusquely. 'But the dear ladies and myself have been anxious to know how you're all faring, and so I decided it was time I came to find out. We're comfortable enough at the Seaview Hotel, but it's not home the way this dear old place was, and we're all looking forward to the day we can come back.'

Donald looked at him dumbly, and then cleared his throat.

'I'm starting to wonder if that day will ever come, Captain.'

'What's that? I never thought I'd find such a defeatist attitude in this establishment, sir! How do you think we'd have fared in the Great War if we'd said the day of victory would never come, heh?'

'We're not at war now, Captain, and I don't have the country's resources behind me. Much as we all loved The Retreat, we're just one small seaside hotel, and if we don't have the money to restore it, then we might as well give up.'

Against his will, he knew he was repeating what the accountant had said. In normal times he would never reveal his personal problems to anyone, but these were not normal times, and after all these years the Captain was an old friend and more than just a paying hotel guest.

'I would hate to see that happen, and so would our dear ladies. We guessed that this would be a difficult time for you, so we've been getting our heads together. Between us we've got a fair bit put by for our old age. And well, not to put too fine a point on it, we all reckon we've reached that time of life by now, if not passed it long ago, so what's the use of hanging on to it for the benefit of relatives we haven't got? So rather than leave it to a ruddy dogs' home, we've decided that we'd far rather invest our savings in The Retreat. What do you say?'

Donald was prevented from saying anything for a moment as Ruth came back with a tray of tea and put it on a table. Her face was flushed, and he knew she must have overheard everything. She leant over and kissed the Captain's grizzled cheek.

'I'd say that's the most generous thing I've ever heard, and I know that when Donald gets his breath back, he'll say the same. Not that we could possibly agree to it, of course, but we do thank you with all our hearts, Captain dear.'

She looked meaningfully at Donald, afraid he would throw the elderly man's generosity back in his face. But he still seemed incapable of saying anything, and the only sound to be heard was the constant grind of the machinery along the sea front as the work on restoring the sea defences went on. The winter weather made it imperative that the work was done as quickly as possible.

'Stuff and nonsense, dear lady!' the Captain boomed. 'Of course you can agree to it, and we three regulars insist on it. We want to invest in the hotel for what's left of our future, as well as yours, don't you see? We're not offering a fortune because we don't have it. But if it's enough to get the work started, then we'll feel that we've done our bit, and the sooner we can come back home.'

Donald gave a sort of strangled gasp then, and the other two realised he was having a hard job to keep control of his emotions. Never one to reveal them publicly except when his temper got the better of him, this time his nerves were near to breaking at what he was hearing. That final word, home, was the one that did it.

'As I said, it's not a fortune, ma'am, so don't get too excited,' the Captain said, turning to Ruth as she busied herself with the tea cups to hide her embarrassment. 'But if it'll help, we intend to put the funds at your disposal as soon as the bank can arrange it.'

Ruth spoke hurriedly. 'It's so very good of you, Captain, and, as you say, if it's the means of having you and the ladies home again at some time in the future, then I think we should accept graciously, providing the investment is put on a proper legal footing. That would be right, wouldn't it, Donald?'

He nodded, even though he knew in his heart that the generous offer would be like a drop in the ocean compared with what was needed.

'We do, and of course our thanks are hopelessly inadequate, but what we can offer you all now is a spot of hospitality one evening. If you don't mind roughing it in this paltry little room, I'm sure my wife would like to give you a special supper as our friends as well as our guests. What do you say?'

It would be a devil of a squeeze in this little sitting-room, Donald thought, but it would salvage some of his pride if they made an occasion of it.

'I say it will be the highlight of our week,' the Captain said. 'Between you and me, the food at the Seaview isn't up to much,' he added confidentially, a remark that brought a smile to Donald's face for the first time in what seemed like years.

Later, Donald finally felt able to tell Ruth of the state of their finances and the way Gilbert Fellowes had spelled it out so baldly. After that he had decided he needed some fresh air to clear his head, and went outside to watch the men and machines at work on the sea defences as he so often did now. She let him go, understanding his need to be alone with his thoughts at such a time.

But Ruth was a practical woman. If nothing could be done about a problem, then there was no use worrying about it and driving yourself mad. It was a sentiment that sometimes worked and sometimes didn't, but she was determined to think positively for the present, and she concentrated on deciding what this special supper for their old regulars was going to be.

In any case, doing something so domestic brought a small breath of normality back to her, and it revived her spirits to be planning something she was good at. Milly had arrived home from school now and was excited about having the regulars back for a couple of hours, and was jollying her mother into baking her favourite apple dumplings and custard for dessert.

Charlotte and Josie came bursting into the hotel together a little later.

'We've got some news for you,' Josie announced. 'I've got a job at Hallam's shop, and

Charlotte's going to work in the stables at Miles's Farm.'

'What?' Ruth said, startled, even while Charlotte glared at her sister for blurting everything out at once.

'We have to do something, Mum,' Charlotte said, almost pleadingly. 'We can't just wait for the hotel to be fully operational again. Besides, we thought if we got jobs, we could give you and Dad some of our wages to help get things back to normal, or at least pay for our keep.'

Ruth hardly knew what to say to this. It was such an obvious thing for them to do, and yet it had never occurred to her that they would simply go out and do it. Theirs had always been such a close-knit family concern, and even taking this sensible course of action seemed the first step to splitting them wide open. And Lord knew what Donald would have to say about it.

She turned back to the gas stove where she had been stirring the stew they were having for supper that evening, her heart jumping at the thought. But she had to put the thoughts into words.

'I don't know what your father will think about you working at Hallam's, Josie, and as for you working in stables with horses, are you sure you'd be suited to it, Charlotte?'

Milly started chanting. 'I know why she's going to work there. It's because she'll be next door to the smithy, and she'll be able to see her boy every day.'

'Don't be silly,' Charlotte said crossly. 'Farmer Miles offered me a job and it seemed pointless to say no when I've got nothing else to do with my time.'

Ruth spoke more sharply. 'I think you had both better speak to your father about this. You shouldn't have taken it on yourselves without consulting him first.'

'Mum, we want to do something to help,' Charlotte insisted. 'We're both old enough to get proper jobs, and most other girls of our age have done so long ago, instead of just having to wait at tables and clean up after strangers.'

She hadn't meant to say so much and she saw her mother's mouth tighten.

'So you don't think being part of a family hotel business is a proper job?'

'Of course I do, and so does Josie, but right now it doesn't look as if much will be going on here for the foreseeable future, does it? Besides, it's too late. We've already agreed, and it would shame us both if we had to go back to Mr Hallam and Farmer Miles and say we weren't allowed to do it after all.'

Ruth slapped down the wooden spoon she had been stirring the stew with, and splashes of hot liquid flew across the room.

'It is not too late, my girl. As for you feeling ashamed, you should be feeling that already by not coming to your father and me first.'

Josie marched out of the kitchen and clumped up the stairs.

'I told you it would be like this,' she shouted

back. 'And we haven't even heard Dad's side of it yet.'

Milly looked from her mother to Charlotte nervously now. The storm had been frightening, but exciting, too; telling the kids at school about how their hotel had almost fallen down and been so flooded that it had nearly drowned them all had been just as exciting (until they started going on about her gran). But she didn't like the way her mother was so cross with her sisters now. Her mother rarely lost her temper, and it frightened Milly in a different way that she didn't understand.

'I'll go after Josie,' Charlotte said abruptly. 'I'm sure she'll want to apologise later.'

'Take Milly with you, and I suggest you all keep out of the way until I've had words with your father,' Ruth said sharply. 'I'll call you when supper's ready.'

Milly opened her mouth to protest, but Charlotte caught her firmly by the hand, and she had no choice but to go upstairs, where they found Josie lying flat on her back on her bed, hands clasped behind her head, her eyes mutinous.

'Go to your own room, Milly,' Charlotte told her swiftly. 'We've got things to discuss.'

'Why can't I stay and listen?'

'Because you can't. Clear off, Milly,' Josie snapped.

'I don't like you when you talk like that. It's the way those rough men at the fair talked. Dad won't like it if he hears you talking like that—'

She ducked as Josie flung a pillow at her, and went out of the room, slamming the door behind her.

'Well done,' Charlotte said mildly. 'Sometimes I think you're just as much of a baby as she is.'

'And you're so wise and sensible, aren't you?'

'No, I'm not. But I'd have tried to be a bit more tactful and handled things better than you did, blurting everything out the minute we got indoors.'

Josie sniffed. 'Oh, well, we all know you've never minded slaving here, but it's the last thing I want to be doing for the next forty years!'

'I don't see myself doing it for that long, either.'

'No, but I want to get out right now. I always wanted to get out, and this storm seemed like a bit of a godsend to me, if you must know. It's given me the chance to do something different, and not be at the beck and call of people who don't mean a thing to me. The regulars were all right, but it's a bit of a pain to have to keep smiling day and night, isn't it?'

Charlotte began to laugh. 'And you think that working in old Hallam's shop is going to be any better? You'll be at the beck and call of his customers just the same, and you'll have to keep smiling at them as well.'

'And you won't need to smile at Farmer

Miles's horses, will you? Milly was right. You'll be able to nip over the fence and see Melvin Philpott whenever you like. It'll be months before I see Tony again.'

She lapsed into sudden misery, and Charlotte stopped laughing.

'Good Lord, you're not still thinking of that fairground chap, are you? It'll be ages before the fair comes to Braydon again, and by that time he'll either have forgotten all about you or found some other girl or moved on somewhere else. You know what these fairground people are like.'

Josie's eyes smouldered.

'I *do* know, as a matter of a fact, and that's why I also know he won't have forgotten me, and that he'll come back, too, because he said he would.'

She refused to react to Charlotte's remark that he might have found some other girl. Of course he wouldn't ... although he probably would. She shivered as the unwelcome thought entered her head, knowing it was probably nearer the mark than anything else. 'Love 'em and leave 'em' came to mind as far as Tony was concerned, and she blooming well wished it hadn't.

'I wish you well of him then,' Charlotte said. 'Now I'd better go and calm Milly down.'

'You're such an almighty saint, aren't you, Charlotte?' Josie snapped. 'One of these days you'll be sprouting wings and a halo.'

Charlotte left her, feeling her lips go tight in

the effort not to yell back at her, which wouldn't help anybody. But a saint she certainly was not. Not when she had the same yearnings as any other girl and, guiltily, she knew that this awful disaster had left her with the same restless feelings as Josie. Not that she wanted to get away from working in the family hotel, because she had never had any qualms about that, and she always enjoyed meeting the guests. But now fate had given her the unexpected chance to be working in close proximity to Philpott's Smithy, and she couldn't deny a sliver of excitement every time she thought about it.

Even Milly had been canny enough to see that but, then, she supposedly had the brains in the family, didn't she?! She tapped on the girl's door and heard a muffled voice tell her to go away.

'It's me, Milly. Can I come in for a minute?'

She didn't wait for an answer, but opened the door and went inside, to where Milly was sitting on the edge of her bed, angrily pulling tufts out of her raggedy old teddy bear.

'I don't know what he's done to deserve that,' Charlotte observed.

'I wish it was Josie's hair! She's always mean to me.'

'You know that's not true. We're all under a bit of strain, Milly, but Mum and Dad won't want to see us fighting when they're so worried about the hotel. We all have to make the best of things, and Josie may not like working in Hallam's shop half as much as she thinks she will. If she's sharp with customers she'll find plenty of them complaining about her.'

Milly gave a small snigger. The little wretch clearly liked the thought of Josie being in trouble with the customers, Charlotte thought.

'I bet you'll like working next to the smithy, though, won't you?'

'Of course I will. Did I ever say anything different?' she said, taking the wind right out of Milly's sails.

'If you and the blacksmith get married, can I be a bridesmaid?'

Charlotte smiled, thinking how easy it was to turn the conversation, even if it wasn't always the way she would have chosen, since she didn't know the answer herself. Sometimes such a possibility seemed like an eternity away.

'Whoever I get married to, and whenever it may be, I shall want both you and Josie to be my bridesmaids,' she said deliberately, and Milly scowled.

'Well, I shall ask Dorothy to be my bridesmaid, because you and Josie will be far too old by the time I get married,' she retorted.

'Thank you very much!' Charlotte said with a laugh as she went out of the room and left her, glad to know that Dorothy was apparently back in favour now.

She paused on the landing, hearing her parents' voices raised more than usual. She didn't want to be an eavesdropper but, even as she thought it, the memory of Josie calling her a saint made her change her mind, and she leant a little further over the banister.

'I don't know what you've got against the girls working outside the hotel,' she heard her mother say in exasperation. 'They've shown initiative and common sense.'

'And you think I'm sticking my head in the sand, I suppose?'

'I think you have to be realistic, Donald. Your mother would certainly be proud of them for trying to be helpful.'

'My mother would probably take it on herself to go out and find a job for herself, and show us up even more,' Donald said, and Charlotte could hear the scowl in his voice.

'She was never as proud as you, although I'm not sure that's the word she would use for your stubbornness.'

Charlotte held her breath. Her mother was always more docile than Donald and frequently able to smooth things over between them, but she was being more defiant than usual.

'So you think Clover would approve of these mad schemes of the girls, then, do you?'

'Of course she would,' Ruth said briskly. 'And so would you if you stopped to think about it. Don't you want your daughters to be independent? You can't expect to have them hanging around your coat-tails all your life.'

'I don't expect any such thing.'

Ruth continued in her gentle, relentless way. 'You only have one small child in the house now, my dear. Charlotte's nearly a young woman, and Josie's not far behind. You can't stop the march of time, Donald, much as I know you'd like to keep them children all their lives.'

There was silence for a few moments, and then Donald gave a heavy sigh.

'You're a good woman, Ruth, and I should listen to you more often, but a father always wants to protect his children, and I'm no different from any other.'

'I know, my love,' Ruth said softly. 'But why don't you go and call them down to supper now, since I'm sure they're all hungry? Let's discuss it all quietly, and you can be sure to let them know how much you appreciate what they've done.'

Charlotte sped back to her bedroom before her father could come clumping up the stairs. He might be the master of the house, she thought, but her mother had cleverly thrown the initiative back to him. He would be the one to be magnanimous about his daughters' decisions but, when it came to important domestic issues, Ruth knew how to use her feminine wiles to manipulate him any way she chose.

Thirteen

Charlotte took a breather from sweeping out the stables. The smell of the horses and the straw in their stalls could be alternately pungent and sweet. She liked horses, even though she had never been in quite such close proximity to them before, but she discovered that there was something oddly vulnerable about the huge animals, who had also taken a liking to her, nuzzling their noses into her hand when she brought them their feed. It was good, too, to be spending her days in the open air, even when the weather was still chilly in the early part of the year, and when exercising the animals meant wrapping up warmly in coats and scarves and boots.

But there was also the bonus of working here. Milly hadn't been so far wrong when she teased her sister about working next to Philpott's Smithy, and she'd be lying if she said it hadn't been an extra incentive to be able to see more of Melvin. Even when they both had work to do, she could often wave to him as he went about his business.

He was also frequently at the farm to discuss matters with Farmer Miles. Those were cosy times, when the farmer and his wife and the two of them sat around the scrubbed wooden table in the big old farmhouse, with steaming mugs of cocoa for their morning elevenses. It was almost like being enveloped in a new family, Charlotte thought dreamily, as if she and Melvin were part of this domestic arrangement, the son and daughter of the house...

At such times, she brought her thoughts up sharply, reminding herself that she already had a family of her own, and that this was only an interlude until her father got the hotel business operational again.

She paused on her broom, brushing back her hair and being aware of the familiar uneasy feeling in the pit of her stomach. So far nothing seemed to be happening at all towards restoring the hotel to its former glory. There were endless heated discussions between her father and the accountant, the bank manager and various other official bodies who all seemed to have a finger in the pie before anything could be decided about the amount of restoration and the cost of it all.

As if they didn't have enough to worry about, Steve Bailey, the *Evening Chronicle* reporter, had made a dramatic account of finding the bones of the dog in the cellars. The account had probably been intended to prove that nothing untoward had been found there, but it had completely backfired. Instead of creating sympathy for the Elkins family, an ongoing series of letters to the editor had been published in the newspaper, suggesting that the hotel was obviously bad luck for whoever owned it. There were even thinly veiled hints in some of the letters about the owner's eccentric mother, who had sometimes been seen during the hours of darkness prancing along the sea front in her nightwear, asking if this was the normal action of a sane woman. Donald feared that the reputation of The Retreat was starting to suffer badly from the unwanted publicity, even before anything was done to restore it. Clover's full name was never mentioned, but the suggestion that bad things were happening in her vicinity was clear to anyone who looked for it.

Before Charlotte and Josie had begun their new jobs, Steve Bailey came to the hotel on several occasions to see how things were progressing and to give his readers an updated report of it all. Donald, as usual, had given him short shrift.

'You're making things worse, man,' he'd told him. 'There's nothing wrong with this hotel except for the ravings of lunatics who imagine things that aren't there. We had bad luck with the storm, and it was more than bad luck when we discovered that the foundations weren't as sound as we'd always believed. But finding the ancient remains of a stray dog was nothing to do with us, or with my mother! It didn't mean there was sinister work afoot.'

'Your mother seems to have created a certain amount of interest, Mr Elkins. Would you care to tell our readers something more about her?'

'I would not,' Donald had snapped. 'Why don't you find something more useful to write about, like the state of the sea-front defences?'

'People's lives are always more interesting to read about, Mr Elkins, and I gather that your mother was something of a lively personality. Your daughters must have thought a lot of her.'

Donald had glared at him, then spoken sharply to Charlotte. 'Please show Mr Bailey out, Charlotte, since we have nothing more to say to him.'

She had done as she had been told and hustled him outside quickly, closing the door behind them before he could hear Donald explode completely at this unwanted intrusion. But she had felt obliged to give a more temperate answer to his comment.

'You're right that we thought a great deal of our grandmother, of course. We all loved her very much, but my father doesn't care to air our personal business. I'm sure you think a lot of your grandparents too, Mr Bailey.'

'Call me Steve, please. And I certainly did when they were alive. Unfortunately they both passed away within six months of each other, just over a year ago now.'

She had blushed furiously. 'I'm sorry. I didn't know.'

'Well, how could you? We all have people in our lives that are special to us, and I'm sure that's how your grandmother was to you, no matter how other people may have seen her.'

She had registered at once how adept he was at neatly turning the question back to her and Clover. She had known she shouldn't prolong this conversation, but there had been a tingling in her veins, and she had felt oddly exhilarated at the thought of playing him at his own game and outwitting him.

'Did your grandparents live in Braydon then?'

'Bristol. And yours? Your grandmother lived with you, I understand. What about your grandfather?'

'He died many years ago; so what of your parents? Are you a native of Braydon or Bristol?'

Steve had suddenly smiled. 'Have you ever thought of working on a newspaper, Charlotte? You'd be good at it. It takes more than an inquisitive mind, it takes a lively personality, too, and you've obviously inherited that from your grandmother.'

She hadn't say anything for a moment and then she had laughed out loud.

'I'm not sure if that's just flattery or the clever journalist talking now, but you won't get anything more out of me in that way, Mr Bailey – Steve.'

'If it's flattery, it's because I find you beautiful and charming. That's not the clever journalist talking, it's someone who would very much like to see you again. In fact – I wonder if you'd care to come to the cinema with me one evening?'

Slightly astonished, she had realised that his voice had subtly changed from the rather brash reporter to a perfectly nice young man asking her to go out with him. She *had been* flattered ... and also suspicious, because this could be no more than a ploy to get more information out of her about her family, and about Clover in particular.

'I don't think so, thank you,' she had said pleasantly.

'That's a pity, but I'm sure I shall ask you again. I don't give up easily.'

If she had expected him to be more persistent she was disappointed. She had turned and gone back indoors with her heart hammering, wondering if his last remark was meant to be cryptic, too. It was a fact that nobody had mentioned Clover by name in the recent letters to the editor, nor said a great deal about her except for her night-time activities. It had probably perpetuated the myth that she was a little strange, Charlotte had thought, but, like all the family, she felt very protective of her memory.

It had been obvious, too, on the evening that the regulars came for supper and they had all had a determinedly jolly meal together, that they had no intention of being disloyal to the family where they had spent so many contented years. Whatever Clover had done in her lifetime was nobody's business but Clover's.

'Why didn't you tell him you already had a

young man?' Josie had demanded later, when Charlotte had related all that had happened between her and Steve.

'Why should I? It's none of his business.'

'Are you sure it's not because you want him to ask you again? I told you he fancied you, didn't I? Do you fancy him, too?'

'Don't be ridiculous,' Charlotte had said crossly.

'It's not ridiculous. You're not engaged to Melvin Philpott yet, and the newspaperman's far more good-looking.'

'Maybe he is, although that's a matter of opinion. Anyway, you don't fall for a chap just because he's good-looking. I might not be engaged to Melvin, but he's still my young man and I've got no intention of going to the cinema or anywhere else with someone behind his back.'

She had been instantly defensive of Melvin, even though she'd had to admit that he was a pretty casual sort of young man except when he had something special on his mind, like walking out on Priory Hill. He had been ardent enough then. She had also agreed that Steve Bailey was far more personable, even if her father would ever allow her to go out with a reporter, which she knew very well he wouldn't. The very fact that she had been arguing over it in her mind was starting to make her angry.

'I'd go out with him if he asked me,' Josie had said mischievously.

'Well, we don't need to worry about that, do

we? Because you're far too young, and I'm sure he'd want a girl who was far more sophisticated.'

For some reason she was thinking about that conversation now, while she was mucking out the stables in the late afternoon. Josie could be a little idiot, but sometimes she hit on the very thing that Charlotte didn't want to think about.

The fact was that she knew she could take a liking to Steve Bailey if she allowed herself to do so. That brief spell of exhilaration, pitting her wits against him while evading all his probing about Clover, had told her as much. He was an intelligent young man, and he used his brains in his job, instead of using his hands in the practical way that Melvin did. She drew in her breath, wishing she hadn't compared them, however unintentionally. Melvin was a skilled craftsman and she loved him, and no smart, good-looking reporter was going to turn her head.

She heard Melvin's voice calling her at that moment, and turned her head sharply as she saw him coming across the field towards her. The working day was nearly over, and she would be glad to get back to the hotel and have a soak in the bath to get the horsey smell from her skin.

'Do you want to come for tea on Sunday, Charlie?' Melvin said casually as he reached her. 'Mum wants to thank you for the card you sent her while she was ill, so what do you say?'

It would be nicer to be asked because she was his girl so that being invited to tea would have more significance, she thought fleetingly, but then she smiled, because this would be the first time, and it had to mean something special, however the invitation came.

'It sounds lovely, so please thank your mother for me, Melvin.'

They were being so very formal, when she knew he'd pull her into his arms if they weren't out in the open, and, as if he had the same idea, he somehow steered her back into the dimness of the stables and quickly pinned her against the wall.

'Melvin, Farmer Miles is around somewhere,' she said with a laugh. 'You'd better not let him catch you in here – and remember my reputation!'

'That's not the only thing I'm remembering, sweetheart. God, it's ages since we've been alone together without somebody bursting into a room and treating us like kids. And you're no kid, are you, Charlie?'

She felt the roughness of his chin grazing hers as his mouth sought hers. Her spirit soared with sudden excitement to be here in the stables with him, with the scent of hay and straw and the earthiness of the animals an evocative mixture. She felt his hand roaming over her breast and didn't try to stop it. Why should she, when it was sending such delicious feelings through her?

'Let's go up in the hay loft for a little while,'

she heard Melvin's voice say thickly. 'Nobody will know we're there, and I need to be alone with my girl.'

She shivered, knowing exactly what he meant. There was a ladder at the back of the stables leading up to the hay loft, and before she had time to argue he was leading her towards it and pushing her in front of him while she giggled, making a weak token protest. But why protest, when all her senses were on fire?

The hay made a soft, sweet-smelling bed and they tumbled onto it together, laughing and giggling. Charlotte felt a new recklessness, hardly knowing where it came from, but just thrilled to be alive, to be with the boy she loved. Her arms wound around his neck, pulling him down onto her, and she heard his gasp of pleasure as she did so. And then she felt his hands pushing up her skirt, and her heart was thumping, remembering the hot, tingling sensations when he had touched her before and anticipating the moment when he would touch her that way again ... and she wanted it so much...

The sound of nearby voices seemed to turn them into frozen statues for a few seconds. Then Charlotte clutched at Melvin's shoulders, frantically trying to straighten her clothes at the same time. He clamped his hand over her mouth. It tasted of heat and metal from the ironwork he had been working on previously, and she tried not to notice how acrid it was.

'Keep quite still, and whoever it is will go away soon,' he muttered.

'They'll be looking for me,' she whispered frantically. 'Why else would they be coming here at this time?'

She didn't dare to lift her head as the sound of voices came nearer. Not just one. Not just Farmer Miles and his wife, but several others, too. She felt sick with fear and shame. If she was caught up here in the hay loft with a boy she would be sent home in disgrace and her father would have to hear of it. She might be seventeen years old, but the threat of his belt would be a very real one then.

She suddenly realised that there was a child's voice amongst the others. She groaned. Not Milly ... oh, surely it couldn't be Milly, sent to fetch her home for some reason. Her legs felt as though they were turning to water, and if she was obliged to climb down the ladder in front of the farmer and his wife, she would simply die from the disgrace.

'It's Farmer and Mrs Miles, and some woman and her kid,' Melvin hissed in her ear. 'Never seen them before.'

Charlotte felt weak with relief. The thoughts spun around in her head. At least it wasn't Milly sent to fetch her with even more disastrous news. The hotel hadn't totally collapsed, and her father hadn't had a heart attack from all the shocks of the past weeks. Nothing else had been discovered in the ruined cellars...

Farmer Miles was speaking in his bellowing voice. 'You'll find we have everything here that the child needs, Mrs Yard. My wife will put her through her paces on the smallest pony to begin with, until she finds her feet – or should that be her stirrups!' He laughed at his own joke, and the others laughed dutifully.

'I'd advise you not to start lessons until the spring though,' Mrs Miles put in. 'Riding's not much fun in the winter months unless you're going in for steeplechasing and suchlike, little lady.'

She screamed with laughter too and Charlotte cringed at the way they enjoyed one another's jokes, if nobody else did. She shifted her position slightly, feeling more and more uncomfortable with a clenching cramp in her leg. As she moved, a sprinkling of hay feathered down from the loft, as soft as a hint of snow.

The movement had made her lift her head a fraction and, although the three adults were busily discussing the child's proposed riding lessons next spring, the small girl suddenly looked upwards, straight into Charlotte's eyes. Charlotte bobbed down again at once, her heart thumping.

Almost immediately, the group turned to leave the stables, having done what they came for and shown the visitors around.

'I don't know where Charlotte can have got to,' Mrs Miles was saying. 'I'm sure she'd have enjoyed showing Dorothy around.'

The voices drifted away and Charlotte went rigid. As Melvin tried to pull her back in his arms again, she pushed him away, making him laugh.

'Oh, come on, Charlie, they're not coming back. That was a bit of excitement, wondering if we were going to get caught, anyway. Now where were we?'

She shoved him harder and struggled to her feet, and his laughter changed to anger as he lost his balance and fell back.

'What's got into you, girl?' he said. 'A bit of danger adds spice to it all.'

'That girl saw me, Melvin,' she whispered.

'So what if she did? She's only a kid.'

Her voice rose in panic. 'She was called *Dorothy*, and she heard Mrs Miles use my name. She'll know it was me.'

She was already scrambling towards the ladder when Melvin caught hold of her arm, his fingers biting into it.

'I don't know what you're getting so bloody het up about. It was only some kid who wants riding lessons in the spring, and she heard your name. So what? You're not setting yourself up as a riding instructor, are you?'

'Oh, you're so *stupid*!' she blazed at him, even while she knew she was being unfair, because he didn't have the faintest idea why she was so upset. 'Dorothy's the name of Milly's friend at school, and it's not going to take long for those two little charmers to put their heads together and work out what I was doing up here without making my presence known, is it?!'

'For God's sake, how do you know it's the same kid?'

'I just know,' Charlotte said stubbornly. 'I seem to remember Milly saying something about Dorothy asking her to have riding lessons as well, and as she doesn't know one end of a horse from the other we took it as just another of her wild fancies.' She and Josie had laughed at the time, but she wasn't laughing now.

'Forget those kids and come back here,' Melvin said persuasively, having no idea how upset she really was. She shook off his hand, rubbing her arm where his fingers had hurt her.

'Are you mad? I have to finish my work, and you have to go. Please, Melvin, don't make things worse than they already are. If Farmer Miles comes looking for me and finds you here, I'll get the sack.'

'Oh, well, if the job's more important to you than me, I might as well bugger off. Don't forget you're coming for tea on Sunday if it's not too much trouble for your highness. My mother's expecting you.'

He swung across from her and slid down the ladder while she was still testing the shakiness of her legs. He looked up, flicked his hand in an arrogant sort of wave and then he was gone, whistling tunelessly.

Charlotte climbed down carefully, filled with resentment. Sometimes he could be so sweet, and at other times he could be hateful;

and sometimes she just didn't know what to make of him. She knew it was the mixture of all those things that made him exciting ... but right now the resentment won.

She tried to calm down and continued with her work in the stables and, sure enough, half an hour later the farmer came striding out to find her.

'I came out here earlier with some visitors, Charlotte, and when I couldn't see you anywhere, I thought you must have gone home,' he greeted her. 'Not tired of the work already, are you?'

'No, of course not! I must have been outside somewhere.'

It was a lame excuse but she couldn't think of a better one, and he seemed satisfied with it.

'Keep up the good work then,' he said. 'But you might as well get off now. The nights are drawing in quite quickly and you won't want to be cycling home after dark.'

She walked back to the farmhouse with him to collect her bicycle and to say goodnight to his wife. And then she got on her machine, and it wasn't only the wind that was making her eyes smart. She prayed that her legs wouldn't wobble beneath her, and wondered how long she was going to have to remain on tenterhooks until Milly came rushing home from school one day soon to say her friend Dorothy had told her a secret. How was she going to react then?

She wasn't in the habit of confiding in Josie

over really personal matters. Josie was still a child in many ways, prone to tantrums, and with a romanticised idea of love. Josie was quite sure that this black-haired, dark-eyed Tony fellow from the fair was going to come back to Braydon in the summer and sweep her off her feet like a knight on a white charger. It wouldn't surprise Charlotte if they never saw him again. Fairground people were transients, going where the work and the whims took them, and, unfortunately, that was the very thing that charmed Josie about them. But now this thing had happened. This thing at the stables, when Dorothy Yard had looked up into the hay loft and her astonished eyes had met Charlotte's. This was too important a worry to keep to herself and, if only Clover had been here, Charlotte would have gone straight to her and asked her what she should do about it. Clover would have understood, and Clover would have had a solution. But she wasn't here, and the only person she could confide in was Josie, however much it demeaned her to do so.

'You mean you and Melvin Philpott were *doing* things?' Josie said in a hushed voice, her eyes as big as Dorothy's had been.

'No, I don't,' Charlotte said. She wasn't confiding everything. 'I mean we'd just gone up there for a bit of a cuddle, that's all, and then these people turned up, and this girl – this friend of Milly's – looked up and saw me.'

'Did she say anything?'

'Not a word. She probably thought she was seeing a ghost, but the others went on talking about her riding lessons and then they went out of the stables.'

'Crikey. How exciting.'

Charlotte sighed impatiently. Josie obviously saw the whole thing as daring and had no concept of the implications yet.

'You do realise what I'm saying, don't you? It was Milly's friend, who is obviously going to tell Milly what she saw. And when Farmer Miles mentioned that he didn't know where *Charlotte* was, the girl would have known immediately that it wasn't a ghost she saw!'

'Why would she think it was Milly's sister?'

'Because, you ninny, knowing how Milly can never keep her mouth shut about anything, she'd be sure to have told everyone that you're working at Hallam's shop now, and I'm working at Farmer Miles's stables. How long do you think it's going to be before they get their busy little heads together and start imagining what I was doing in the hay loft?'

'I don't know, but if Dorothy didn't see Melvin, they couldn't prove anyone else was there, could they? You'd just have to say you were too scared to come down because *you* thought you'd heard ghosts!'

Charlotte didn't say anything for a moment, gradually realising that it was such a daft and unlikely idea that it might just work. And, besides, Dorothy might not even say anything to Milly, and she might be worrying over nothing. She was letting her imagination get the better of her, and the only thing to do was to wait and see what happened.

How stupid she was, and how sensible Josie was for once. Because, of course, if Dorothy had only seen one face in the hay loft, there was nothing to prove, and nothing to say that Melvin Philpott had been anywhere near Miles' Farm that day at all. And she had forgotten until that moment how very careful Melvin had been to stay hidden, but she wasn't going to think anything about that now, except to be very thankful that he had.

'Josie, I could kiss you – but I won't,' she added at her sister's startled look. 'There is a tiny brain inside that noddle of yours, after all, and we obviously don't need to do anything.'

She wished now that she had thought it all through for herself and not involved Josie at all. Not that she thought for a moment that she couldn't trust her, but she couldn't help thinking of something Clover had once told her. It was brief and to the point. She could almost hear Clover saying it now.

Once a secret was shared, it was no longer a secret.

Fourteen

Josie enjoyed working at Hallam's shop. She was quick-witted and pretty, and the customers liked her. If it wasn't such an awful thing to admit, she knew she was almost glad of the storm that had done such damage to The Retreat, because it had meant she could get away from a family business and be as independent as other girls of her age. She could earn her own money, and it made her immensely pleased with herself when she handed most of it over to her mother at the end of the week, which she always did when Donald was elsewhere, in order to save his pride. This particular evening he had taken Milly, as promised, on a brief visit to the regulars at the Seaview Hotel.

'You know you don't need to do this, and your father doesn't like it,' Ruth always protested, when both she and Charlotte gave her their wage packets, expecting no more than pocket money in return.

'We do need to do it, Mum,' Charlotte told her. 'It makes us feel that at least we're not totally useless, while you and Dad are so worried about the future. How ever long is it going to be before we can go ahead with the rebuilding work?'

Ruth sighed. 'Heaven knows. One minute the building inspector says we can get workmen in to start on restoring the foundations to their original condition, and the next there's a lengthy discussion on whether it wouldn't be wiser to fill in the cellars completely, impossible though it sounds.'

'Well, why not?' Josie said with a shiver. 'We've never used them, and I'm sure we wouldn't want to after what happened!'

'No, but the cost of such a massive amount of work is almost impossible to conceive. If that is what's decided, then we just don't see how it can possibly go ahead.' Ruth hesitated, seeing the unease in their faces. ' I know your father doesn't care to discuss finances with you girls and, sweet though you're being with your wages, I'm very much afraid it's all looking rather hopeless, my dears.'

They looked at her in growing alarm. Ruth was always the optimist, the one who bolstered them all up, but they couldn't miss the despair in her voice now.

'Perhaps we shouldn't anticipate anything until we know the outcome of all the enquiries, Mum,' Charlotte said nervously. 'We could always stop Milly eating so much and save a few pennies that way, and at least she's got tired of those ghastly piano lessons so we don't have to listen to that any more,' she added, trying to bring a smile to her mother's wan face.

It also meant that Donald no longer had to

pay for the lessons. And the way things were going, any hope Milly had of going to that posh school she once hankered over seemed to be in question, too.

'If those pennies could be turned into pounds, and a great many of them, then I'd agree with you, my love,' Ruth told her.

'This is awful,' Josie said, when they had gone upstairs to wash themselves in time for supper. By now they were sitting on Josie's bed and looking gloomily at each other. 'I didn't know things were as bad as Mum suggests, did you? I just thought it was taking a long time to decide where to begin, but what do you think Dad will do if he can't find enough money for the repairs?'

Charlotte spread her hands helplessly. 'Sell up, I suppose. What else can he do? That is, if anyone wanted to buy a wreck of a hotel. I expect it would take a thousand pounds or even more to put it to rights, and I don't know anyone with that sort of money, do you?'

'I don't even know what a thousand pounds looks like.'

Neither did Charlotte, and nor did she have any idea if such a sum would be remotely enough. It already sounded like an impossible figure to them both.

'Perhaps somebody would buy it for the land it stands on,' Josie said uneasily.

'Why would they want to do that? Without the hotel here I don't suppose it's worth much. In any case where does that leave us?'

They hardly knew what to say to cheer each other up. They had never had to think of such things as money before. It had simply always been there, part of the fabric of their family life. The thought of not having what they needed in the future was suddenly terrifying.

'The Captain said Dad could get a job anywhere, managing some other hotel,' Josie said suddenly. 'He said any hotel owner would be glad to have him with all his years of experience, don't you remember?'

'I'm sure he could, but what about the rest of us? A man doesn't apply for a job and then say, "Oh, and by the way, my wife and three daughters will be coming along too"!'

Josie looked at her with frantic eyes. 'What will we do then?'

'I don't know, Josie. I just don't know.'

Milly burst into Josie's room at that moment, making them both jump.

'Mum says you're to hurry up and come down for supper, and Dorothy told me she saw you at the stables, Charlotte. You were up a ladder looking down at her and she said you looked all red and funny. I'm going to ask Dad if I can have riding lessons there with Dorothy, but you're not to make fun of me when I do!'

She tore out of the room again like a little whirlwind, and the two older girls stared at one another and then burst out laughing. As if they could afford riding lessons when they were wondering how they would even survive, Charlotte thought, almost hysterically.

And all her earlier worry over what Dorothy Yard would tell Milly, and what those two little schemers might have made of it, dissolved into nothing now. Clover would have called it a storm in a tea-cup ... but in any case, they all had a much bigger storm to worry about.

After supper, while the washing-up was being done, Donald said he wanted them all to join him in the little sitting-room later as he had something to say to them. He looked more ashen-faced than usual, and they knew he had been having discussions with people again that day. It was almost an everyday occurrence now for important-looking strangers to arrive at the hotel with notebooks and measuring equipment, and then to go away without any firm decisions ever being made. The Elkinses' fate seemed to be in the hands of these unknown officials who took no consideration of the strain it was putting on the family.

'Are you sure you want Milly here?' Ruth murmured to her husband.

'Not really, but it's unfair to banish the child to her bedroom.'

'If you want to get rid of me, Dorothy said I can go to her house any time I like,' Milly piped up. 'She's got some magazines about horses, and we're going to talk about riding lessons. She only lives in Stuckey Way, so can I go now?'

'Of course not, it's getting dark,' Ruth said at once, seeing the frown on Donald's face when riding lessons were mentioned.

'I'll take her if you like, and check that she can stay for a while,' Charlotte offered. 'I can be back from Stuckey Way in ten minutes or so and I'm sure Dorothy's father will bring her back, providing you're sure about this, Milly.'

She was assured that it was all right, and it was tacitly agreed that it was far better for Milly to be elsewhere if Donald had something important to tell them. A few minutes later the two girls had put on their outer clothes and were walking the short distance to Stuckey Way.

'Why were you up a ladder at the stables the other day?' Milly asked suddenly, catching Charlotte off guard.

'I was fetching some fresh hay for the horses,' she invented quickly.

'Dorothy said you looked scared.'

Charlotte spoke smartly. 'So would you if you were busy and then you heard strange voices floating up towards you. I thought it was a ghost for a minute.'

She blessed Josie for putting the thought into her head as Milly skipped along beside her.

'A ghost! I bet you thought it was Gran, coming to find out what you were doing on a farm.'

'Well, it could have been, couldn't it? She always liked to know what we were all doing.'

And if Clover was somewhere up there now, looking down on them and chuckling, she hoped she would forgive all these little white lies.

'Now, which house is it?' she said as they neared the end of Stuckey Way and diverting Milly's attention from ghosts and stables and Clover. 'I'd better speak to Dorothy's mother first, just to make sure you can stay for an hour.'

'She's nice,' Milly said. 'She always smells of cakes, like Mum does.'

Charlotte laughed. She presumed that Dorothy's mother spent a lot of time baking, like Ruth, and it was a warm and cosy way for a mother to smell.

The evening was quickly organised, and Charlotte left her sister in the Yard family's care and went back to the hotel with jitters in her stomach now. She had managed to keep them at bay all the while she was walking with Milly, but now they were back as she tried desperately not to anticipate what Donald had to tell them that evening.

'You'll know that I had words with the Captain this afternoon while the Misses Green entertained Milly at the Seaview Hotel,' he began. 'And you all know that the regulars had offered us some of their savings to invest in the hotel repairs.'

'Not that we wanted to accept, of course,' Ruth put in swiftly, seeing how demeaning he was finding the whole situation. He wouldn't want to spell it out in front of his daughters, either, but the fact that he wanted them here told them all how very serious this was.

'You're quite right, but nor did I want to offend them by refusing outright. But after today's meeting with the accountant and the other officials whose names I won't bore you with, I'm afraid, my darlings, that the situation is completely hopeless. Even if we took everything they had – and I would never consent to that – it wouldn't restore The Retreat. Our business here is finished.'

Charlotte noted how her mother's hands were gripped tightly together now. She guessed that she would dearly love to put her arms around her husband in a vain effort to protect him from the inevitable. But Ruth would know, just as Charlotte did, that Donald was far too proud to want any outward show of emotional support.

Josie was the one who burst into uncontrollable tears. Josie, who had never been satisfied with what she saw as a menial job waiting on strangers, but who now saw their whole way of life disintegrating in front of her.

'You can't mean that, Dad?! But we can still stay here, can't we? We still have this part of the hotel to live in, don't we?'

'Josie, pull yourself together,' Ruth said sharply.

'Leave her, love,' Donald said. 'She's too young to appreciate the full meaning of it all.'

'I'm not a baby!' Josie lashed out now.

'We're both trying to understand, Dad,'

Charlotte said, 'so can you tell us exactly what's going to happen?'

'Josie's right about this part of the hotel being sound, and there's room enough for us, just. But the original old part of the hotel has to be demolished and, in doing that, there's a great risk of this part being undermined as well. In any case we would be ordered to evacuate while the work's going on. The noise and the dust would be impossible to live with, as well as being far too dangerous.'

'So what exactly are you saying, Dad?' Charlotte said in alarm. 'Are we going to be homeless?'

She could hear Josie still sniffling alongside her. No doubt in her sister's naively romantic mind, the opportunity of joining the fair would be stirring in order to save the family's fortunes, she thought bitterly.

While in hers ... she couldn't help the shameful thought that Melvin Philpott might not think quite so much of a destitute young girl as he did of the daughter of a successful hotel owner. She wished the thought had never entered her head, but it had, and she couldn't get rid of it.

'Of course we won't be *homeless*,' Donald was saying stoutly now. 'But we will no longer be able to live here, and I've taken advice from Gilbert Fellowes and our solicitor. The most sensible thing we can do is to sell up for whatever we can get for the land the hotel stands on and move to Bristol, where I would almost certainly find a good position in a hotel, and somewhere for us all to live. It's not going to happen immediately, so none of you need think we're going to be thrown out on the street. There's still a great deal of discussion and paperwork to be gone through first.'

No one said anything for a few minutes, and then they all spoke at once.

'*Dad*, we can't move to Bristol. It's horrible and the river is so smelly, and besides, we've always lived in Braydon!' Charlotte exclaimed.

Josie wailed loudly, 'I don't want to live in Bristol. I'll never see my friends or anyone I know ever again.'

'You don't *have* any friends,' Charlotte turned on her. 'All you're thinking about is being in Braydon when the fair comes again in June.'

'Whatever you girls think, we all have to do what your father thinks is best,' Ruth said loudly, seeing the way Donald's face was darkening at this squabbling.

'Oh, well, best for him, but not for us,' Josie said rudely, and was rewarded by a slap from her mother.

It was anyone's guess who was the most shocked. Ruth had never hit any of her daughters before, and Josie's face was stricken as she rubbed at her sore cheek.

'I'm sorry I felt compelled to do that, Josie,' Ruth said tightly. 'But this is one time when I will not tolerate any arguments. Your father has been through a traumatic time these last weeks, and we will all do exactly as he says. Is that understood?'

Hearing such decisive words from their normally placid mother, Charlotte moved to her sister's side and put an arm around her, since Josie was now too dumb to say or do anything.

'We do understand, Mum, and of course we'll do whatever Dad thinks is right. But we don't have to like it, do we?'

Donald cleared his throat, and it was very clear that throwing his pride to the wind was very painful to him.

'None of us likes it, Charlotte, my dear, and if there was any other way, I promise you I would take it. If we could rebuild The Retreat to its former glory no one would be more delighted than me. Leaving here will be like tearing out my heart and abandoning all the memories of my girls growing up. But I fear this place has come to the end of its days.'

Josie suddenly went limp against Charlotte and the tears flowed.

'I'm sorry, Dad,' she sobbed against her sister's shoulder. 'I didn't mean to be so disrespectful. I know it will hurt you as much as it hurts us.'

The look that passed between her parents said that it would hurt them so much more.

'What of Milly?' Charlotte said suddenly. 'She'll have to be told, of course.'

'Not yet,' Ruth said firmly. 'There's no need until we know precisely when things are moving here. Only then will your father go to

Bristol to find a suitable position and a small house for us all.'

'It can't be that small for five of us, can it?' Josie muttered. 'And it would have been six, if Gran had still been alive.'

Donald gave a deep sigh. 'We'll have to buy what we can afford, my dear. I don't care to discuss finances with you girls because it's my concern but, from now on, we must accept that things will never be so easy again.'

'They might, Daddy,' Charlotte said, unconsciously using their old childhood name for him. 'You might find a hotel in Bristol that appoints you manager instantly and offers living accommodation for all of us!'

'Of course I might, so let's put the smiles back on our faces and refuse to be downhearted,' Donald agreed, thinking that such a hope was very small indeed.

By the time Milly was brought back to the hotel they had recovered a little from the shock of Donald's announcement. They were all determined not to betray what was likely to happen until it became absolutely necessary, and had agreed that the discussion would go no further than the four walls of the small sitting-room.

Between themselves, though, Charlotte and Josie couldn't deny what a blow this was to themselves as well as to their parents.

'He's right in saying that nothing will ever be the same again,' Josie said aggressively, back in her bedroom again to ponder on things. 'I know you think I'm shallow and silly at times, Charlie, but I have grown-up feelings, too. And I *did* want to see Tony again at the fair. I was banking on him seeing me a year older, too.'

She looked so miserable that Charlotte couldn't be angry with her for being so selfish. Besides which, she had to admit that Josie *was* growing up. She would be sixteen before the fair arrived back in Braydon, and her body was already more shapely than that of the gawky girl she had been a year ago. Tony whoever-he-was would have seen a difference in her. As he still might, Charlotte amended, refusing to accept the inevitable until it actually happened.

'You do think I'm stupid, don't you?' Josie went on sharply, when Charlotte didn't reply.

'No, I don't. If you must know I was thinking that you're growing up fast, Josie, and there's no reason at all why you shouldn't have feelings for someone.'

'His name's Tony.'

'All right, Tony then. But if you think you're the only one who dreads the thought of leaving Braydon, you're wrong. Clover would have hated it, so I suppose it's a blessing she's not here to know what's happening. I'm sure Mum feels just as badly about it as Dad, and heaven knows what Milly's going to say when she hears the news.'

'Well, Dad's right not to let on to her just yet, because she's such a blabbermouth. The whole town will get to know about it soon enough, and you'll be dreading it as well, although you always manage to cope with things much better than I do.'

Charlotte bit her lip. So far she had managed not to think too closely about what it was going to mean to her to leave Braydon. It wasn't just the town, of course. It would mean leaving Melvin, too. The normal, halcyon months of courtship she was so looking forward to would come to an abrupt end, because it would be impossible for them to see one another when they were living miles apart. She was far too young to think seriously about marriage and, in any case, her father would never hear of it.

Besides, she thought, suddenly steeped in her own misery, would Melvin be so interested in her now? Such a thought had occurred to her before, but now it was far more than a passing one. Now, it was almost a certainty that the question would have to be answered. She had wondered if he would still want her without the prestige of being a hotel owner's daughter. If she was to be living in Bristol, without that sort of security cushion around her, how could he want her then? If she thought that Josie's Tony was the sort who believed in out-of-sight, out-of-mind, then why should Melvin Philpott be any different?

'Oh, Charlie, I can see I've upset you now, haven't I?' Josie muttered. 'As usual I go blundering in, always thinking about myself, and never anybody else.'

'We're all thinking about ourselves, Josie,

and that's only natural. We're all going to be affected in one way or another.' She swallowed the lump in her throat and went on, 'But we must try to put our own feelings aside as much as possible, and remember what an awful blow this is to Mum and Dad; and don't you dare call me a blooming saint for saying so, either,' she finished almost viciously.

Josie hugged her quickly. 'I know you're not, but sometimes I just wish I could be more like you, Charlie.'

Charlotte wrinkled her nose in mock disgust. 'Do you? I can't think why. I'm no angel! Just remember that we have to be extra careful to keep our family business to ourselves now, don't we?'

'What do you mean?'

'I mean that we have to do exactly as Dad said. He would be mortified if he thought anyone outside the family knew what he has in mind before he was ready to let people know. That means you don't go confiding in Mr Hallam or any of your shop customers when they ask how things are getting on.'

'I wouldn't!'

'Maybe not deliberately, but it's all too easy to let something slip, and you know how Dad would hate to have people talking about us any more than they do already. It goes for me too, of course,' she added, with a sinking feeling.

'You mean you're not going to be able to say anything to your love-bug.'

Charlotte laughed at her sister's expression, but her heart sank even more. 'That's just what I do mean, and how I'm going to pretend everything's all right between us when I'm aware that we're soon likely to be parted for ever, I don't know.'

Josie put her arm around her clumsily for a moment. 'Cripes, Charlie, I didn't think you could be so melodramatic.'

'There's a lot you don't know about me,' Charlotte murmured.

'Is there?' Josie said, her eyes alive with interest now.

Charlotte got up from her bed. 'And a lot that's private,' she said firmly.

She moved across to the window and gazed out at the sea front. The waters of the Bristol Channel were gently rippling now, sparkling like diamonds in the light of the full moon, and the only reminder of that terrible night of the storm was the continuing daily chug-chug of machinery as the sea wall was in its final stages of repair. Soon, the only visible reminder would be the devastation that had overcome the hotel, and the ruin of the family who owned it.

'I wonder what Clover would have made of all this,' she murmured. 'I sometimes picture her picking her way daintily along the promenade in the dead of night, and then dancing with her Tommy to some favourite melody that only they can hear, without a care in the world.'

'Charlie, don't say such things! You're

scaring me!'

She turned around, realising that Josie's voice was higher pitched than usual now, and she gave her a reassuring smile.

'I'm not going crazy, and I don't mean that I actually *see* her, you ninny. I just remember her the way she was, and I don't ever want to forget her. She may have seemed slightly mad to outsiders, but those nights when she wandered along the promenade really meant something special to her.'

'I know that,' Josie said crossly, 'but other people thought she was plain daft. Look how Milly's school friends upset her by calling Clover a witch.'

'They've come around now though, haven't they? Now that we're practically homeless and sort of poor relations?!'

This made her worry again over what Melvin might think of their new situation, when it eventually had to be told. On Sunday she was going to have tea with him and his family, and it had seemed such a joyous invitation at first. Now, everything had changed and she knew she would have to watch every word she said. Suddenly she felt the need to be on her own for a while before they went downstairs to face their parents again. Her father's worry was far more important than hers, but she wouldn't be human if she didn't think of herself, just a bit.

She left Josie and went into her bedroom, shutting the door firmly behind her, gazing out of her own window towards the sea front.

Unconsciously she stroked the ugly black and white china dog on her window sill, which Josie had got from the fair and had finally given to Clover after all. The texture of the china was cool and smooth and somehow comforting.

'I'd give anything if you were here to give us the answer to our troubles now, Clover,' she said unsteadily. 'Somehow you always managed to put things right.'

Although she didn't see how even her beloved grandmother could have solved this one.

Fifteen

Charlotte had never been to Melvin's home before, and she felt ridiculously nervous as she cycled towards it. On any ordinary day, she would have been feeling excited because, despite the fact that it was Melvin's mother who had invited her for Sunday afternoon tea, it was still an invitation to her young man's home, and that had to mean something.

But this was no ordinary day. This was the first Sunday since her father had dropped what amounted to a bombshell, telling the family that their days at The Retreat, and in Braydon itself, were numbered. The very fact that they had no idea how soon that day would come was adding to the tension they all felt. It coloured everything they did from now on.

Rushing into everything as usual, Josie had even started throwing out some of her old magazines and keeping her bedroom tidier than its usual chaotic state, in preparation for leaving.

'Why are you doing this already?' Charlotte had blazed. 'Can't you see it will only make Mum more unhappy if she thinks you're so eager to leave?'

'No, it won't,' Jose had retorted. 'It'll make her think I've turned over a new leaf in deciding to keep my room tidy at last.'

'Well, don't do too much of it. Any great show of throwing out unwanted belongings will only arouse Milly's suspicions that something's going on that she doesn't know about.'

But Charlotte had to admit that once Josie accepted the inevitable, she had the capacity for making the best of things, while she herself chose to hold on to the past for as long as possible. It was only a small gesture of defiance, but Charlotte refused to move a single item in her bedroom, preferring to believe that they would remain there for ever. Common sense told her such a thing couldn't happen. Nothing stayed the same for ever, and everything changed. People grew up, got older, moved away ... and if she got what she desired the most, then one day Melvin

Philpott would propose to her and she would move away from her old home anyway, and live happily ever after.

Sometimes she wondered if such things ever happened except in story books. All the furniture from the guest bedrooms and anything that was still serviceable from downstairs had now been put into proper store. Removal men did the job, and the family was now forbidden to leave their own living quarters. It made them feel as though they were living in a ghost town.

Charlotte shivered in the cool afternoon breeze as she leant low over her handlebars. Marrying Melvin *was* what she wanted, and she had wanted it for so long now that she couldn't imagine wanting anything, or anyone, else. Only occasionally, especially listening to Josie going on and on about her blessed fairground chap, she wondered what it would be like to love someone else ... but it was such a disloyal thought that she always dismissed it at once.

The smithy was in sight now, and behind it was the old stone house where the Philpott family lived. The house was solid and square, smoke curling leisurely from the chimney with the promise of a cosy fireside indoors. It occurred to Charlotte that she had never lived in a real house where she didn't have to do her share in the family business. Here, the family didn't have to attend to anyone else's needs but their own. How odd that she had never thought of it that way before.

'I thought you'd forgotten,' she heard Melvin greet her the minute she knocked on the front door of the house and found it opening immediately.

'I wouldn't be so rude. Besides, I've been really looking forward to it.'

'So's Mother. She and Dad are in the parlour but they can wait a minute until I've had a good look at you.'

'Why?' Charlotte laughed. 'Have I got a smut on my nose or something?'

Melvin squeezed her to him. 'No, you goose. I just want you to myself for a minute, that's all. Once Mother gets you in her sights, she'll be giving you the Spanish Inquisition.'

'About what?' She knew she sounded dense, but she wanted to fend off the moment when Mrs Philpott would start asking questions about the hotel and how things were going with the rebuilding prospects. It would be natural and polite for Mrs Philpott to enquire about the family's troubles, and it was the one thing Charlotte desperately didn't want to talk about.

Melvin nuzzled his chin against her cheek. His skin was rough, but not unpleasantly so, and normally it would have sent a thrill through Charlotte's veins, but somehow she couldn't respond to it at all today, and he sensed it at once.

'What's up?' he said.

'Nothing. It just makes me feel awkward, standing here like this, when your mother will be very well aware that I've arrived. We should go inside, Melvin.'

He grinned. 'Good Lord, do you think my mother expects me to behave like a monk when my best girl's coming to tea?'

'Your best girl? I thought I was your only girl!'

'So you are. Bloody hell, Charlie, I thought it was your sister who picked holes in everything anybody said. Come on then, let's go and face them.'

She moved forward, his arm still around her. She couldn't have said why she felt so unsettled now. It wasn't just because he felt no compunction in swearing when his parents might well be within earshot; it wasn't that he still smelled of the smithy, despite his tidy clothes, because that would make her seem so prissy; it wasn't because his last words made her feel as if she was walking into a lions' den. It was none of that, and yet it was a mixture of all of those things.

Mrs Philpott stood up to greet her when they walked into the parlour, while her husband remained in his armchair, complacently smoking his pipe and apparently finding no reason to stand on ceremony because they had a visitor for Sunday tea.

Charlotte found herself wondering how many other girls Melvin had brought home to tea, and hated herself for even thinking of such a thing. What was *wrong* with her? This was what she had wanted, the first step to a proper recognised courtship, and here she was finding fault with everything about it.

'Come and sit yourself down on the sofa, Charlotte, dear,' Mrs Philpott said. 'I've got a nice bit of ham for our tea and I've made one of Melvin's favourite jam sponge cakes for afters. He'd never forgive me if I didn't do the usual honours on a Sunday. You've got a good appetite, I hope?'

'Oh, yes, thank you,' Charlotte said faintly.

Was this the Melvin she knew? The one who couldn't wait to get his hands on her, and would take their relationship a great deal farther if she gave him the chance, but with no mention of an engagement.

Was this – this *Mother's pet* – she wished the words hadn't entered her head, but they had done so now and she couldn't get them out – the Melvin she knew?

'Its good to see a young girl with a bit of meat on her,' Melvin's father commented lazily, his gaze making her slightly uncomfortable. 'Some of them tarts you see in the picture papers nowadays are nothing but skin and bones.' He finished his words with a small belch.

'Now then, Father, we want none of that smutty talk this afternoon,' his wife chided him. 'Would you like to come to the kitchen and help me prepare the food, Charlotte, dear? We can leave these two to themselves while we chat and get on with the women's work.'

Charlotte followed her in a daze. She had never expected Melvin's mother to be so *twee*, nor for her to be practically a slave to the wants of the two hefty men sprawled out in the parlour now.

Perhaps it wasn't the usual way of things, she thought generously. Perhaps it was only to put on a show for Charlotte's benefit ... She really hoped so, for if this was the normal way of things in the Philpott household, she found herself pitying the girl who Melvin would eventually marry, if she was brought to live here. She hadn't even considered it before, but Melvin would continue his craft with his father, and his wife would probably be expected to simply move in with the rest of them and be absorbed into the family.

She had never believed in warning bells going off in anyone's head before. She had always thought such a phrase was one of those silly things you read in penny dreadfuls. But she knew how very apt it was now.

'So how are things going for your family, dear?' she heard Mrs Philpott say once they were in the warm and cosy kitchen with the door closed behind them. 'Is the hotel anywhere near to having the repairs done to it? I'm sure your father will be anxious for it to be back in working order before the summer visitors start arriving, won't he?'

Here it came then. The warning bells were thundering in Charlotte's head now. Melvin's mother was as keen on gossip as the next one, but Charlotte had no intention of telling her anything that was her family's private business. And then the nerves calmed. She remembered the game of wits she and Steve

Bailey had played and, if there was ever a time to put such an art into practise again, this was it.

'That's what we're all hoping for, of course,' she agreed. 'But you can't hurry officials.'

'But surely they've given you some idea of when it can be started?'

'If they have, I'm not privileged to know it.'

'Your father won't want to be losing business any longer than he can help, though. I've seen your Josie in Hallam's shop, and Melvin says you're working in the stables next door to us now, so it's good to know you and your sister are being dutiful daughters and helping out.'

'Oh, we're just doing our best to keep out of the way,' Charlotte told her, keeping the smile firmly fixed on her face. 'And is this jam sponge cake really Melvin's favourite? It smells delicious and I would love to have the recipe.'

'I'll write it out for you,' Mrs Philpott said absently, her mind clearly still on other things. 'But what about your regular guests? I expect they're anxious to return to the hotel, aren't they?'

'Of course, and we'll welcome them back as soon as possible.'

Putting it in the present tense was only a little white lie, Charlotte thought defiantly; there was no way she was going to let this gossipy woman know how dire the situation was for the Elkins family. She wondered if this had been the sole reason for inviting her for Sunday afternoon tea. There was nothing special about it at all, but far from feeling hurt she felt a strange lightness inside in knowing that she hadn't been brought here just to be inspected as a prospective bride for the son of the house.

Of course, that was what she still wanted, she added hastily, and she still loved Melvin but, if marriage ever happened, it would be on her own terms, and not in order for her to become a kind of parasite to the Philpott ménage.

Charlotte was startled by her own reactions but they didn't alarm her unduly. She was glad she didn't feel she had to put on a show to be accepted into this family. She didn't want to ingratiate herself with Melvin's mother and, as for his father, she saw him as a great oaf, apparently too ill-mannered to stir himself when guests arrived for tea. It was quite an eye-opener. Like the father, like the son, perhaps, a small voice whispered inside her head.

'When's tea going to be ready, Mother?' she heard Melvin's father yell from the parlour. 'Me belly thinks me throat's been cut.'

His wife smiled indulgently at Charlotte. 'That's a man for you, always thinking of his innards. You'll need plenty of good recipes to please one of your own, Charlotte. Now help me get this bread sliced and buttered, and we'll take the ham into the parlour before those two elephants expire with hunger.'

By now, Charlotte thought she had the

measure of Mrs Philpott. She had a far quicker brain than Melvin's mother and parried off any mention of the hotel business, finding it easy enough to divert her attention to recipes for stews or pies or fruit cakes. The entire household seemed to revolve around food, and both Melvin and his father devoured the mountains of bread and ham with alarming speed.

'You won't want to be working in Miles' stables for ever, I daresay,' Mrs Philpott put in when they were on to the jam sponge, and Charlotte gave up being surprised at seeing the two men lavishly cover their portions in cream to eat as if it was a pudding.

'Oh, no, not for ever. I much prefer working in the hotel.'

She did too. She didn't have Josie's objection to waiting on tables. Some might say it was far healthier to be working in the open air as she did now, but you couldn't get much conversation out of horses, and she had always enjoyed the comings and goings of the hotel guests and meeting different people.

The grandfather clock in the parlour struck seven o'clock, and Charlotte said she had better be going before it got too dark.

'Melvin, where are your manners? Aren't you going to see the girl home?' his mother said, when he made no move.

'There's really no need,' Charlotte said hastily. 'I can be there in no time on my bicycle, and I've really had a lovely time, Mrs Philpott.'

She couldn't honestly say that she had, but she had been brought up to be polite and, even although she had expected Melvin to take the chance for a time alone with her, she was relieved when he didn't press it.

'Well, I'll walk you to the end of the lane anyway,' he said. 'Perhaps we could go to the pictures one night next week.'

'That would be nice,' she said.

She said goodnight to his parents and received a grunt from his father, already immersed in the newspaper. Once outside the house, she let out a huge sigh of relief. It was partly because she had been so careful not to give anything away about her family's circumstances, but she knew it was also because she was glad to get away from the stifling atmosphere of that house. If she ever married Melvin, she told herself firmly, she would insist that they lived well away from his parents, and she didn't analyse why there was even a tiny suggestion of doubt in her mind about that now.

'Mother can be overpowering, can't she?' Melvin said with a grin once they were out in the lane and breathing in the early evening air. 'Dad's all right, though. He don't say much, providing he gets his victuals on time.'

'That goes for you too, doesn't it?'

'Well, that's what mothers are there for, isn't it? If she didn't have us men to cook and clean for, I don't know what she'd do with herself all day. But we don't want to waste time talking about her, do we?'

'Is that what you think wives are there for, too?'

She didn't know why she was goading him in this way, or even if that was what she was consciously doing. It was just that these past couple of hours had seemed to show up both their families in such a different light, and in ways she had never even thought about before. Her own parents were far more of a partnership in all that they did. The hotel had been a joint concern, involving both of them equally, and involving their daughters, too. Whatever went on in the Philpott household seemed to be strictly divided between the men and the skivvy. Charlotte wished she hadn't thought of that word, even though it seemed so horribly apt. The worst of it was, they all seemed so smugly satisfied to keep things that way. Neither of them had lifted a finger to do anything to help Mrs Philpott, and nor had she expected it of them.

'You're in a funny mood all of a sudden, Charlie. I thought you were pleased when Mother asked you round for tea,' Melvin said.

And why have I never noticed what a petulant-sounding little boy you can be at times...?

'I was pleased. But you said yourself I was going to get the Spanish Inquisition.'

Melvin laughed. 'Oh, that's just Mother's way. She always likes to know the whys and wherefores of people. You shouldn't let it bother you. Come here and give us a kiss and a cuddle before I send you on your way.'

It wasn't that she had *wanted* him to see her home, Charlotte thought resentfully, and she had been the one to say it wasn't necessary. But if he'd thought anything of her, he might have insisted on it, anyway.

She melted into his arms, giving in to his hugs and kisses, because she did love him, despite the fact that she was finding all kinds of things to annoy her about him tonight that had never seemed so obvious before.

He let her go, giving her a smack on the rump as he did so.

'Off you go then, girl, and I'll pop over to the stables during the week to arrange about going to the pictures. The back row sounds favourite, doesn't it?'

'Lovely,' Charlotte mumbled, her eyes stinging with sudden tears at his off-hand manner. Where was the tenderness, the affection, the *romance* that every girl had a right to expect from her boy?

She got on her bicycle quickly and pedalled away from him without looking back. She hadn't expected to leave the smithy this early. She had thought there would be some sort of socialising, asking about her job, chatting generally, or perhaps playing card games; and she hardly thought such an activity would be frowned on in the Philpott household, even if it was Sunday.

Now, she couldn't wait to get home, even if she had to share the small sitting-room with the rest of her family. Either that or go to bed early, and that would only raise comments.

She hardly knew why she felt so out of sorts, but she had to admit that this day had been a great disappointment. Seeing Melvin at home had told her a great deal more about him than she had known previously, and perhaps it was a good thing, said that irritatingly insistent small voice inside her. A man who was so pampered by his mother, like his father before him, would certainly expect the same from his future wife. Not that he had asked her yet ... but if and when he did, it would need thinking about. It definitely would.

Deep in thought, she realised she had reached the long stretch of promenade, softly lit by gas lamps now that dusk had fallen. The sea was moonlit, calm and beautiful without the treacherous wind that could whip up high tide into a frenzy and ruin lives.

She stood down from her bicycle, gazing out to sea, and her breath caught on an involuntary sob, thinking how quickly things could change. It was such a short time ago now that her adored Clover had danced along this very promenade, lost in her memories and none the poorer for that.

Her eyes blurred, trying to imagine that she could see her now. Wishing that she could conjure her up out of the ether or wherever she was now, even if the thought of such an image scared her half to death, as it assuredly would.

She heard a faint noise in her head. She fancied it was some sort of a tune, and her heart hammered with fear, immediately taking back the wish to see any kind of ghostly presence, no matter who it was!

The tune came nearer, and she realised it wasn't proper music at all, just a rather tuneless whistle, and at the same time as her eyes flew open she felt something soft and wet nuzzle her hand. She smothered a scream as she looked down to see a large dog, his tail wagging with furious pleasure at this unexpected encounter. Her first thought was of the wild dogs that used to roam along the sea front, but she immediately knew that this wasn't a wild dog. He had a collar around his neck and his owner was whistling for him to come back now. The man came nearer, and she almost collapsed with relief when she recognised him, followed quickly by anger.

'If this is your dog, you should keep him under proper control and not allow him to frighten the wits out of lonely females at night!' she spluttered.

Steve Bailey bent down to fasten a lead on the animal's collar and looked at her coolly.

'Well, I swear that I never saw such a competent lonely female as you, Miss Elkins! What are you doing out here after dark? Meeting a lover?'

The sheer cheek of him almost took her breath away.

'It's not dark yet and, whatever I'm doing, it's none of your business,' she snapped.

'You're quite right,' he said, his voice less aggressive. 'But you took me by surprise, just as Rex took you by surprise, I'm sure, and we both apologise for that.'

'Thank you,' she muttered.

She felt oddly nonplussed. Plenty of people walked their dogs along the promenade at different times of day, but she had never seen him doing so before. As if to put her straight on that score, he smiled.

'Actually, I've only acquired this mutt in the last couple of weeks, so we're both still getting to know one another. His previous owner used to take him for walks every evening so I feel obliged to do the same, especially until he stops fretting over losing old Bob.'

'Old Bob?' She began to feel like a parrot.

'His old owner. He died from pneumonia and it was a case of either having the dog put to sleep or somebody taking him in. Rex is an old 'un himself, but there's still life left in him yet, isn't there, old boy?'

'What are you, some sort of good Samaritan?'

'No. Just a friend.'

Charlotte knew she had sounded ungracious but, now that her heart had slowed down from the shock of seeing the man and the dog, she bent down to ruffle Rex's head and was rewarded by a riotous licking.

'You see? We all need a friend, and I'd really like to be yours, if you'd let me, Charlotte.'

'It's probably not the wisest thing to do to make friends with newspaper reporters,' she said without thinking.

'Only if people have got something to hide. But even if they did, what makes you think a reporter would be any less of a friend than anyone else? Would you have me remain friendless for ever more?'

He was teasing her now, as if her thoughtless comment hadn't made her feel foolish enough already.

'I'm sure you've got plenty of friends, and it's time I went home before my father sends out a search party for me.'

Not that he would. He'd think she was being brought safely home by her young man. The thought made her even sharper with Steve Bailey.

'Please let me escort you,' he said quickly.

'No, thank you. It's not necessary,' she said, mounting her bicycle again.

'Then perhaps I'll see you along the prom again sometime,' he called after her as she pedalled off. 'It's obvious that Rex enjoys your company, too.'

Charlotte wasn't sure if that was meant to imply that he certainly did. She didn't reply as she headed off in the direction of The Retreat. In the half-light it looked gaunt and forlorn, with only the family extension showing signs of life now. It used to be a blaze of welcoming lights, advertising that here was a successful business, but those times would seem to be gone for ever.

She swallowed the lump of sadness in her throat and rearranged her features before she went indoors to the welcome smiles of her family, all wanting to know if she had an enjoyable time and to ask what Melvin's home was like.

She told them as much as she thought would satisfy them, trying not to compare the two different young men with whom she had spoken that evening. One whom she loved, but could still find plenty to criticise about; and the other, whom she didn't really know, but whose talk always managed to strike a spark inside her. Tonight he had shown unexpected courtesy to her, and made it plain that he would like to see her again, but she wouldn't entertain such a thing, of course.

In any case, what was the point of getting to know anyone new, when all the signs indicated that she might not even be living in Braydon for very much longer?

Sixteen

Josie was finding it hard to keep the news to herself. She was alternately upset and intrigued about the prospect of leaving Braydon. She was upset because she might never see Tony at the fair again, although who knew whether their departure would happen before June, anyway? Nothing much seemed to be happening at all, and her father was forever going off to meetings that seemed to come to nothing. She was intrigued because she always liked new things, and she was canny enough to know that Tony wasn't the only attractive young man in the world.

In fact, she had always thought the Elkinses' world was a very insular one, and she didn't have the same interest as Charlotte in hotel guests. Even working at Hallam's Food Supplies had shown her a different environment, and it would be exciting to be out in the world and away from this dreary little seaside town. She knew better than to say as much to her parents, of course, but unfortunately she had made the mistake of writing that thought in her diary, and Milly had found it.

'What are you doing in my room?' she shrieked on the morning when she found Milly snooping.

'Mum sent me to fetch the dirty washing,' Milly shrieked back. 'Why have you put your diary in your laundry basket, anyway?'

'So that nosey little kids like you won't find it when you go snooping in my bureau,' Josie yelled, grabbing it back. But it was too late.

'What do you mean about going away from this dreary little seaside town?' Milly bawled, quoting her word for word. 'Where are you going, anyway?'

'None of your business, and you had no right to spy in my private things, you little sneak,' she hissed.

Before she knew what Milly was going to do, the girl had whirled around and was flying out of the bedroom, forgetting the reason she had come now that there were more important things to think about.

'Mum, Josie's going to run away!' she heard Milly shriek next, and her heart stopped, realising all too late how her sister had interpreted the dramatic words in her diary. She flew downstairs after her, and found her mother in the kitchen, comforting the distraught child.

'Of course I'm not going to run away, you idiot,' she snapped.

'Well, that's what you wrote in your diary. You said it would be exciting to be away from this dreary little seaside town.'

Milly had always been good at memorising things, Josie thought bitterly, which had encouraged her teachers to say she would easily pass her exams for the new school next year.

'Is that what you wrote, Josie?' Ruth said quietly.

'Diaries are meant to be private,' she replied savagely. 'You write your thoughts and feelings for yourself, not for little sneaks like her to read!'

'All the same, did you say that it would be exciting to be away from here?'

Josie stared at her mother, unsure what she was getting at. She wasn't aware that she had done anything wrong in writing down her feelings. It was one way she tried to keep them under control without letting fly at everyone around her – and not always very successfully.

'I may have done,' she said, sullen now.

Ruth turned to her small daughter. 'How

would you feel about that, Milly? Moving away from Braydon, I mean. Josie thinks it would be exciting, and you'll be going to a new school next year, so things will be changing for you in any case.'

Josie's breathing slowed, realising that her mother was taking the initiative now. Her father hadn't wanted Milly to hear of their likely future plans until it was impossible to keep them from her any longer, but everything had changed now.

It wasn't her fault, she told herself. *It wasn't her fault.* If Milly hadn't been so darned nosy, this would never have happened.

'I don't know what I think,' Milly said, wriggling away from her mother and glaring resentfully at Josie. 'Why?'

'Darling, we still don't know what's going to happen about the hotel,' Ruth said gently. 'Of course we hope that it can be rebuilt and then everything will go on as before. But it may not be possible, and we just have to wait and see.'

She was being as tactful as she could be, but Milly saw through her at once. Without warning, her small face crumpled.

'But where will we go? I'll never see Dorothy again if we have to go away.'

Josie snorted. Leaving Dorothy Yard was the least of their worries, although to Milly it was clearly one that was very important. She smothered her impatience and tried to make amends.

'It won't be so bad, Milly. You'll soon make

new friends.'

'No I won't, and I *hate* you!' Milly shouted. She ran out of the kitchen and up the stairs, banging every door on the way.

'Well done, Josie,' her mother said. 'Now we have to tell your father what's happened, and hope that he can find the words to calm her down, since it's obvious that neither of us can do it.'

'Oh well, Saint Charlotte might.'

After a moment's silence, Ruth spoke quietly. 'I'll overlook what you just said, Josie, since I can see this whole business has upset you. But if I ever hear you say it again I won't be responsible for my actions. This family has enough problems without you showing your jealousy of your sister.'

'I'm not jealous of her!'

'Then try not to be so bitchy, there's a love.'

Since Josie had never heard her mother use such a word before, it was enough to stun her into silence. Coupled so oddly with the endearment it quickly turned her anger to shame, and she hugged her mother mutely before going back upstairs to see if she could repair some of the damage that had been done to Milly – even if she had been the one to start it all.

But Milly simply refused to speak to her, and it was only some time later when her father insisted that she come downstairs that she appeared, blotchy faced and red eyed, expecting to be firmly scolded for reading someone else's diary.

Josie and Charlotte were already there in what seemed to Milly suspiciously like the preparation for a family council meeting in the small sitting-room, and it was clear from everyone's faces that they knew what had happened that morning.

'Now then, Milly, it seems that we've underestimated you,' Donald said.

'I know I did wrong, and I won't do it again,' she said shrilly.

He shook his head gently. 'From the look of you, I believe you mean it. Being found out and facing up to what you did is probably punishment enough, so we're going to say no more about it.'

She looked at him nervously, knowing that wasn't really the end of it, since everyone looked so serious. Donald cleared his throat, hardly knowing how to begin and yet knowing now that this had to be said and understood.

'Milly, love, I want you to be very grown up about what I'm about to say. Your mother has already given you a hint of it.' He might have known she would cotton on at once.

'You mean about leaving Braydon, don't you?' she squeaked, her eyes wide and scared.

'I'm afraid I do, love. And now that we're all here, I'm going to tell you what I propose. It's no longer possible to keep the news to ourselves, and rumours have already started flying about the town. I don't mean all that nonsense about the hotel being cursed, or about Clover's nightly wanderings. I mean about what's going to happen to the hotel now. And the bad news is that it has to be pulled down and we will have to leave here,' he finished baldly, hardly able to contain his distress any longer. Ruth put her hand on his arm, offering mute support, and he continued after a moment.

'I don't want any more rumours so I intend to put a notice in the local newspaper to the effect that once the hotel is demolished the land is for sale. We must get what we can for it, however little that might be. In the meantime I want you girls to answer any questions with dignity but, as work will begin in the near future, it's no longer possible to keep the news to ourselves. I will shortly be going to Bristol to find suitable accommodation for us all and to find other employment.'

Milly was crying softly now and Josie simply stared at the floor. Charlotte's heart ached for her father, but she knew he was too proud to want any of his daughters to sympathise too openly. She swallowed hard.

'Shall I make some tea, Mum?'

The usual panacea ... and Ruth nodded with barely a smile.

'I'm sure we could all do with some, my dear.'

Charlotte fled to the kitchen, glad to get away from that sad little scene. Her hands shook as she filled the kettle and put it on the hob, and yet in a way it was something of a relief now that the decision had been made. They could all move on ... even if it meant moving away ... she avoided thinking too much about that at the moment, relieved at least that she no longer had to hide anything from Melvin. The customers at Hallam's shop could have their curiosity satisfied, and poor Milly could try to make her peace with the luckless Dorothy, who would be losing her best friend. They would all have changes to make and, despite Josie's misery over not being in Braydon when the fair came around in June, Charlotte had no doubt she would be the one to find the transition the easiest of all.

'I'll help you,' she heard her sister's voice behind her. 'That was a turn-up, wasn't it? Suddenly making the announcement like that, I mean.'

'I think Dad probably had to do it like that. He couldn't have kept it all inside him much longer or he'd have burst.'

'I wonder if your Melvin will want to go out with a poor relation?!'

Charlotte banged the cups and saucers down on a tray and glared at her.

'What a spiteful thing to say. Why should it make any difference to him?'

'Well, you won't be such a good catch now, will you? I've heard his mother often enough in the shop, bragging about her precious son walking out with my sister. It's a feather in her cap, but I bet she won't feel the same when she knows we don't own a hotel any more, and we're left with nothing.'

'I won't listen to such rubbish, and in any case I'm walking out with Melvin, not his mother! Now help me take this tea into the sitting-room before I throw something at you.'

Although, remembering the cloying atmosphere of that smithy house last Sunday, and the way Mrs Philpott had pampered to her menfolk, Charlotte felt a cold shiver run through her. The sooner she told Melvin the better, and before her father put the effective notice in the newspaper too.

Donald wasted no time in doing just that. Enough time had been wasted already, while he desperately tried to hold on to his home and his livelihood, but now the whole town would know that the Elkins family faced real disaster as a result of the storm. He fashioned out the gist of the notice himself, and relied on the experienced folk at the newspaper office to word it appropriately.

He was almost humbled by the way his girls had shown themselves to be real troupers in the end. He had told them they were at liberty to tell whoever they chose now that they would be leaving Braydon when the family affairs were settled. It was the simplest and most dignified way of putting it, he admitted, and he was still a man to cling on to as much dignity as he could.

Even young Milly, whom they had so dreaded telling, had finally gone off to school full of importance to inform her best friend that they must make a vow never to forget their friendship, and that once she had a new address to give her, they must always keep in touch by letters even when they were far apart. Clearly, the thirty miles or so between here and Bristol would seem like an ocean apart when you were only ten.

Josie would be adaptable, but Charlotte would be upset at being parted from her young man. Donald frowned. He had never thought a great deal of the blacksmith's son but, if Charlotte cared for him, and providing the chap respected her, that had been good enough. No, Charlotte would be the one to have her life disrupted the most when the day came to leave. As well as himself and Ruth, of course ... not for the first time, he counted himself a very fortunate man to have such a loving and supportive wife by his side, just as his father had before him.

Charlotte watched as Melvin came striding across the field towards Miles's stables, her heart pounding. She couldn't put off telling him any longer, and nor did she want to, since the newspaper notice advertising the sale of their land was imminent. It would be unthinkable for him to see that before she had told him herself.

'How's my best girl today?' he said with an easy smile, his arm moving around her waist and sliding down to squeeze the curve of her buttocks as he pulled her to him. She wasn't in the mood for responding, and she stood rigidly as his mouth sought hers. He reacted at once.

'You're not going all stand-offish on me, are you, Charlie?'

She wriggled away from him. 'Is that all you ever think about?' she snapped. 'I do have other things on my mind besides you, you know.'

'Oh yes, like what?' he taunted. 'If you think mucking out these stables is more exciting than a bit of slap and tickle, then I might as well find a girl who's more fun.'

Her eyes stung with mortification that he could reduce their courtship to *a bit of slap and tickle*. And was fun the only thing he wanted, when she thought he really loved her?

'Didn't you ever love me at all, Melvin?' she said in a choked voice.

'Of course I love you. I've told you often enough, haven't I?'

'Not really. Only when you want something.'

He moved back a pace. 'Well, that's nice, that is. If you're going all prissy on me now, girl, I seem to remember you never made any bloody objections when we went up on Priory Hill.'

God, he was so insensitive! Couldn't he see how distressed she was becoming? 'Don't you *ever* think of anything else? Don't you think there's more for people to worry about than fooling about on Priory Hill?'

'Well, what have you got to worry about now?'

She was suddenly pummelling his chest,

and the words burst out in a rush. 'Only that our hotel's going to be pulled down and my dad has to sell the land for what he can get, and we're practically going to be paupers with no home, and we'll have to move to Bristol so he can find work.'

He caught at her flailing hands and held them tight.

'Christ Almighty, girl, why haven't you told me any of this before?'

'Dad told us all not to until there was no other way. But everyone will know soon, because he's putting an announcement in the paper.'

'My God, he won't like that. Everybody knowing, I mean. That'll be a blow to his pride, won't it? He won't like being poor, either.'

'Is that all you can say? Don't you have any thought for his feelings?'

'I thought that's what I was doing.'

Her nerves were stretched to breaking point now. But she had to know.

'And what about me. What about us?'

He was still ready to tease. 'Well, it'll be pretty hard to go walking out on Priory Hill if you're living on the breadline somewhere in Bristol, won't it?'

'You mean you'll have to find somebody else to take home for your mother's approval, I suppose?'

As if Melvin finally realised how very brittle she sounded, he pulled her close to him again. Her heart was breaking, and he seemed to be only just aware of it.

'God, Charlie, you know I wouldn't want to do that. But unless they leave you behind when they go, I'm not going to live like a monk for the rest of my life.'

As she heard the sound of Mrs Miles's voice calling her into the farmhouse for their cosy morning elevenses, she disentangled herself again.

'I think you'd better go now, Melvin. I've got to tell Mrs Miles that they'll have to find somebody else to muck out their stables when I leave.'

' I'll come and see you again when you're in a better mood, then. You're still my girl, Charlie. You always will be.'

Until the next one comes along, she couldn't help thinking. But she let him kiss her goodbye and held her head high as she walked towards the old farmhouse, and then she let all the tears and anger flood out of her in the comforting arms of the farmer's wife.

The notice in the local newspaper sent ripples of shock around the town. By then Donald had made several fruitless journeys to Bristol seeking a hotel position, although several had made tentative promises. He was very conscious of having to provide for a large family, even if his two older daughters insisted that they would be seeking work themselves once the move became a fact.

Charlotte had taken to walking along the sea front in the early evening, just to get the smell and taste of the stables out of her lungs, and with no wish to see Steve Bailey again. The thought may have been more of a subconscious one, however, when the big dog that she remembered came bounding along towards her one evening, nuzzling his nose into her hand, and she turned with her heart beating rapidly to see Steve close behind.

'You know all there is to know now then,' she greeted him, her voice daring him to make any futile platitudes over her family's misfortune.

'Oh, I wouldn't say that, and good evening to you, Miss Elkins.'

She turned away and continued leaning on the renewed sea wall, biting her lip and wishing their own repairs could have been done so efficiently.

'Sorry,' she muttered. 'I'm not very good company lately.'

'I'm happy enough to be a friend if you want to talk.'

'Isn't that the way all reporters worm their way into a person's confidence?' she countered.

He was thoughtful. 'You don't seem to have a very good opinion of us, Charlotte. I wonder why that is? Have you ever had bad publicity through a newspaper report, or is it just that you dislike me personally?'

'I don't dislike you personally,' she said crossly. 'I don't even know you.'

'I wish you'd allow me to put that right. I'm not a bad fellow, really, and not one for betraying confidences. I have all my own teeth and strong legs; isn't that the requirement of those horses you look after?'

She couldn't resist a laugh, although she hadn't felt much like it recently.

'That's better,' Steve said. 'I was beginning to think we'd got off on the wrong foot completely, and I like you too much for that.'

She felt her heart flip. 'You don't know me!'

'The more you keep saying that, the more I want to. I wish I could do something to help, but I'm sure your father has done everything possible to save the hotel and it's a real shame the way things have turned out. The Retreat has been a landmark building here for a very long time.'

'You really do sound genuinely sympathetic,' Charlotte said slowly, ruffling his dog's head absently and moving away from the sea wall now.

'And you sound really surprised,' Steve grinned. 'Can I walk you home if you're ready? Or we could stand here and talk all night, of course.'

'You'd better walk me home, then.'

It was the most bizarre thing, to be walking home beside a tall young man she had half thought of as one of the enemy, and his affectionate dog. When they reached the family part of the hotel she paused awkwardly, not quite knowing what to say, when the door opened and her father peered out.

'Do we have company, Charlotte?' Donald said.

'It's Mr Bailey, Dad,' she said hastily. 'Steve Bailey from the newspaper.'

Steve spoke quickly. 'I happened to meet your daughter along the promenade, sir, and offered to escort her home since it's growing dusk and a little chilly.'

Before any of them could guess what was going to happen, Rex had pulled his lead free of Steve's hand and burst inside the kitchen, where Ruth was preparing supper. The dog sniffed the air appreciatively and, having heard the exchange at the door, far from being annoyed Ruth was laughing at his antics.

'The poor thing doesn't exactly look half starved but, if you care to wait a moment, Mr Bailey, I'll give you some scraps for him. In fact—' she looked from him to Charlotte and back again — 'if you have nothing to rush home for, would you care to have a bite of supper with us?'

'That's very kind of you, and we both thank you,' Steve said with a smile.

The other girls came through from the sitting-room, astonished to see a stranger and a dog in their midst. Milly was instantly charmed by the boisterous Rex, and the minute Josie could get Charlotte alone she pulled her to one side.

'What's he doing here?' she hissed.

'Having supper with us and, before you ask why, perhaps it's better to be aware of the enemy you know rather than the one you don't.'

She didn't quite know why she'd called him the enemy again. Here in their own home and in a far friendlier atmosphere than the one he'd encountered here previously, he was no more than a charming young man who had clearly got the approval of her mother, at least.

Inevitably the talk got around to the eventual departure of the Elkins family, and once again Steve voiced his regret without being overly inquisitive. He merely said that The Retreat had become as good as an institution here, and how much they would be missed in the town, and Charlotte felt the heat in her cheeks as he glanced her way when he said it.

Donald cleared his throat and then said something to astonish them all.

'You know, Bailey, it seems to me you're right. Our family has left its mark on the town in no small way and people are naturally going to be curious about us when we leave. I know how you fellows work, so how would you feel about having an exclusive interview on our past and future plans? What do you say?'

'I say it's a marvellous idea, and not one that I would ever have dared to broach myself, sir. The last thing you want is an intrusion into your privacy, but it would certainly allay any unnecessary rumours.'

'My feelings exactly,' Donald said. 'We can get started just as soon as you like – tonight, if you wish, and no story of The Retreat can be complete without mention of my mother. I'll show you a photograph of her with my father. She was a real character, was Clover, and missed by us all.'

'Clover, you say! Now I remember where I heard that name before! I've been racking my brains,' Steve commented as he followed Donald into the sitting-room, leaving Rex in the adoring arms of Milly, who was now declaring that if she couldn't have a dog when they moved to Bristol, she wasn't going to go at all.

Seventeen

Melvin was incredulous. 'You don't mean to say your dad let that newspaper chap get a story from you, did you? He must be off his head. Those buggers are like leeches once they get hold of a story, and God knows what will be printed about your family now, especially your crazy grandmother.'

'Clover wasn't crazy!' Charlotte said hotly. 'She was eccentric and adorable, and she meant the world to me.'

'You make her sound like a cocker spaniel.' Melvin could barely hide a sneer now. 'But no matter how you dress it up, Charlie, everybody knew she was mad, wandering off in the night the way she did.'

'I'm surprised you even want to be associated with anyone who had a crazy grandmother, then!'

'I won't be able to, will I, once you get out of Braydon?'

Her eyes prickled. This wasn't meant to be happening. She had finished work for the day to find him waiting for her at the end of the lane and, as he took her bicycle to wheel it for her, for a few sweet moments she could imagine that everything was the way it used to be; before Clover died; before the terrible storm; before everything literally came crashing down about her family's ears. Now it was all spoiled.

'Oh, come on, Charlie, let's forget it. My mother's expecting me back for supper in half an hour, and I'd better not be late, so let's make the most of it. Let's go over to the empty barn in the next field.'

'No thanks. It's dirty and smelly.' And she didn't want to think he'd be mentally counting the minutes so he could be back in time for supper so he wouldn't disappoint his mother. It might be cutting off her nose to spite her face, but she couldn't respond adequately with thoughts of his mother hovering with his supper.

'You never used to be so fussy until you started seeing that smart reporter chap, all done up in a suit and tie like a dog's dinner.'

'I have not been seeing him, as you call it, and whoever saw a dog in a suit and tie! Steve

Bailey came to the hotel a couple of times for interviews with Dad and to borrow some old photos of Clover and my granddad. I wasn't even there the last time.'

She was surprised that Steve had wanted the photos but it gave her an unexpectedly warm feeling to know that Clover and her Tommy were going to have their photo in the paper, all these years after it was taken. It was a kind of continuity that Clover would never have expected, either, but she would have loved it all the same.

'Well, it seems to me you're getting too damn friendly with the leech.'

She stopped walking, forgetting that he was holding on to her arm with one hand and wheeling her bicycle with the other, and she nearly fell over before his momentum slowed.

'Will you stop calling him by that stupid name?' she snapped. 'And if we're just going to keep bickering I can't see much point in going anywhere together.'

'Right. If that's what you want.'

Before she knew what was happening, he had flung her bicycle to the ground and marched back towards the smithy, leaving her with her heart thumping and wondering how things could change in an instant. She wanted to call him back, to tell him not to be so daft, and of course it wasn't what she wanted, but she had her father's pride, too. He had never begged for favours and neither would she. Instead, she picked up her bicycle, checked that the wheels weren't buckled, and rode off towards home without a backward glance.

'Have you finished with him then?' Josie asked, when she had wormed the gist of it out of Charlotte.

'None of your business. I'm not likely to see much more of him soon, anyway, so it's probably best this way.'

She couldn't deny how much it hurt, though. She didn't want to finish with Melvin, even thought the practicalities of their removal to Bristol would make it inevitable. She certainly didn't want to finish with him like this, in a temper and with him flouncing off like a girl. The thought brought an unwilling smile to her lips.

'I don't think you mind so much after all,' Josie said, seeing her small change of expression. 'In fact, I think this has given you a good excuse to be rid of him.'

'You don't know what you're talking about.'

'Oh no? What about this reporter chap, then? I reckon you're falling for him.'

'Of course I'm not. I'm not falling for anybody. What I mean is I've already fallen for somebody. Well, not just somebody. Melvin, of course. And we're having a little minor setback, that's all.'

Josie giggled. 'Gosh, Charlie, anyone would think you were trying to convince *yourself!*'

'And you're an idiot,' Charlotte retorted. 'When you're mature enough to have real feelings for someone, you'll know what I mean.'

'I'm not an infant.'

'You're not a grown-up, either.'

They glared at one another and then laughed simultaneously. What was the point of standing here arguing over nothing?

'You know what? We're starting to sound more like Milly and that friend of hers now,' Charlotte said. 'Let's call a truce, shall we?'

The trouble was, even by the time she went to bed that night, she couldn't quite forget it. At least, not her sister's shrewd remark about herself falling for that reporter chap, as Josie referred to him. Steve. Steve Bailey. Without warning, she had an instant picture of him in her mind. Dark hair, nice eyes, friendly manner. And the rest ... all his own teeth and strong legs ... his own words came back to her, making her smile in the darkness.

But he didn't mean anything to her. Melvin was the one she loved, despite their differences, and when she had to leave Braydon, she didn't know how she was going to live without him. The enormity of it all washed over her, and her throat felt choked. She didn't want to leave here, any more than the rest of her family, but it seemed that fate, or God, or whatever, had decided otherwise. It wasn't fair. It just wasn't fair, and she buried her head beneath the bedclothes, the way she had done when she was a little girl, shutting out the night demons.

The family knew they would have to brace

themselves for questions as soon as the newspaper announcement appeared that the land on which The Retreat stood would be sold as soon as the buildings were demolished.

'Or sooner, if anyone was daft enough to put in a sensible bid,' Donald told them grimly.

He was finding it hard to put on a brave face, but he knew he had to do so for the rest of them. As the man of the family, he constantly reminded himself that he had to be strong, while assuring them they would come through this crisis in the end. They were survivors ... even if he frequently had grave doubts about it himself.

As a piece of public interest, a week after the shock announcement of the proposed sale of land in the newspaper came Steve Bailey's account of the Elkins family history. He had done them proud, according them maximum dignity and stating several times what a loss the family would be to the town, as well as the commercial loss of the landmark sea-front hotel, as he kept referring to it.

'You can't fault it, can you?' Ruth commented, when, like all of them, she had read it several times. 'He really is a very nice young man, with none of the crassness sometimes attributed to reporters.'

Charlotte wasn't really listening. She was still reading several touching little anecdotes about Clover and Tommy, which her father had obviously related to Steve. He had declined to have the family photographed, saying that folk in the town knew them well enough, and those that didn't, didn't matter. But there was a splendid photo of Clover beside Tommy. He was resplendent in his military uniform, while she looked young and vital and attractive, and as exotic as ever. No wonder Tommy had loved her, Charlotte thought. No wonder they all did.

Donald had evidently informed Steve that Clover had been born Clover Dunwoody, a fact that none of her granddaughters had even been aware of. It made Charlotte realise how little they had really known of those past times despite all Clover's tales, and it was sad to think that now she was gone, the memories were gone too.

'Gran looks quite normal in that photo, doesn't she?' Milly said with a giggle, looking over Charlotte's shoulder.

Ruth chided her. 'Of course she does. She was a lovely young woman, Milly. People aren't born old.'

'Me and Dorothy don't want to get old and wrinkly. I expect I shall die when I'm about thirty years old,' she announced.

'That doesn't say much for you and Dad then, does it, Mum?' Josie chuckled.

'And I bet you won't be saying that when you're twenty-nine,' Charlotte told her, and then hid a smile at seeing how the thought of being as old as twenty-nine sent a look of horror to Milly's face.

She continued reading the newspaper account. It was surprisingly long, and probably meant that there was little else of interest to report in the early months of the year, Donald had said cynically. It made only a brief reference to Clover's eccentricity, merely calling her a well-known, colourful figure in the town. It detailed the fact that she had died shortly before the disaster that had struck the hotel, and what a double blow fate had dealt the family.

By the time she came to the end of it, Charlotte hadn't wanted to read any more. Theirs had been such a happy, comfortable life until a few months ago. Common sense said Clover couldn't live for ever, and yet to her granddaughters she had been somehow invincible. This newspaper report, so accurate and sympathetic, still seemed to emphasise the yawning gap between that other life and the uncertain one they were all living through now.

'I'm going out for a while, Mum,' she said, feeling as if the house was suffocating her. 'I won't be long.'

She didn't know where she was going. She certainly didn't want company. In a strange way the newspaper report had made it all seem so much more real, as if reminding the world that this Elkins family, who had thought so much of themselves and their hotel, were no longer of any importance. She knew it hadn't been meant like that, and probably wouldn't be taken like that, but her feelings were so raw and sensitive now that she couldn't see it in any other way. She found herself walking along the promenade, wrapped up warmly in the chill air, remembering that this was what Clover always did whenever she had problems to solve. Not that anything could solve the insurmountable one they had now.

Charlotte didn't want to get into conversation with anyone and face their sympathy. To avoid other walkers, she climbed down the small stone steps to one of Clover's favourite coves beneath the sea wall. The tide was a long way out now and the pebbly cove was littered with rocks on which to sit. Just as Clover had done. Just as they had found her one night, singing to the dolphins...

Charlotte smothered a sob, feeling totally out of sorts and as bewildered as Milly at that moment, wondering why everything had to change. There were no dolphins here. There was no Clover. There was only a new way of life that they didn't want, and which wasn't even open to them yet.

Her mother was being so stoical about it all. Clover wasn't Ruth's own mother, but they were alike in many ways. Clover had followed Tommy, no matter where the military life led them, and Ruth would be prepared to go wherever Donald decreed. Ruth had been so brave through all of this, even if none of the other females in the family were so inclined. Milly didn't want to leave Dorothy. Josie wanted to stay at least until the fair came again in June. And she didn't want to leave Melvin.

She felt suddenly spineless. If she had as much independent spirit as Clover, why wouldn't she consider staying behind when the family moved? Asking to be taken in as a lodger somewhere, perhaps on Miles's Farm, where she could see Melvin every day. And a fat chance she had of her father ever agreeing to that! She wasn't eighteen yet, and she knew it was pointless to ask.

By now she was sitting on a flat piece of rock, polished smooth by the ebb and flow of countless tides, the rock that Clover always made her special place when she came here to think or dream. If only Charlotte could absorb some of her grandmother's essence, she thought futilely, but that bright spark had gone for ever.

'Hey, Charlotte!'

She heard a voice call her name and turned sharply to see Melvin leaning on the sea wall on the promenade, overlooking the cove. She waved to acknowledge him, not too sure if she was in any mood to be sociable, and not wanting another bout of bickering. He was her love, but right now she felt as remote from him as if she was on the other side of the Channel. She waited as he came scrambling down to the cove and crunched across the pebbles to join her.

'I called to see you and when your mum said you'd gone out, I guessed you'd be down here. This is where she used to come, isn't it?'

She squinted her eyes in the small burst of sunlight that parted the clouds and gazed out to sea.

'I didn't think you'd remember.'

'Why not? You told me enough times. What are you doing here? You'll catch your death of cold sitting on that rock.'

'Now you *sound* like my mother.'

'God forbid. Come for a walk. Or if you're chilled already we could go to the beach café and have some tea. My treat. Unless you've really gone off me for good, Charlie. Have you?'

She turned back to look at him properly then. He had always seemed so brash, so sure of himself, but there was a touch of uncertainty about him now. As if he was the one who was afraid of losing her, even if he'd never said as much in so many words.

'I haven't gone off you,' she said huskily.

'Come on, then.' He held out his hand and pulled her off the rock and into his arms. 'This is better than squabbling, isn't it?'

'Much better,' she said, reluctantly disentangling herself as several other people came into view above.

They climbed back up the stone steps and walked along the promenade to the road where there was a small beach café. She didn't object when Melvin tucked her hand in his arm. Let everyone see they were a courting couple, she thought recklessly, while they still had the chance.

'I suppose you've seen the paper?' she said when they were sitting in the café with two steaming cups of tea in front of them.

'Couldn't miss it.'

'So what did you think?'

'Well, my mother was very impressed.'

'Good Lord, is that all you've got to say? Josie always said you thought you'd gone up in the world for walking out with a hotel owner's daughter!'

She didn't know what made her say it, but the words were out before she could stop them. His face darkened.

'Is that all you think of me?'

'I didn't say I thought it, and anyway I wanted to know what you thought about the paper, not what your mother thought.'

He shrugged. 'Well, I thought it told me that you'll be leaving here soon, so I might as well find myself another girl.'

She scrambled off the chair so fast she nearly knocked it over. Her eyes were blazing until she saw that he was laughing, and then his arm shot out to hold her.

'I'm joking, sweetheart. Why would I want another girl when I've got you?'

'But you won't have me for much longer, will you? That's the whole point,' she said passionately. And she had no doubt that out of sight would be out of mind as far as Melvin was concerned. He had an eye for the girls, even if he professed that she was his only one – for now.

'What we need is a miracle,' he said, trying to jolly her up. 'If your old gran was here, I bet that's what she'd be saying.'

'Yes, she would, but they don't always

happen to order, do they?' Even if she had to admit that she'd done her share of praying for one in these past weeks. All to no avail, of course.

Melvin sat back on his chair and folded his arms, impatient now. 'Well, if you're just going to sit here looking gloomy I might as well have left you where I found you in the cove.'

'I'm sorry! It's hard to be cheerful when my whole family is so worried.'

'Your Josie doesn't seem to be. My mother said she was laughing and joking in Hallam's shop the other day. She overheard her telling one of the other girls that she'd probably get a job in a posh dress shop in Bristol and find herself a millionaire sugar daddy. I reckon she can't wait to get away from here.'

This was all news to Charlotte but, since Josie always had her head in the clouds with wild ideas, then if it stopped her moping, what did it matter?

'Well, that's Josie and this is me, and we'd better get out of here,' she said reluctantly as the waitress hovered around them when they had finished their tea, obviously wanting to clear the table.

They walked back to the hotel without finding much to say to one another and, when he left, he went off whistling as if he didn't have a care in the world, Charlotte thought resentfully. As if he wasn't going to miss her at all...

* * *

Milly was in the habit of spending Saturday afternoons at Dorothy's house now, and the two had become thicker than thieves. Today, Milly had got home minutes before Charlotte. She was jumping up and down, bubbling over with excitement, and involving the whole family in it.

'You've got to say yes, Dad! Me and Dorothy are going to work ever so hard so she can pass her exams and go to the grammar school with me next year. You will say yes, won't you Dad? You *will* make him, won't you, Mum? Please. *Please!*'

Josie was laughing her head off at her sister's antics, while her parents were looking faintly bemused at the torrent of words and trying to calm Milly down.

'What's going on?' Charlotte said.

Josie turned to her. 'She's got this daft idea that Dorothy's parents are going to let her live with them when we move to Bristol so she can continue at school here until she takes these blessed exams next year, and not have her lessons disrupted.'

'It's *not* a daft idea!' Milly rounded on her at once and stamped her foot, her plaits flying around her face as usual. 'Dorothy's mother is ever so nice and Dorothy hasn't got any older sisters to laugh at her all the time, so there!'

'For goodness' sake, Milly, slow down,' Ruth said. 'We don't even know these people, and it's a big responsibility to have someone else's child living with them. I'm sure they didn't mean it, even if they suggested it.'

'They did mean it, and Dorothy's mother is coming to see you tomorrow to talk to you about it, so there.'

'Stop saying those stupid words, Milly,' Donald put in irritably. 'If this is a genuine offer, then we shall have to think seriously about it, but I can tell you right now it's unlikely.'

'That means no,' Josie said in an aside to Charlotte. But Milly heard.

'I hate you! I'll be glad when I'm not living with you any more,' she said, her eyes starting to stream.

'Now look what you've done,' Ruth said at once. 'Milly, love, if Mrs Yard is coming to see us tomorrow afternoon, then of course we'll listen to what she has to say. But are you sure you'd like to be so far away from all of us? You wouldn't be able to run home down the road whenever you and Dorothy have a falling-out, would you?'

'I know,' Milly said in a muffled voice now.

'She hasn't thought about it at all,' Donald said. 'You'd better sleep on it, Milly, before you fancy yourself living in somebody else's house for ever more.'

'I didn't say it was going to be for ever *more*.'

All the same, when she went upstairs later, Charlotte found her furiously putting some of her books and toys into a box.

'What are you doing?'

'Josie was packing some of her things ages ago and now I know why. I'm doing the same, only I'm not going to Bristol with her. She hates me.'

'Of course she doesn't hate you. You're the one who said you hate her, and I'm sure that's not true, either. Is it?'

'It is sometimes.'

Charlotte put her arms around the stiff little figure. 'Oh, Milly, you wouldn't really want to live away from all of us, would you? We'd miss you all the time, and you'd miss us, too, especially at night without Mum to come and tuck you up.'

'Well, me and Dorothy thought it would be nice, and her mum didn't seem to mind when we were talking about it. We'd be like sisters,' she said uncertainly.

'You've already got sisters.'

Milly didn't have an answer to that, and Charlotte left her to it, more depressed than ever. This was something none of them had thought about. None of them wanted to leave Braydon, but at least they were still going to be together. This was breaking up the family and the old way of life even more. First Clover, and now Milly ... and she remembered guiltily that a short while ago she too had wondered about staying behind. Milly had had more courage than she had, facing up to her father, but only because she was too young to know it would never have worked.

Before Dorothy's mother was expected, the girls had been told to make themselves scarce, leaving their parents to discuss the matter. The three of them went for a walk along the sea front, meeting the familiar afternoon walkers and being invited to join in the games of throwing balls and sticks for their dogs.

If Charlotte found herself seeking a certain person with a dog called Rex, she wouldn't admit it to herself, and certainly not to the others. In any case he didn't make an appearance that afternoon. She shouldn't care, and she didn't. The only reason she thought about Steve Bailey at all was because he was far more sympathetic to what was happening to her family than Melvin seemed to be.

'Catch, butterfingers!' Milly yelled at her, as one of the tennis balls came bouncing her way. She put out her hands automatically and threw it back to its owner.

By now Milly's cheeks were glowing and she was in a high state of excitement. Charlotte suddenly ached for her. If she wanted this so much, how could they drag her away from Braydon if she had the chance to stay in the place where she had lived all her life? Yet how could her parents bear the thought of leaving her behind with some other family? Even Josie, who complained about her nosiness so often, would really miss her. And so would Charlotte.

'It won't be the same without her, will it?' she asked Josie.

'It'll be more peaceful. That can't be a bad thing, can it?' But she looked uncertain now, as her sister raced around after one of the dogs. ‘Oh, I know she gets on my nerves at times, but if you want to know what I really feel about it, Charlie, I think it would be awful to leave her behind. If we have to go then we should all go. I don’t want our family to be split up, and I’m darned sure Mum and Dad don’t want it either. Dorothy’s mother should never have suggested it.’

‘*If* she suggested it. Did you never think that it may be just an idea that those two cooked up? You know how dramatic Milly gets, and she can probably twist Dorothy around her little finger by now.’

Being the youngest, Milly could often get what she wanted, but this was different. This wasn’t a new toy or a small outing. This was changing their lives. And by the time they all returned to the hotel, hot and bothered from the games, it wasn’t only Milly who was on pins to know what had been decided that afternoon.

Eighteen

They heard the sound of voices coming from the sitting-room and went inside tentatively. Their parents were having cups of tea and biscuits with a pleasant-faced lady who Charlotte recognised at once, and instantly prayed that she wouldn't recognise her. But why would she? She hadn't been the one to glance up with startled eyes at the hay loft in Miles's stables. Charlotte let out her breath.

'These are our older daughters, Mrs Yard: Charlotte and Josie,' Ruth said at once. 'And this is Dorothy's mother.'

'Come over here, young lady, and confess to your mother and me just what you've been up to,' Donald spoke directly to his youngest, cutting across the niceties and looking at her keenly.

Milly blushed to the roots of her blonde plaits.

'Me and Dorothy thought it would be a nice idea, that's all,' she mumbled.

'Well, nice ideas don't always work out so well in practise, and you're too full of them for your own good. And what makes you think Dorothy's parents would be willing to have someone else's child living with them? What if you were ill and calling for your mother? How would these poor people feel then if we were far away in Bristol?'

Mrs Yard held up her hand to stow his flow and spoke more gently. 'It's not that we don't like you, Milly, because you know we do, and Dorothy is very fond of you. But your place is with your family, dear. If you were away from them, even for one night, I'm sure you'd be very homesick. We needed to get this sorted out straight away and your parents agree that of course you must stay with them. They would miss you terribly if they had to leave you behind.'

Seeing how red-faced Milly was becoming now, Ruth added, 'But you and Dorothy can always write to one another, darling, and tell one another what you're doing. You're good at writing, Milly, and it will be excellent practise for when you become a proper writer.'

For once, Josie didn't snigger. Milly had looked momentarily crushed, but her mother's words had already started a new idea spinning in her fertile brain.

'I suppose we can do that,' she conceded. 'That will be all right, won't it, Mrs Yard?'

'I think that's a lovely idea. Dorothy's not half as good at writing as you are, so it will help her, too.'

'Well then, if you don't mind I think I'd better stay with my family, even if we do have to go to horrid Bristol to live.'

'I think you've made the wisest decision,

Milly,' Mrs Yard said gravely, as if it had been all Milly's own.

So that would seem to be that. Another storm in a tea-cup was successfully dealt with, and if only the larger one could be smoothed over so easily, thought her father, there would be no problems.

Charlotte related it all to the farmer's wife in the farmhouse kitchen the next day, being sure of her discretion.

'Dad would never have let her do it, of course. The two little devils had planned it all by themselves, but I'm sure Milly was the brains behind it.'

'That child will go far,' Mrs Miles remarked. 'And what about you, Charlotte? Are you quite happy to leave Braydon?'

'I'm not happy about it at all, but I wouldn't dare suggest I did anything else. It would break Dad's heart if he thought another of his girls was thinking of splitting up the family.'

She kept her eyes lowered, knowing it was such a temptation, even now, to ask if the comfortable farmer's wife wanted a permanent lodger.

'You're a loyal girl, Charlotte, though there are plenty of folk who will miss you in the town, especially one who's not too far from here. What does Melvin have to say about it?'

'Oh, you know Melvin. He'll soon find somebody else, and it's not as if we're engaged or anything, is it?'

She deliberately said the words, even

though they smarted. She would dearly love to be engaged to him, to make it all official, but what would be the point, if they couldn't even see one another very often, if at all?

'You know, during the war when me and my Bert were engaged, we had to spend a couple of years apart while he was off fighting the Hun. It meant a lot to me, wearing his ring on my finger, knowing he was coming back to me someday. It was a sort of talisman.' Mrs Miles gave a short laugh. 'But just listen to me, going on so daft, when all you see is a couple of old duffers who've forgotten the meaning of romance!'

'I don't think that at all!' Though she couldn't deny she was startled, having never heard Mrs Miles talk like this. But if it was meant to make her feel any better, it failed, because to be comforted by having an engagement ring on your finger, it meant somebody had to ask you first. And Melvin hadn't.

When the elevenses were over, Charlotte left the farmhouse and went back to the stables to finish mucking out. If she had any sense she'd put all thoughts of marriage out of her mind, because Melvin obviously didn't have them. He loved her in his own way and she was in no doubt that he wanted her in a masculine, physical way, but not enough to beg her to stay in Braydon, or to ask her to marry him.

'A penny for them,' he said at the end of the day, when he waited for her at the end of the lane as he usually did now. She'd been so deep in thought she almost ran into him with her bicycle.

'They're not worth a penny.'

'Sixpence, then.'

She laughed 'Don't be daft. What's got into you? You don't normally throw your money around just to hear what I'm thinking about!'

'Only when it seems to be something important. Is it, Charlie? Is it about what you said the other day about your Josie's opinion of me? You ought to know by now how I feel about you, and it's not just because you're the daughter of a hotel owner like your dippy sister said. In fact, now that you're no longer a rich man's daughter, I love you all the more.'

She caught her breath. Oh, why hadn't he said all this so much sooner, when there was still a chance for them to be together? Why now, when they were so soon to be apart? Already her father had been scouring Bristol for a suitable house for them all and, even without the immediate security of a hotel position for him, she knew they would be leaving here soon.

'I'm still leaving Braydon, though, and when I'm gone you'll find somebody else,' she said unhappily. 'I know you will, Melvin, and I suppose I wouldn't blame you if you did.'

It was the nearest she could come to giving him her blessing, because she simply couldn't do that. She *loved* him, she thought passionately, and she couldn't bear to think of him being with some other girl.

His arm was around her waist and he squeezed it tightly. There was no one about, and the day was mild for early spring. With a quick glance around, he kissed her cheek and her face automatically turned towards him so that his lips found hers. She felt the familiar flutter as her heart began to beat faster, because this was the young man she had loved for so long, and she was so soon to be parted from him, and it was breaking her heart.

'You don't have to go home yet, sweetheart,' he whispered against her mouth. 'Let's go into that empty barn for half an hour. Nobody will miss you for that long.'

When he had suggested this before, she had usually said no. Now, as if in a dream, she knew she was not going to say no to whatever he asked of her. They would probably have so few chances to be alone together from now on, and they had to snatch their chance of happiness while they could. If the thoughts filling her head were more like those of a cheap penny dreadful, or the romantic nonsense Josie might write in her diary, she didn't stop to think about them. All she wanted was to be with Melvin and to be assured of his love.

'I'd better not be too long then,' she said huskily.

The barn was cool inside and smelled none too sweet. It wasn't unpleasant though, and there was enough straw on the floor to make it comfortable. To be extra sure, Melvin removed his coat and lay it down on the bed of straw with a flourish, making Charlotte giggle and tell him he looked like Sir Walter Raleigh.

'So come and lie with me, my lady, or should that be my lusty wench?' he said, his voice thickening with desire.

She giggled more nervously as she lay down, snuggling into his coat and warmed by his body heat inside it.

'I think you're the lusty one,' she whispered, as he stretched out beside her, his hands reaching out for her at once. He covered her face with kisses, and she felt the familiar thrill at the masculine texture of his skin against her own. His fingers strayed at once to inch up her skirt, and she knew she was going to do nothing to stop him.

'Isn't that what you like?' he said, his voice becoming more urgent as he felt her limbs relax and part. 'Isn't that why we're here?'

'As long as you love me,' she almost moaned as his fingers reached their goal and moved into her flesh. 'You do love me, don't you, Melvin?'

'Of course I do. I wouldn't get like this if I didn't love my girl.'

Before she had any idea of what he was going to do he had thrust her hand downwards until she could feel the hard swelling inside his trousers. She swallowed, her throat suddenly dry as she realised fully what was about to happen. It was going to happen now, today, and she couldn't deny that she wanted it ... his seduction may be swift and lacked finesse, but since it was the only one she had experienced, she assumed this was how a man behaved. He wanted her and he took her...

'Get it out, Charlie,' he said hoarsely. 'It won't bite you.'

She flinched. The words were crude, but not frightening. She realised that her whole body was shaking now, but not so much with pleasure as with the finality of what she was doing. Once she made love with Melvin, in what the Bible called having carnal knowledge of a man, there was no turning back. She would no longer be the girl she was.

For some reason her grandmother's words began floating around in her head. She didn't want them there, she thought, momentarily angry. This wasn't the time ... but Clover had always said that a girl should keep herself pure for marriage. Not for a quick fumble in a smelly old barn, but in the sweet intimacy of the marriage bed.

'What are you waiting for?' Melvin almost snarled. 'Or maybe you want me to do it for you?'

His fingers left their warm searching and scrabbled with the buttons of his trousers. And in that moment, Charlotte threw herself away from him, getting to her feet so fast that her head swam and she nearly fell over. But this was wrong. It shouldn't be happening and it wasn't going to happen. If he loved her enough he would be prepared to wait. She tottered towards the opening of the barn and out into the fading daylight.

'What the bloody hell's the matter with you?' Melvin yelled. 'Come back here, you silly bitch! You can't leave me like this!'

She didn't dare to question what he meant. She grabbed her bicycle from where it had fallen and, with her heart racing now, she sped away from him, out to the lane and on towards the road. He wouldn't follow yet. He couldn't, in the state he was in. Her face red with mortification, she knew very well what he would be doing now. She had gleaned that much of the ways of men.

Almost sobbing now, she rode home furiously. She was never sure if she actually believed in guardian angels but, if she did, she was sure that Clover was hers, and that she had been watching over her at that moment. It both comforted her and humiliated her. If she thought Clover had actually been watching what was about to happen in that barn, then it would be one of the worst moments of Charlotte's life.

She tried to be realistic, telling herself it was her own common sense that had stopped her. It was easier for a boy to be carried away by lust, and up to the girl to stop him. Besides, she didn't want to think it was nothing more than lust that made Melvin want her, but she wasn't even sure of that any more, either. It was easy, too, for a boy to say he loved a girl, especially when he thought he was going to get his own way.

But deep inside, she knew she felt just as passionately as he did. The desire to know a lover properly, in the biblical sense of the word, was not exclusive to a man. She longed for him ... but one of them had to be sensible, and it was a sure thing that it wasn't going to be hot-headed Melvin!

'My God, Charlie, what's wrong with you? You nearly ran me over!' she heard Josie's voice yell at her as she rode straight into the hotel yard without looking where she was going.

She blinked hard, realising Josie had been walking home from Hallam's shop and had almost stepped right in front of her bicycle. Or rather, Charlotte had almost ridden into her.

'Sorry! I wasn't looking where I was going,' she gasped.

'Where's the fire, then? You're not usually in such a rush to get home. Had a row with lover-boy, have you?'

It was so far from the truth, and yet so dangerously near, that Charlotte found herself laughing hysterically. Josie sounded alarmed now.

'Charlie, stop it! Whatever I said, I didn't mean it!'

Charlotte put her bicycle away in silence, trying to stop the hammering of her heart and the sick feeling inside her. Melvin would be finished with her for good now. He'd think her a silly little fool or, even worse, someone who was no more than a tease. She shouldn't care, but she did. He might not be a gentleman in the accepted sense of the word, but he was exciting, and she loved him. She still did, and if that made her a silly little fool, then that was what she was.

Before she could think what to say to Josie, the door of the hotel opened and her mother looked out, obviously having heard the noise outside.

'Come inside, you two. Your father has something to tell you.'

They looked at one another now, everything else forgotten. Ruth's voice was not so much calm as resigned. It had come then, the moment they had all been dreading. The decision to move had been made long ago, but they had never really believed it until now. Never wanted to believe it. But they knew Donald had been in Bristol all day, and now he had something to tell them. It could only mean one thing. He had found a new job and somewhere for them to live.

When they were all gathered in the sitting-room, they quickly learnt that only one of the assumptions was right.

'Before you ask, I haven't been able to get a new position yet,' he said heavily, always using the same words as if to give them their proper dignity. After being a hotel owner for so many years, and a noted figure in the town, working for someone else was bound to be a come-down, Charlotte thought swiftly, and she ached for her father's embarrassment.

'But I have found us a very nice little house,' he went on brightly, trying to lighten gloomy faces. 'Since the move affects us all, I would like us all to see it before I make any firm commitment on the place. So I've arranged for a proper viewing next Saturday, and I have got the loan of a car to take us there.'

'I have to work in the shop on Saturdays,' Josie said at once.

'I'll be playing with Dorothy all day,' Millie said resentfully.

Charlotte hesitated. It would be so easy to say she too had to be at the farm on Saturday, but she knew she didn't, and it would seem like another slap in the face to her father if none of them went with him and Ruth to see the new house. Which house they lived in would ultimately be her parents' decision, but she could see he needed this family support and, if neither of her sisters was prepared to give it, then she must.

And not for a moment was she going to think that this was the first step towards taking her away from Melvin. Once they found a house to suit them, she had no doubt the move would be swift. And probably better so.

'I'll come with you and Mum, Dad,' she said. 'It'll be quite an adventure.'

'I will too, then,' Milly said after a moment, clearly liking the thought of an adventure. 'Dorothy won't mind not seeing me for one day.'

They looked at Josie, sitting with tightly folded arms. She shrugged defiantly.

'I'll leave it to the rest of you. It won't make any difference what I think, will it? And Saturday is always our busiest day in the shop.'

She made it sound as if Braydon was a great metropolis instead of a small seaside town where nothing much happened – except when the sea surged over the sea defences and ruined a family's lives. But she had a week to think about it and, by then, she might have changed her mind, Charlotte thought, wondering if her sister had any idea how important it was to their parents to pull together in this.

'You are a selfish little brat, aren't you, Josie?' she said mildly when Josie came into her bedroom for a late-night chat. 'Can't you see how much Dad wants us all to go to Bristol together next Saturday? And I thought you were all for it.'

'Well, now I'm not, so why should I pretend I want to see a rotten house? If I'm a selfish brat, then you're a hypocrite, because you don't want to go either, do you?'

'No, I don't, but you have to see it from their point of view. They've had all their dreams shattered and I, for one, am not going to make things any harder for them. Besides, I thought you had some grand idea about working in one of the bigger posh shops in Bristol?'

'I did – I do – but I'd still rather stay here

where I belong.'

Her bravado suddenly collapsed and her face crumpled, and within seconds Charlotte had put her arms around her and was hugging her tight.

'Maybe it won't be for ever,' she said unsteadily. 'Maybe one day we can all come back to Braydon. Don't you think it's what I want more than anything? How do you think I feel, with the thought of never seeing Melvin again?'

'I don't know,' Josie said in a muffled voice. 'You always seem so much more capable of accepting new things than I do. You never make much fuss about it, so I didn't think Melvin Philpott meant that much to you after all.'

Charlotte drew in her breath. If only she knew. If only any of them knew how very hard this was going to be for her. When there was no answer, Josie pulled away from her and stared into her face.

'Does he mean a lot to you, Charlie? You never tell me anything.'

'That's because you're my little sister,' she said automatically.

'I'm not little! I'm nearly sixteen, and I'm old enough to know what goes on. I've got feelings too – so have you and Melvin done things yet?' She shot the last words at her sister, hoping to shock her into telling.

It only made Charlotte laugh and shake her off. 'If you think I'm giving away any secrets so you can write them in your diary for Milly to find, you can just think again! Some things are private and personal, and best kept that way.'

'I bet that means you have then!'

'It doesn't mean that at all, and if you can't talk about anything else then go to bed and leave me alone. I'm tired, if you're not.'

She was also depressed and disinclined to talk to anyone. The future had once looked so bright, and now it was all going wrong. She didn't want to live in Bristol any more than the rest of the family. She didn't even want to go there to view the house that her father had found for them, but she knew how desperately he wanted to keep them all together, which was why she had agreed to go.

What they needed was a miracle, she thought sadly, but everyone knew that miracles didn't happen to order, if they happened at all. It wasn't the first time she had thought it, and it wasn't the first time they had needed one, either. But it hadn't appeared to save the hotel, so what hope did they have of one appearing now?

Nineteen

The letter arrived on Monday morning, amongst a batch of other mail that Donald didn't care to inspect too thoroughly. It all had to be dealt with, the bills and statements and other documents that couldn't be put off indefinitely. He had always been an efficient businessman in his dealings, but the thought of facing yet more officialdom in disposing of the home he loved was filling him with dread.

He assumed that the letter with the Bristol postmark on it was merely to confirm the arrangement with the estate agent for the house viewing on the following Saturday morning. It could wait, with all the rest, until after midday when he might feel more like coping with them.

Donald knew what he was doing to his family, even if it was through no fault of his own. The disruption to all their lives was something he grieved over every day. He knew he had Ruth's unwavering love and support, and for that he was more grateful than she would ever know. But his girls shouldn't have to go through this.

Charlotte was being a brick, but he knew how she would miss her blacksmith, even if

Donald didn't entirely approve of him and would prefer to see her settle eventually with someone else. Josie was just being resentfully adolescent over everything, and she would have to get over it. Poor Milly would have to change schools at a critical time of her school life, which was something else still to be organised, he reminded himself.

He took the letters into the sitting-room after the midday meal and began to open them. As he expected, most of them were the sort he didn't want to see. Bills seemed to be never ending. He left the one with the Bristol postmark on it until last, since he had already guessed what it contained.

He slit open the envelope and unfolded the letter inside, frowning at the unfamiliar heading along the top of the printed document. The names of Redman and Searle were certainly not those of the estate agency he was dealing with. And then he blinked, seeing that they were the names of solicitors with a whole row of letters after them. He began to read the letter rapidly, finding his heart beating crazily fast as he did so.

Dear Sir,

We would be grateful if you would call at these Chambers at your earliest convenience, as we believe we are holding certain documents to your advantage. Please telephone these Chambers to make an appointment as soon as possible. We require you to bring proof of identity to the effect that you are indeed Donald James Elkins, presently residing at The Retreat Hotel, Braydon, Somerset, and that you are the son of Thomas Ralph Elkins and Clover Elkins, née Dunwoody. Please also bring proof of these two persons named, such as their birth and/or death certificates.

We remain,
Yours respectfully,
J. D. Redman and O. V. Searle

The scrawled signatures over the printed names was indecipherable but, by then, Donald realised he had been holding his breath for so long he felt he was near to exploding. His immediate thought was to contact his own solicitor to find out what the letter could possibly mean, and what documents they could be holding that were to his advantage. But he knew he would far rather find out for himself.

He didn't dare to hope ... but he suddenly found his voice and went hollering out to the kitchen, where Ruth was rolling out pastry for the evening meal.

'Good Lord, Donald, you made me jump. What on earth's wrong now?'

'I don't know that anything's wrong,' he almost rasped. 'But you'd better read this, woman, and tell me what you think.'

He thrust it into her floury hands regardless. She tut-tutted, shook the powdery spray off the letter and began to read, her eyes widening long before she reached the end.

'What do you think it's all about?'

'I don't know, but I'm going to find out,' he said grimly. 'When solicitors say there's something to your advantage it usually means one thing. Somebody's been left some money, and in this case it must be us!'

Ruth stared at him, her own heart jumping around in her chest.

'Well, don't get your hopes up too much, my dear. I mean, who could have done such a thing? Did your parents have any long-lost relatives that we never heard about? There's Clover's sister Mary and her daughter living on Exmoor, of course, but they didn't even reply when we wrote to them about Clover's death, let alone come to the funeral. Perhaps Mary died and left you a few pounds.'

Donald's heart slowed. Perhaps that was it. The thought that this was the miracle they had all been praying for vanished from his mind as quickly as it had appeared. But then he reasoned that these solicitors wouldn't have mentioned his parents by name if they didn't have something to do with whatever documents they were holding to his advantage. He shook his head.

'You're wrong, love. I'm sure this has nothing to do with Aunt Mary, whether she's died or not. This is something between my parents and me. I'll go to the post office and telephone these people to make an appointment with them as soon as possible.'

'Maybe next Saturday when we go to view

the house?' Ruth said.

He shook his head again. 'I need to know what this is all about before then. I don't have your patience to wait another week! For all we know, we could be millionaires without even knowing it.'

The idea was so farcical that it started them both laughing, and before they knew it they were inventing all kinds of wild fantasies about being left a king's ransom, and a few minutes later Charlotte came in to the kitchen to find her parents hugging one another helplessly, covered in flour and talking nonsense.

But since this was something that might affect them all, even though Donald still didn't dare let himself dream that it would make any difference whatsoever to their future plans, he related the contents of the letter to his daughters later. By then he had made the appointment to go to Bristol the next day, and he would see Messrs Redman and Searle at three o'clock.

He admitted to himself that he was nervous about it. He was a businessman, and perfectly confident in his own domain, but he was also a down-to-earth fellow and he didn't relish the prospect of having to meet the sort of snotty-nosed people who worked in *Chambers*. He had another, more basic meaning for those!

'You'll be fine, Donald,' Ruth assured him, when he was smartly dressed in his best suit the next morning and preparing to catch the train to Bristol.

He certainly hadn't intended to hire a car for the journey today. It was something he did only occasionally, and today he knew he would be far too jittery to drive safely.

Donald arrived at the imposing offices of Messrs Redman and Searle, which he remembered to refer to as Chambers, and glanced at the highly polished name-plate on the wall. Then he counted to ten, pushed open the heavy oak door and gave his name to the prim woman at the reception desk inside. He was early, and he was asked to sit down until he was taken through to the Chambers. He was becoming more nervous by the minute and wished he'd had the gumption to rush in at the last minute, however flustered it would have made him. It couldn't have been worse than the way he was feeling now.

The receptionist finally rose and asked Donald to follow her. He clutched the envelope containing the documents he had been asked to bring, wishing he'd thought to use a fancy briefcase ... if he had one.

The grey-haired gentleman in the pin-striped suit rose from behind an imposing desk and came forward to shake his hand, introducing himself as Jeremy Redman. He immediately asked the receptionist to bring some tea and biscuits for their visitor, making Donald feel more nervous than ever. He was being treated almost like some kind of royalty, which was completely absurd, when the information he was about to be given couldn't be anything very grand ... A small bequest from a long-forgotten relative could not make the slightest difference to the Elkinses' fortunes...

An hour or so later he was on the train back to Braydon, his head spinning, his mind stunned. He still couldn't take it in, and he wasn't even going to try until he was in the security of his own home, with his wife and family around him. He remembered someone once saying that great hardship and great good fortune were one and the same when it came to unravelling the senses. It was exactly the way he felt now.

When the train arrived in Braydon, he stepped out of the station still feeling as if he was in a dream. If it wasn't for the letters of authority in the official envelope that he clutched so tightly now, he would assuredly think that this was what it had been. Once more, he felt as if he had been holding his breath for a very long time and slowly, in the clean salt air of his home town, he began to let it out and to breathe more easily. It would be the worst irony of all to expire now, he thought, with a feeble stab at humour.

As he reached The Retreat, seeing the lights from the extension where the family lived and the gaunt reminders of the building that was so soon to be pulled down for ever, he felt a great lump fill his throat. Tattered as the old building was now, it was bathed in the soft golden glow of the lowering sun that stretched across the mellow waters of the Bristol Channel. That glow seemed to reach out and touch him, reminding him that here was love, here were so many golden memories.

He swallowed, knowing he was being a sentimental old fool, but knowing, too, that some things were more precious than gold. He pushed open the door, knowing the family would be anxious to know why he had been summoned to the solicitors' Chambers in Bristol. They were all there, all the people he loved best: Josie and Milly squabbling as usual; Charlotte helping her mother at the stove; and Ruth, his sweet-faced Ruth, momentarily unaware of his presence, until she turned and looked at him, questions in her eyes.

'I think we'd all better sit down,' he said huskily.

Fleetingly, he thought he knew exactly how the good fairy in all the storybooks must have felt, knowing she was the bearer of good news.

'What is it, Donald?' Ruth said quietly.

The girls were silent now, knowing something was about to be said that was going to affect them all, but not yet knowing what it was. Faced with such unusual patience, Donald allowed his face to break into a smile. It dawned on him that even with good news, the shock of it was sometimes too great even to smile ... until the time came to share it.

'It seems that Clover left us more than just trinkets and memories,' he said, his voice not quite steady.

Everyone clamoured at once then, and he had to throw up his hands and tell them to be quiet or they'd never hear anything. Ruth came to sit close beside him on one of the cheap kitchen chairs, her hands clasped together.

'Please don't keep us in suspense any longer, darling.'

He drew out the precious bulky envelope he had been carrying home with him so carefully. Even now, he could hardly believe it.

'We all know how dotty Clover had got in her last years,' he said, 'and I make no excuse for saying so. She was my mother, and I loved her as much as the rest of you, but eccentric was hardly the word for her. You girls only ever knew her when she was floating off somewhere in one of her fantasies, but I have to tell you that she was always a delightful dreamer, and it was probably why my father loved her so much, too.'

'Daddy, are you ever going to get to the point?' Charlotte burst out. 'We all know how Clover was, and none of us ever thought less of her because of it.'

'I'm getting there,' Donald said. 'I just wanted to build up the background picture for you, my loves. You all knew her for the eccentric old lady she became, but my father knew her for a beautiful young woman who would go anywhere with him, no matter how dangerous. Despite all that, he recognised how flighty she was – I don't mean that in a bad way, but rather how much of a dreamer she always was. And one of them had to be the sensible one, the one to provide for the future.'

'Go on, darling,' Ruth said, when he hesitated, clearly affected by speaking of his parents in this way, which he so rarely did. In fact, none of them had ever thought much about Tommy at all. None of them had known him except Donald, and his childhood memories of the upright military man in the sepia photographs must surely be very sparse.

'Was Gran secretly a Russian princess – or a lady spy?' Milly asked excitedly, obviously having inherited Clover's gift of romance.

'No,' Donald said with a laugh. 'But she was far richer than any of us could ever have guessed, and the secret might have been lost for ever had it not been for Steve Bailey.'

'The newspaperman?' Charlotte exclaimed, startled. 'What on earth does he have to do with any of this?'

'It was the piece he wrote about our family, and the photograph of Tommy and Clover than I loaned him that started it. He has a friend who works for a Bristol newspaper, and the other man thought it was worth a small mention in his paper as well. It was only a small piece, together with the photograph, but the solicitors who wrote to me saw it and were struck by Clover's unusual name. They did a bit of searching in their archives and came up with a long-forgotten will of Clover's.'

'But she always said she never believed in making wills, and that it was unlucky and tempting fate,' Ruth said. 'She just left a few letters for us all, saying what bits of jewellery and so on that she wanted us to have.'

Donald drew out the fading document from the envelope. 'So she did, but you can see from the date on it that this one was made many years ago, before I was even born. I suspect that it was my father who insisted on them both making wills, knowing the risks they took in their colourful lives. His is also here but, like Clover's, it was never claimed. After he died, she must either have forgotten it or been too distressed to do anything about it. In any case she would have been well provided for with the military pension my father received. These wills were simply forgotten and have lain in the chambers of Messrs Redman and Searle and their predecessors for all these years.'

'So what do they say, Dad?' Josie could contain her impatience no longer. 'Are we fabulously rich after all?'

Charlotte couldn't say anything. Unlike her impatient sister, she was more moved by the romance of it all. The love story that was obviously Tommy and Clover's, and the fact that so many years later that love story was to touch them all in some way.

'I rather think, my loves,' Donald replied slowly, 'that we are.'

He was nearly deafened by the whoops from Josie and Milly, the gasps from Charlotte and Ruth, and the demands for him to tell them everything *immediately*, and that he was being very mean to keep them in suspense any longer.

'All right,' he said. 'I'll go into the finer details later, but the main thing that has emerged from all this is that many years ago, when they were in South Africa, my father invested some money in a small diamond mine, hoping that one day it would make some modest returns. As you know they then travelled all over the place, and any dividends that might have come his way were simply deposited in a South African bank for safe keeping. That diamond mine became far richer than anyone could have hoped. Tommy left everything to Clover, of course, and this forgotten will of Clover's leaves everything to me.' He paused for breath. ' So yes, my loves, I think we can say that when everything is finally proven, we are rich.'

The stunned silence echoed the way he himself had felt earlier, but then everyone was talking at once again.

'So we don't have to go to rotten Bristol to live!' Milly squealed.

'We'll be here all summer and for ever more!' Josie said, her first thought clearly on the annual fair that would return to Braydon again in a couple of months.

'So Clover sent us her miracle, after all,' Charlotte said softly, thinking that her fanciful assumption that Clover was her guardian angel might not be so very wrong after all. Because now she didn't have to say goodbye to Melvin, and perhaps someday soon he would propose to her ... which would be wonderful, providing they weren't expected to live in his mother's house, she amended.

'But Donald, what about the hotel?' Ruth tried to be practical. 'You've already offered the land it stands on for sale.'

'I shall withdraw it at once,' he said, authoritative now. 'You can all examine these documents later, but you must be careful with the old wills, because they're quite fragile. They're such important documents, and not just because of the inheritance. They're our past, as well.'

'I didn't know you could be so sentimental, Dad,' Josie teased.

'But he's right,' Ruth said. 'Everyone's past is what shapes their futures, and we have the evidence of that right here.'

Donald went on briskly, before they were all overtaken by emotion again.

'So let's look on the practical side for a moment. I have a letter of authority from the solicitors, endorsing that there will be ample funds being transferred to my account from a South African bank very soon. Do I have the family's approval that we pull down the old hotel and make plans for a new hotel to be built on the same site, once the area is made safe? Is it what we all want?' He was left in no doubt of the approval of this plan.

'Then I'll go to the bank tomorrow with all this information together with the solicitors' letter and give the manager the shock of his life when I ask for a substantial loan and assure him it will be honoured. I'll arrange to see the accountant, too, and put an announcement in the newspaper to say the land offer is withdrawn. You do all realise that before the old place is completely flattened and plans for the new one drawn up and building begun, we'll have to move out of here, don't you? What I propose is that we rent a house here until we can get the hotel furniture out of storage, and buy whatever else is needed for us to be back is business again.'

No matter how practical he had to be, he couldn't hide his pride and delight in saying the words. Then they were all hugging one another and Milly was screaming that she had to tell Dorothy that she was staying in Braydon after all.

'You don't tell her anything yet, young lady,' Donald warned her. 'This is family business, and it's private.'

'But we won't be able to keep it private, Donald,' Ruth protested. 'And I'm sure Milly's not the only one who'll want to tell people of our good fortune. From the way they have been so sympathetic towards us in the past I know they'll be pleased for us now.'

'I suppose you're right,' Donald said, 'but at

least let me see the bank manager first, or they'll think you're all making up one of Clover's fairytales.'

'That's almost what it is, isn't it?' Charlotte said, her throat catching. 'But doesn't it prove that sometimes fairytales do come true?'

A little while later she felt a great need to get out of the house and be by herself. By then Josie and Milly were gabbling away like idiots, planning what they were going to do with their new-found wealth, and her parents had gone away to their bedroom to be alone, to discuss and to plan, and probably to weep a little at the way things had turned out.

The sun had dropped onto the horizon now, filling the sea with the richest of rosy sheens. To Charlotte the bay had never looked so beautiful, made even more so by knowing that she wasn't going to have to leave here after all. She had never realised how fiercely she loved this place where she had been born, until the time came when they had forcibly had to face leaving it.

Now all that was changed, and it was Clover they had to thank for it. Dear, darling, dotty Clover, the grandmother she had always adored ... she whispered her inadequate thanks into the soft, swirling breeze and up into the ether.

Out of the corner of her eye she saw a figure in the distance. Her heart stopped for a moment but it wasn't ghostly and it wasn't dancing daintily along the promenade. It was tall and male, and the shaggy dog bounding at his heels came scampering towards her as he recognised her, and her heart raced again as the man came nearer.

'I'm glad to see you again, Charlotte,' Steve Bailey greeted her. 'Rex and I always look out for you on our walks, but you've been quite elusive lately.'

'Have I?' She didn't stop to wonder why Steve Bailey should always look out for her. There was far too much else bursting inside her to be said. 'Steve, I'm going to tell you something that's private and personal but, since you started it all, even if you don't know it yet, I just have to tell you.'

'Oh, dear. Have I done something terrible?' he said cautiously as her words started stumbling.

The brilliance of her smile made him draw in his breath. 'Not at all. Oh, not at all! It's absolutely the *best* thing! I know my family will want to thank you, but now that I've seen you, I just have to tell you what's happened.'

She realised she was clutching his arm in her excitement, but he didn't seem to mind. He steered her to the splendid, newly constructed sea wall, where they sat close together with Rex lying patiently beside them. Then she began to talk, and it all poured out, all the joy and the happiness that was in store for her family now; all the love and affinity she had always felt for Clover.

Once she had finished, and before she knew what was happening, Steve's arms had closed around her, holding her tight. Then he was kissing her very hard, and the moment was so perfect, with the weirdest sensation in Charlotte's mind that Clover was giving her silent blessing, that she gave no thought to pulling away.

Alert and excited at their feet now, Rex began leaping up and down and barking like a mad thing, as if to imply that whatever might be happening between his two favourite people, he approved of it, too.